Karys

SECRETS &
PHOTOGRAPHS

ECCC '24

A. K. RAMIREZ

SECRETS & PHOTOGRAPHS

MARISSA AMBROSE WITNESS SERIES BOOK 1

4 Horsemen
Publications, Inc.

4 Horsemen Publications, Inc.
1497 Main St. Suite 169
Dunedin, FL 34698
4horsemenpublications.com
info@4horsemenpublications.com

Cover by J. Kotick
Typeset by S. Wilder
Edited by Joseph Mistretta

Library of Congress Control Number: 2022941299

Print ISBN: 978-1-64450-663-9
Hardcover ISBN: 978-1-64450-664-6
Audio ISBN: 978-1-64450-992-0
Ebook ISBN: 978-1-64450-662-2

Acknowledgments

To the Queen of Salt Mountain, who convinced me not to give up. This book would not have seen the light of day without your support.

To the Girl Gang who helped with the plot bunnies

And to my family, who supported my borderline unhealthy writer habits, even when it was rough.

Table of Contents

Chapter 1

*M*arissa felt cold. She couldn't see anything, a blindfold tied tightly against her eyes. Music blared against her ears, the throbbing in her head synced with the beat of the music. The cold, rough concrete burned her bare legs, and every time she attempted to adjust them, she felt sharp sensations rush through. She was stiff and cold and tired. Her right hand was handcuffed to something that felt heavy and unbreakable, though she tried to pull away. Time had blurred, and her mind swam, unable to focus on anything. She was thirsty, hungry, and tired. Marissa had never been so frightened in her life.

Someone grabbed her by the arm, squeezing tight as they unlocked her cuff from whatever she was attached to and ushered her along. She whimpered in protest and tugged away from the fingers that dug *into her. She thought she heard a laugh in her ear over the music before that hand shoved her hard. She nearly toppled over but fell into another set of hands that caught her in their arms. These weren't as rough and didn't grip her as tightly. They held her up as she pulled her legs back under her, and one of the hands rubbed her arm where the other had aggressively gripped. She could feel his breath on her neck as his lips touched her ear, whispering something she couldn't quite hear.*

She gasped, sat up with a start, and sighed, acknowledging she was safe in her room. Ellie was lying on top of her legs, her cold nose poking at her in concern. She rubbed Ellie's ears, feeling her heartbeat slow to normal. Her chest heavily convulsed as tears fell down her cheeks. Pulling the dog in close, she hugged her tight—a solid reminder she was no longer in that place but inside her bedroom, in her home. Safe.

"Good girl," she whispered, gripping Ellie's fur. The shepherd leaned in close, burying her cold nose into her neck.

Leaning back, Marissa glanced over at her clock. It was nearly five.

"Come on. Let's go downstairs."

With a heavy sigh, she shifted as Ellie bounced off the bed and toward the door. Marissa swung her legs over the side and winced, aches traveling through her body from her heels as they hit the floor.

"It's going to be a day," she mumbled and forced herself to stand.

It was still dark outside, and she was sure the air outside was cold, but the old house was warm. It may have been old, but her mom had updated everything except for the walls. Marissa wandered into the bathroom; she could still hear Ellie bouncing in the hallway, excited to start her day. She did not share the dog's enthusiasm.

She washed her hands and stared at the reflection that stared back at her. Her dark hair was a tangled mess, and dark circles were under her eyes. Marissa remembered when she took pride in how she looked, brushed her hair several times a day, and had a whole skincare routine. She had been a beauty queen when she was younger. It all seemed so pointless now. Her eyes drifted from her face down to her shoulder with the long, dark scar. Then they drifted to the scar that ran from the bottom of her collarbone across her chest. Her tank top covered most of it, but she knew the rest ran down her side and to her back. She was full of scars now.

She turned the light off and followed Ellie to the hallway, stopping at the top of the stairs. It was the same every morning: the stairs were always daunting. Her ankles locked up like they usually did, forcing her to take slow and precise steps. Once she reached the bottom, she headed to the kitchen and opened the back door, letting Ellie bound out into the dark yard. Sunrise was still a way off, but the sky was beginning to lighten.

She went to the cabinet above the sink and dug out her meds. Since her recovery from the events at the warehouse, Marissa had received a long list of diagnoses: fibromyalgia brought on by trauma, panic attacks, PTSD, and arthritis. Not to mention a rapid heart rate they couldn't pin down, chronic migraines—so many meds.

Putting on her tea kettle, she set up her teacup and waited for the water to boil. It had taken some time, but Marissa had made her childhood home her own again. Her mom had signed the house over to her while she healed, which gave her full rein to do as she pleased with the place, taking the opportunity to downsize without selling. Port Townsend was not where Marissa thought she would be, especially after so many years in Seattle. She loved the city: the noise, the crowds, the food. The fact that almost everything was open until at least midnight. Not like this tourist town, which felt like it had a town-wide bedtime of 9 p.m. It was known as a charming, quaint town by the sea, and as far as she was concerned, it had lost its charm decades ago.

Slowly but surely, the house was coming together. She sighed, grabbed her hoodie off the hook by her back door, and threw it over her head while letting Ellie back inside. Her mom had done all the hard stuff, remodeling the upstairs and downstairs to an open-concept floorplan and updating the plumbing and electricity. Marissa could see her front door, the living room, the dining room, and a study from the kitchen. Below the stairs was a full bathroom.

As the tea kettle screamed, she poured the water into the cup and watched the steam rise. This was not where Marissa expected to be at thirty-six. Growing up, all she wanted was to get the hell out of this town. She would be married to her high school sweetheart with kids, living in a big city, and making detective. The funny part was, Marissa had married her high school sweetheart. Twice. They'd also had two divorces. She had been living in a big city, owning not one but two properties in Seattle. She had made detective, reaching incredible heights as one of the youngest promoted in her unit. And now, she was back in her childhood home, divorced and alone, still a detective but benched for the unseen future. It felt like a punishment.

Of course, some of it was her doing. She had pushed Jared away and moved back home. Her nightmare wasn't only when she slept. Her precinct had done all but call her a liar during her recovery when she told them there was more than one assailant. She couldn't see, so it was simply her word. She had undergone so much; she couldn't have been sure. That was what her unit had said because it didn't fit into the profile the SPD had given. People she had trusted with her life didn't have her back.

She paused for a moment before retrieving the hidden key from her hutch and carefully climbing onto her counter. Despite telling herself she wouldn't, most mornings she would pull down the box. She winced, pain stretching through her leg as she reached the top of her cabinets to recover a lockbox. Once it was on the counter, she paused as her feet hit the ground. She hoped that one day, something new would stand out. Some tangible clue she could hold in her hands. Ellie came right alongside her and whined, sensing her discomfort. Marissa stretched a hand down, scratching her ear as she unlocked the box and let the photographs pour out onto the countertop. There were candid shots of her going about her day, walking down the street, leaving the bakery, checking her mail. A good stack of them was just Jared. Sometimes they would arrive weekly, and sometimes she would go a few weeks without receiving anything. Or maybe it was just a good reminder of why this was her life now. Why she had chosen to be here, alone. A reminder that her life was in danger.

Local cops and SPD, while agreeing she was a victim of a stalker, wouldn't connect it to that case because before the warehouse, Marissa hadn't received any photos. She had been given police protection across the street, but she knew no one had taken her seriously. In the eyes of the law, she hadn't been threatened and couldn't identify anyone. She only had pictures that appeared on her doorstep or in her mailbox. She kept them safely locked away, spending most of her days trying hard to forget them. But too often, she found herself thumbing through them. It had become an almost daily ritual.

Once she was satisfied the tea had steeped long enough, she returned the photos to the box and put everything back in its place. Her former partner, Tom, would tell her dwelling over the same pieces of evidence wouldn't get her anywhere. He had always given her advice like that. He had been so much like the older brother she'd never had, having been the oldest of three sisters. Taking her mug with both hands, she headed out to the backyard, not bothering to turn the light on. She stretched out on her swinging bench and scrolled through her socials. Occasionally, she found her eyes wandering over the backyard, watching for anything or anyone out of place. She knew there was always an officer across the street, watching over her and her home, but they hadn't proven very helpful yet. They hadn't managed to see who or how things were being left on her doorstep.

The early morning air was chilly and quiet. The only noises she could hear were Ellie's panting as she plopped herself down next to Marissa and the occasional breeze blowing by. She glanced at the clock on her phone. Barely any time had passed. Putting her feet up, she finished her tea, put the empty cup down on the side table, and looked out into her dark yard. She needed to rest, but she knew sleep would keep eluding her. She didn't want to sleep anymore; the nightmares had worsened.

If she had stopped to think about it, she would have realized why. All that mattered was every time she closed her eyes, she was back there again.

Chapter 2

Marissa leaned back into the couch and sighed heavily. She had almost canceled today's session but canceling was becoming a habit. And if Marissa wanted to go back to work, she had to make these appointments. Ellie was on the floor, below her feet, already twitching as she napped.

"So, how are you feeling today?"

The sound of a woman's soft voice broke through her thoughts. Dr. Seaver sat in a large leather armchair across from her, her legs crossed neatly, a pen in her hand, and her notebook on her lap. Her blonde hair was pulled back tightly, her mouth in a stiff smile.

Marissa adjusted again, maybe the fourth time since sitting down, curling her legs beneath her, and offered a slight shrug. "Fine?"

"Are you asking me if you feel fine?" Dr. Seaver stared at her expectantly, seeming wary of Marissa's attitude. When Marissa didn't respond, she continued. "Today marks the second anniversary, right?" Her tone shifted, becoming softer and gentle. And the glare she had been giving a moment earlier had also softened. No matter how much Marissa hated her, there was a reason she was considered good at her job.

"Two years yesterday," she answered, letting her eyes fall back on the window. Putting the words into the space between them made her feel naked and vulnerable.

"When we first started meeting a year ago, you told me that you wouldn't forgive yourself for what happened. Your words. You wouldn't forgive yourself."

There wasn't an obvious question, but she paused, waiting for Marissa to answer. Uncomfortably, she nodded. "That's right."

"Do you still feel like the blame should rest solely on you?"

Marissa just stared, blinking at the other woman.

"When you say, 'I will never forgive myself,' this implies that there is something to forgive. That you were somehow to blame for what happened."

So much for just sailing through this session as she had planned.

"Do you still feel that way?" she asked matter-of-factly, pen in hand, ready to take note while Marissa sat and stared dumbfounded.

"I—" Somehow, Marissa hadn't considered it this way before. Her mouth opened and closed several times before the doctor verbally prodded her again.

"Do you feel like what happened was your fault?"

Grateful for the forwardness of the question despite the discomfort rising in her stomach, she silently nodded. She could feel the wetness of tears and her face burning.

"Why?" Her voice was even softer than it had been a minute ago.

"It was my lead—"

"That you discussed with your partner, Tom Disher."

"Yes—"

"And he agreed with you that it was a solid lead?"

Marissa just nodded her head.

"And who made the call for backup?"

"I did."

"And who didn't wait."

"Well—"

"No, Marissa. Who went in instead of waiting for backup?"

"Tom did." She dropped her eyes back to the floor.

Tom had argued, saying that by the time backup arrived, they would be long gone. He went into the warehouse, and Marissa waited fewer than five minutes before running after him. It had been too late. She entered the warehouse just in time to watch the gunfire and see him fall to the ground, lifeless. And then someone had struck her from behind, and everything went black.

"The point here, Marissa, is you are blaming yourself for something you had no control over. You ran in after your partner because he was in danger. You called for backup; you wanted to wait. You didn't do anything wrong." She passed over a box of tissues that Marissa accepted. "You need to give yourself some grace. Stop blaming yourself."

The hour-long session felt like an eternity. As Marissa tried to regain some semblance of composure, Dr. Seaver offered her a new box of tissues. Ellie wasn't pleased with Marissa's discomfort either, now on the couch with her head resting on Marissa's shaking leg.

"We've been meeting for nearly a year, and this is the first time you've been honest with me. I know it hasn't been easy. You have kept so much on the inside, and you are letting it swallow you from the inside. I'm here to listen. I'm not here to be your friend; I'm not here to put judgment on you. I'm here to give you the support you need to pick yourself back up." She smoothed out her white knee-length skirt and gave a small smile. "Be kind to yourself this week, and I will see you next Friday."

Marissa would have continued talking around everything if it had been up to her, but the doctor earned her paycheck. She hadn't planned on even acknowledging what this week was. *Be kind to yourself* was such a loaded statement.

Marissa shoved her hands into her pockets and looked down the street. Ellie walked alongside her, shaking her service dog vest back into place after lying down for so long. It was a quiet, cold day with gray skies and the roads were bare. It was pretty typical for a September day. The tourist town was slow during the later months of the year.

Patting her side, Marissa called Ellie to her and headed down the street, deciding the smell of fresh baked goods was just what she needed.

As she opened the door, the chime went off over her head, and her sister waved happily from behind the counter, finishing up with the customer at the register. The smell of pastries and baked goods filled her nose. Seeing her sister had quite the line, she walked over to an empty booth by the window, motioning for Ellie to lie down beneath the table.

For Goodness Bakes had been their mom's shop. And from the very beginning, their mother had let Mel work her way up, so by the time she was in high school, she was running the place. And when Melanie was pregnant with Bridget, their mother had signed the whole bakery over to her. Her little sister had quite the gift for cooking and baking. She was absolute magic in the kitchen, especially when it came to baking. It was a gene that Marissa did not share. She was a general disaster in the kitchen.

"Aunt Rissa!" An auburn-haired girl ran over and threw her arms over Marissa.

"Bree!" She gave her niece a big hug. "Oh, this is what I needed! How did you know?" The little girl giggled, and Marissa couldn't help but smile. "And how is the birthday girl today?"

"Amazing. I'm eleven now, you know." She giggled again and glanced under the table. "Can I take Ellie for a walk?"

Marissa grinned and glanced over at Mel. "As long as it's okay with your mother, it's fine with me."

Moments later, Brianna came over to gather up Ellie and take her for a walk.

"Remember, take her vest off. She isn't working when you walk her."

Bree looked so much like Melanie when she was her age. Growing up, Marissa had always assumed that she would be the first to get married and have kids. Melanie had been married for twelve years now, with four kids. And what was crazier, Melanie had married Marissa's ex-husband's brother. Back when they were kids, Brian and Mel couldn't stand each other. Of course, when they were kids, Marissa and Jared were inseparable. Now he wouldn't even take her calls. But again, it was of her own doing.

"You are making it so I have to buy my kid a dog, you know." Melanie sat down across from Marissa, sliding her a plate of cookies. "You look like you need some cookies," she added with a grin.

Marissa raised an eyebrow before taking a warm cookie off the plate. "Well, every kid should have a dog." She paused. "And today is even her birthday!"

"Yeah, maybe for Christmas," Melanie said with a sly smile before furrowing her brow. "What's wrong?"

Marissa sighed and took another bite of the cookie. The cookie tasted like magic and smelled even better. "Nothing."

Mel just continued to stare.

"I just came from Dr. Seaver's office."

Melanie's frown deepened. "I still don't understand how this is ethical."

She wasn't wrong. It was bad enough that she already had to see a psychiatrist once or twice a week. Still, Marissa wasn't allowed to carry her badge or gun without the sessions. That was frustrating. But then there was the fact that the only psychiatrist in a twenty-five-mile radius was Laura Seaver. Laura Seaver was three years older than Marissa, and while they were never friends or enemies, they had run in the same circles. She dated Allison, one of Marissa's best friends in high school. A fundamental problem with small towns.

Mel took one of the cookies off the plate and took a bite. "You okay?"

Marissa just shrugged. "Always." She gave her sister a wry smile. Marissa loved Melanie so much that she wouldn't share any of the grim or awful details of the things she went through. Without even giving it a thought, she always worked hard to give her sister a brave face, whether she believed it or not.

Melanie raised an eyebrow but didn't say anything.

"Sessions with her are just draining," Marissa added.

That seemed reasonable enough, as Melanie took another cookie. "You're coming to Bree's birthday party tonight, right?"

"I wouldn't miss it for the world!"

Even though Marissa never missed a single important milestone, Melanie looked uncertain.

"Why?"

"Well, you know Jared will be there."

Marissa held back a sigh and had to work to keep her face neutral. "Of course," she said before taking a bite of her cookie, trying to hide any signs of her feelings.

"I guess he's bringing his new girlfriend," Melanie said slowly, watching Marissa closely.

"That's cool." Marissa had to force the words out. For Melanie, Marissa put on all the works: They were just in different places. They tried to make it work for so long, but she needed to focus on herself. It was all a load of shit. So, she pretended not to care, or at least to care less. Even though just hearing his name made her heart sink.

Melanie made a face. She didn't necessarily buy Marissa's excuses, but she also didn't pry. "That's not going to be a problem, right?"

Chapter 2

"Of course not. I'm happy for him." Marissa had done all but told him she didn't love him anymore; of course, he would move on. It had been six months. That seemed good enough for Mel. "Good. I'm super excited—we're doing cupcakes instead of a cake, per her request, and the theme is mermaids..." Marissa zoned out. She didn't mean to, and she continued to nod and respond, but her heart wasn't in it. Her mind wandered to her ex-husband, whom she hadn't seen since she told him she wouldn't be going back to Seattle with him.

After her recovery and physical therapy, Marissa came back home to finish healing. And for a year, Jared would come down and spend weekends with her. A whole year. Fuck, she missed him. She missed his voice. He had been her best friend since the second grade. Now he wouldn't even take her phone calls, wouldn't respond to texts. Not that she could blame him. From his point of view, she had been a selfish bitch. She made him put his life on hold for over a year for nothing.

"So we'll see you tonight around six?" Melanie's voice broke back through her thoughts.

Forcing a smile, she nodded. "Absolutely."

The timing was perfect, as Bree ran back through the door with a happy Ellie right on her heels.

"Good timing, kid. I've got to go." She stood, slipping Ellie's vest back on, and gave her niece a big hug, lifting the girl off the ground. "I'll see you tonight." Turning to Melanie, she gave her a quick hug and kiss on the cheek. "Thanks for the cookie, sis. I'll see you later."

Marissa took a big, deep breath as she hurried across the street and looked out on the water. For Goodness Bakes was right on Main Street, across from the dock: only two blocks away from her therapist's and only a ten-minute walk from her quiet neighborhood. But Marissa wasn't ready to go home yet. As though on cue, her phone buzzed in her pocket. It was her mother. She wasn't in the mood for a chat with her mom either. Her calls had become more frequent lately, always wanting to know how she was doing, what she was doing. She couldn't help but vocalize her concern, and since she had given her the house, Marissa felt obligated to answer. But not right now. She would likely see her tonight at the party anyway.

"Let's go for a run, baby." She looked at Ellie, who offered a toothy grin back happily at her. It was her new go-to when she could stomach it. Despite the chronic pain that plagued her, Marissa was in incredible physical shape, at least from an outsider's eye. She would run until she could run no more. Her doctor had advised against such behavior—she was thinner than she should have been—but if she could push through the pain, running always left her feeling in some kind of control. And her abs looked phenomenal.

Marissa started at an easy jog, clenching her jaw as her heels hit the ground with every step. *I just need to push through. This will pass; I am safe,* she told herself. It was always her go-to when she had to force herself to keep going. She repeated it to herself as she made her way from downtown to uptown and along the path to Fort Worden State Park.

As she left the buildings and people behind and made her way into the state park, Marissa went from a jog to a full run, and she didn't stop until she made it to the Point Wilson Lighthouse. She nearly collapsed against the old building, looking down the steep incline. She stood and breathed heavily, her chest wheezing. Ellie was also feeling it as she lay down beside Marissa's feet, head up and alert but panting.

"Sorry, girl." She rubbed the dog's head. She huffed before sliding to sit down beside the dog, pulling her knees up and wrapping her arms around them, just watching the waves. It was windy and cold, and the water was choppy. She could taste the salt in the air. This was one of the few things about Port Townsend that she did love: the smell of the sea always in the air. It made up for its cliche small town vibe that the little town fully embraced.

Looking up at the sky, she sighed. It looked like rain was incoming. She pulled her phone from her pocket and stared at it for a long moment, studying the wallpaper. It was a much happier time; a trip Marissa and Jared had taken to the mountain. A selfie in the snow. She kept meaning to change it but couldn't bring herself to do it. Opening her contacts, she called the first person on her list.

"Hey, Rissa. What's up?" The voice on the other end of the line was unsurprisingly cheerful.

"Hey, Allie. I know you have to work soon, but do you think you could come to grab Ellie and me?"

There was a pause. "Where are you at?"

"We're at the lighthouse. We went for a run and ended up much farther than I planned."

Now there was a sigh. Marissa could picture her friend's disappointed look now. "Yeah, give me fifteen minutes. I'll be right there."

After she hung up, Marissa looked at the clock. She'd left Mel's nearly an hour ago. Leaning her head back against the old wall, Marissa sighed, glancing down at her phone again. She scrolled through her contacts and stopped at Lydia Disher's number. She had been meaning to call for weeks now. She wanted so badly to check in on Lydia and Evelyn, but whenever she heard Evelyn's laugh or saw Lydia's face, all the guilt came rushing back. Backing out of her contacts, she went to her voicemail and stared at the only saved message in her inbox. The message was just over two years old, but Marissa hadn't been able to bring herself to listen to it still. She couldn't bring herself to hear Tom's voice. Closing her phone, she wiped her eyes and looked out into the water, wishing she could think of anything else.

Marissa was still lost in her thoughts when Allison tapped her on the shoulder, causing her to jump. "Hey, lady."

"Hey," Marissa said softly, taking a deep breath, smiling at her dark-haired friend, having to shield her eyes from the sun.

"You need some help?" Allison offered her hand out, and Marissa accepted. "Did you seriously run from your house?"

"From the bakery."

"Jesus." Allison looked like she was about to give her a lecture but held back. Marissa was grateful. "The car is right over here."

Marissa clenched her jaw as she walked. She had pushed herself too far, and they both knew it. So, they took the five-minute drive in silence. Marissa was sure Allie was trying to think of what to say. But she kept her lips set until she pulled up behind Marissa's Cooper.

"Listen. You need to try and take it easy. We both know that was way too much. I don't know what is going on right now, but you need to take better care of yourself." Marissa sighed heavily. "And that's all I'm gonna say on the matter."

Marissa opened the door and let Ellie jump over her and run to the front door of the house. She turned her head back to look at Allie before stepping out of the car. "I appreciate it."

"You know I'm here for you, always, my love." She flashed her big smile. "I'll be working at the bar tonight if you need me."

"Thanks, Allie. I'll call you later."

Marissa watched as Allison pulled out of the driveway and headed out of the neighborhood. When she was out of sight, she sighed heavily and turned toward her front porch. As Marissa walked up the four steps, she scanned the porch floor, furrowing her brow. But as she reached the door, she breathed a sigh of relief that the porch was empty. She looked down both ends once more before unlocking the door and heading in.

"Medicine and a nap." Marissa nodded, responding to herself.

She had a few hours to try and take it easy, and then she could take a shower and get herself to Mel and Brian's. Marissa walked straight to the kitchen to the medicine cabinet. She thumbed through her pain pills, looking for something that would be effective. She was going to have to refill her meds soon. Eventually, she found the one she was looking for and popped two oxys.

"Fuck," Marissa grumbled, the ache rushing through her body. She made her way to the couch and all but collapsed. She had planned only to rest her eyes, but the exhaustion washed over her.

Chapter 3

Marissa woke with a start, feeling Ellie's cold nose pushing her arm. "What, baby?" she asked before realizing her phone was ringing. She nearly fell off the couch, trying to grab her phone from the coffee table. It was Mel. "Fuck, what time is it?" The call dropped and showed two missed calls from Melanie. The time in the top corner read 7:21.

"Fuck!" Marissa snapped and jumped up, immediately regretting the fast movement. She felt her heart beating hard against her chest as she wobbled in place for a moment. So much for that shower she had planned on. She started stripping off her clothes as she made her way up the stairs to look for something she hadn't run four miles in. Less than ten minutes later, Marissa was hurrying back down the stairs after changing her clothes and washing her face. It was really all she had time for.

"Come on, Ellie, we've got to go." She slipped the dog's vest on and darted out the door, locking it behind her.

Thankfully, Brian and Mel only lived two blocks away, although it was uphill. The cool night air helped invigorate her, making the brisk walk in only a few moments. Her phone was ringing again as she walked into their open yard, kids running all over the place. She spotted Melanie instantly, tapping one foot with her hip out, looking just like their mother at that moment, the annoyance painted across her face.

Shoving her hands into her jacket pockets and putting on a sheepish expression, she walked up to her sister and sighed. "Sorry, Mel."

"Don't say sorry to me." She stared at Marissa for a moment before her expression softened. "It's fine. You haven't missed much. We're getting ready to grab the cake. I think we have a few straggler kids coming in."

Marissa nodded and turned to look at her niece's birthday turnout. An insane number of children of varying young ages ran all over the place, screaming and taking part in a massive game of tag. Parents were spread out. Brian was chatting with other dads nearby, beer in hand. They really had a grip on the whole idyllic life.

"Aunt Rissa!" Suddenly, all of her nieces appeared, taking turns to give her the biggest hugs.

"My favorite girls!" She knelt down, admiring all of their dresses as Bethany, who was only four, jumped into her arms.

"Come on! Andy's it!" a dark-haired girl announced to the sisters as she ran by. The three older girls ran off to join the game without hesitation.

Bethany held on to Marissa, giving her a kiss on her cheek. "I missed you more!"

Marissa couldn't stop the smile. "No, I missed you more!" She held on tight to the four-year-old as she stood back up, genuinely smiling.

And then, as though on cue, Marissa saw them coming up the hill before she heard Melanie muttering under her breath, "Look who else decided to show up."

A big grin stretched across Jared's face as he headed toward them. The sight of him still took her breath away and, in turn, annoyed the fuck out of her. He stood tall, wrapped in a black leather jacket and a pair of jeans, baseball cap backward on his head. He was laughing, arm locked with a petite blonde thing beside him. She wore a dark jacket with a bright pink top low enough to show off her enormous bust, which complemented her tiny waist and super-tight jeans, with a pair of sneakers. She was laughing along with him, her perfect cheeks flushed. Her hair was thrown up, probably meant to be some kind of messy bun, but it sat on top of her head perfectly. Marissa turned to the table behind her and surveyed the food, fighting the lump growing in her throat.

"Hey, Mel." Jared kissed Melanie on the cheek before stepping back to introduce his date. "Melanie, this is Kirstie. Kirstie, this is my amazing sister-in-law." He paused, causing Marissa to turn.

When Bethany saw him, she squealed and threw her arms wide open. "Uncle Jared!"

"Is that my favorite Bethany?" He beamed at the little girl.

Marissa put her down so Bethany could run up to him and took a slow breath through her nose.

"And this is Mel's sister, Marissa."

Marissa blinked as Kirstie extended her hand. Marissa shook it, but she barely processed anything the blonde said. Her eyes drifted up to Jared, who only looked back for a second with his cold, green eyes before turning his attention to Brian, who had walked up at some point. Marissa hadn't even noticed. She felt as though she had been slapped across the face.

"Excuse me." She took Brian's entrance as her escape to head inside. She barely even noticed Ellie shoving her nose into Marissa's leg; the dog alerted to her raised heart rate. She darted to the bathroom and locked the door behind her. Marissa stared at her reflection for a long minute, blinking. They had spent nearly every day of their teens together and their twenties married to one another, and now she was just "Mel's sister?" A physical pain twinged through her.

The next hour felt like forever. Marissa smiled and sat through the presents and the birthday cupcakes, although she didn't partake in the food. She was grateful their mom wasn't in town; otherwise, she would have been all over Marissa with the lectures and comments about how skinny she was. But Marissa wasted no time in her exit after giving her niece a big hug and promising a slumber party very soon. She gave her sister a quick hug, gave Brian a look she was sure he would mostly understand, and just left.

When she was halfway down the block, she looked back. Brian and Melanie's house usually seemed pretty big, but in the evening, with their backyard lit up and dozens of children running all over the property, it seemed enormous. Glancing back the other way, she looked toward her own house and sighed heavily. She could go home . . . or not. It didn't matter, so long as she had gotten out of there. So, wrapping her arms around her, she started walking, Ellie trotting alongside her.

Glancing around and behind her, Marissa could hear Tom's voice in her head, scolding her for not being careful. Because she knew this wasn't being careful. Pushing the thoughts of her partner aside, she took in her surroundings as she walked, slowing her pace. She had ended up down at the bottom of the hill, in the direction of the Mansera Hotel. She checked the time on her phone and let out a huff. It was better than being by herself. Allison was working tonight, so the drinks would be good.

Shoving her phone into her back pocket, she made her way to the restaurant entrance that would take her straight to the bar, Ellie keeping pace beside her. It was, of course, packed. It was a Friday night. People were hanging out along the sidewalk just outside, chilling in the parking lot, waiting for seating. When she opened the doors, she was hit first by the noise. Giving a tight smile to everyone, she pushed through, no one really paying her much mind. She grinned as Allison darted by with drinks in her hands. Allison grinned back at her friend with bright eyes before sweet-talking the table where she'd dropped the glasses off. Her dark hair was pulled up into a messy bun on top of her head, and she had just the faintest hint of makeup on her face, making her big blue eyes pop. Allie wore a red crop top that Marissa was not a hundred percent sure was hers, with a denim skirt and black knee-high combat boots. And she was busy working those good looks, stuffing tips into her bra as she made her way back.

Allison was one of Marissa's oldest friends. When they were in elementary school, they lived across the street from each other. And not much changed once Allie moved across town. They still talked every single day, often getting in trouble and grounded together. Their first school dance, rather than getting dates, they just went together. They had been through all the times together, good and bad. Marissa was there for Allie when she came out to her parents as bisexual, and Allie was there for Marissa for each breakup and divorce.

Allie motioned over to the bar while she scurried to the backroom, probably to grab food. Looking around, Marissa didn't see the usual staff, Lee or Rachel, out on the floor, which seemed unusual considering how crowded it was. At the bar, she stood close to the backroom, trying to stay out of the way while she patiently waited for Allie to have a minute.

"Here, Miss," She heard a gentle voice in her ear and felt a soft tap on the shoulder.

Turning, she saw a charming man smiling at her. He gestured to the bar chair he had pulled out for her.

"Oh . . ." Marissa blinked, surprised. The first thing she noticed was his striking blue eyes. He had sandy-colored hair and slightly darker, short facial hair. "Thank you," Marissa said slowly, sitting down in the offered seat. Ellie moved behind the bar and laid down on the dog bed Allie had set up for her, seemingly feeling she was no longer needed.

"May I buy you a drink?" The handsome man stood off to the side, still smiling, offering her his full attention.

Marissa considered him for a moment and flashed him a smile. "Thank you so much." She tossed her hair over her shoulder. A moment later, Allie returned with Rachel, Lee, and a girl she'd never seen in tow. Allie grinned at her and disappeared again with the new girl, leaving Lee to take her order.

Once their orders were in, Marissa extended her hand to the man in front of her. "I'm Marissa."

"It is a pleasure to meet you, Marissa. I'm Jack." His southern accent rose above all the background noise.

Moments later, Allie slid alongside Marissa, giving Marissa her drink.

"I believe this is for you." Allie gave her a subtle smile before turning her attention to Jack. "The friend you came in with might be getting sick in the parking lot. There's a free drink in it for you if you can get him back to his hotel room. He's scaring away customers."

"Of course, ma'am." He nodded his head and flashed Marissa another smile. "I hope to see you when I get back."

She nodded her head, giving him a small smile. "We'll see." She picked up her glass and took a sip, nibbling on the straw. "Thank you for the drink."

"I'll buy you another one when I come back." He promised before heading off into the crowd.

Once he had turned the corner to head out the door, Marissa turned to Allison, who was grinning from ear to ear.

"Well, he was cute." Allie gave her a playful look.

Marissa adjusted in her seat and pulled her phone from her back pocket to fully sit in her chair, offering nothing more than a shrug.

"Oh, come on. That accent? Those eyes." Allie gave her *that* look. "And he did not see anyone else once you walked into the room."

"Now you're just making shit up." She slurped down her favorite drink, wasting no time emptying the glass.

"Having a night, are we?" Allison watched Marissa before sliding the now empty glass to Lee, who had taken cover behind the bar. "Another Dirty Julius. And start her a tab."

Lee nodded, staring at them blankly for a second before looking at the glass. "What's in that again?"

Allison's impatience was written all over her face. "Orange juice, rum, vanilla, and sugar. Orange slice. It's literally the same drink she always orders."

"I'm sorry, Allie. This is why I'd rather stick to food," he grumbled while making the drink.

Marissa bit her lip to keep from laughing while Allison watched him with serious detail. Once he passed over the drink, Allison waved him off. "Go.

Take orders. Tell Rachel it's time to get Emma behind the bar."

Grabbing Marissa's hand, she dragged her over to a new empty table.

"So talk to me before the cute boy comes back. You've got that 'Fuck my life' look."

Marissa frowned, playing with her straw with a huff. There wasn't any point in trying to lie; she would just know.

"Jared showed up to Bree's birthday party with his new girlfriend. To introduce to the whole family." She stabbed the orange slice with some aggression. "He introduced me as 'Mel's big sister.' And that was the only time he spoke to me. And it wasn't so much to me as it was towards me."

Allison gave her a sympathetic look and motioned at Rachel to bring her own drink. She continued to stare, waiting for Marissa to go on. She made sure to suck down most of her glass before meeting Allie's gaze. The second drink was definitely more potent than the first.

"I'm not saying I didn't expect him to get a girl-friend." She paused to think about her words. "She looks like she just graduated high school. With double D boobs. That I'm not really sure are real."

"Tell me more," Allison said patiently, taking her time with her own martini.

Marissa got to the bottom of the glass before glancing at the crowded bar. "She's blonde. Her name is Kirstie. And did I mention she looks like she's twelve?"

"You might have." Allison was giving her a small smile for what Marissa assumed was the encouragement to continue.

She started to say something but clamped her mouth shut. The desire to talk about her had passed. "Tell me about you. How is your night going?"

Allison looked disappointed at the change in topic and shook her head. "Uneventful." She shook her head and glanced down at her phone before looking at Marissa. It was then that Marissa noticed her friend's body language and how very carefully Allison was watching her phone. Raising an eyebrow, she leaned on her elbows.

"Are you waiting for a call?"

Allison waved Rachel back down, finishing her own drink, ordering both of them a new one, and huffed back at Marissa.

"Don't profile me." She pointed the finger at her. "I was just looking at the time."

Marissa wasn't buying it. Everything about her friend's posture said she was anxious, her knee bouncing continuously. But it was clear it wasn't something Allison wanted to share, so she wouldn't pry. For now.

"She's like twenty-fucking-four."

Allison looked relieved before giving Marissa a sympathetic look. "Maybe this is a good thing," she offered, ignoring Marissa's skeptical nose twitch.

"Hear me out. You know I love Jared. And I love you. And I love you together—when you work. But how often is that, really? Maybe this is the push you need to start moving forward."

Marissa bit the inside of her cheek and just shook her head. "I have moved forward. It's fine. I was just ... surprised." That was at least honest. She had been completely surprised.

Thankfully, she didn't have to go into much more detail as Jack returned.

"Good. Now I don't have to feel guilty about leaving you alone. Emma needs help at the bar. Lee is useless." Allie grinned and winked at Jack. "Keep her happy for me, will you?

"I will certainly try, ma'am." He did have a charming accent.

They spent the next half hour talking over absolutely nothing with drinks until Jack ordered them a flight of tequila shots. Marissa hesitated—tequila, while one of her favorites, was hard for her to stomach. But with some encouragement and a charming smile, Marissa took several shots. Followed by several more. After that, her entire world started to wobble.

Marissa grinned at something Jack said, nearly falling over her own feet. "Oh shit."

"Here." Jack reached out and grabbed her by the arms, and Marissa saw red. She yelled and pulled away, grabbing Jack by the arm, and shoving it behind his back. He yelped as Allison ran over to

Marissa's side, taking hold of her. Ellie suddenly reappeared at Marissa's side and grumbled at Jack.

"Here we go." Allie pried Marissa's fingers off Jack's wrist and pulled her to the side. "You'll have to forgive her. Tequila is kind of her vice."

Marissa grumbled and nearly fell into Allison.

"I'm gonna take her to go get some rest. I hope she didn't hurt you, did she?"

Jack just smiled. "Not at all. I'm sorry I may have indulged in all of the tequila shots." Marissa saw him look at her before he looked back at Allison. "Is she going to be okay?"

"Oh yeah, she'll be fine. These guys will take care of the rest of your night and tab. I'm going to take care of her." She made sure she had a firm grip on Marissa before smiling at him. "It was lovely to meet you, by the way."

Marissa's surroundings had become blurry, and the ground was spinning below her feet. Still, before realizing what was happening, Allison sat her down on a bed. "Where did the bar go?"

Allison couldn't hide her amusement, sitting down next to her. "We are in my late-night work-room." Marissa just stared blankly before Allison continued. "I get my own room for those nights I work really late, so I can just crash."

"That makes sense." Marissa blinked. "Because we are in a hotel!"

"That is correct."

"Bathroom?" Allison squeaked, an unexpected fire building in her throat.

Allison pointed. By the time she went to say something, Marissa had already jumped up and bolted into the bathroom. She barely made it to the toilet before everything came back up.

"Fuck tequila."

Allie stood in the doorway, leaning against the frame, her arms folded in front of her. "So, I don't want to be that bitch friend who gives you a mom speech or anything, but you have got to stop with the self-destructive behavior. You know you can't hold tequila. And correct me if I'm wrong, but didn't you divorce your husband the last time because he was drinking way too much?"

"I don't drink nearly that often," she said without taking her head out of the toilet.

"No, but you also aren't eating. You're pushing yourself too far, like today—running four miles." She stepped toward Marissa and brushed all the hair away from her face. "You're not taking care of yourself."

"What's the point?" she mumbled into the porcelain. If Allison heard her, she had no response.

After a few moments, when Marissa had stopped heaving, she heard Allison start the shower. "Come on. I think you got some of it in your hair."

Groaning, Marissa all but crawled to the shower and climbed right in, still fully clothed. She curled

36

up, pulling her knees to her chest, letting the water hit her face while she sat there.

"Okay, strip in there and pass me your clothes. I can run them down to the laundry room later."

Marissa did as she was told, complaining the whole way.

"You're not in your twenties anymore, you know. You can't shoot an entire bottle of tequila."

"That was you in your twenties, not me." She wiped the water away from her eyes and turned her head. "I was too busy getting married and divorced in my twenties. You know, back when I had a sex life. You were the partier."

Allison was quiet on the other side of the shower curtain for a long time. Marissa closed her eyes, feeling like maybe sleep was coming.

"So what happened out there anyway?" There was hesitation in her voice. "I mean, I've seen you pull away from someone before, but that was a little extreme."

"I don't know," Marissa said quietly, opening her eyes. "I don't like being grabbed. Even though I know he was just trying to help me balance. I just panicked."

"Well, you didn't hurt his impression of you at all. He was really sort of smitten with you." She laughed lightly. "I'm pretty sure you could have broken his arm, and he wouldn't have cared."

Marissa didn't say anything. There was nothing to say. With such a severe reaction to an innocent, helpful touch, she couldn't even begin to imagine how she would handle any intimate kind of contact. This was why running had become her substitute for sex. Chronic pain or not, it would continue to fill that need until she could run no more.

"Marissa, you better not be falling asleep in there."

She groaned and shifted uncomfortably. "Did you say there was vomit in my hair?"

"A little, yeah. There's some shampoo in there you can use."

With a heavy sigh, Marissa stared at the shampoo and finally stood up and lathered her hair. It was a half-hearted attempt. Her head was already throbbing, and it felt like there was a stone in the pit of her stomach. Her muscles ached from the heaving, and her arms felt impossibly heavy. Once she was satisfied there was no vomit left, she turned off the water.

"Do you have a towel?"

And just like that, a towel appeared through the curtain. Wrapping the towel around her body, Marissa paused before stepping out. Thankfully, Allison offered her hand to help with stability.

"Come on. I have some pajamas that will fit you." Taking Marissa by the arm, she led her to the doorway and motioned for her to stay while she grabbed the clothes. "Here. Yell if you need any help."

Marissa gave her a weak smile and took the clothes. "Thanks." She took her time getting dressed, still reeling. She had purged most, if not all, of the alcohol she had consumed, but it hadn't made her feel any better. It had killed her buzz, though. Ellie laid there on the bath rug watching her, full of judgment but ready to help steady her if need be.

Once she was fully dressed, she wobbled out of the bathroom and plopped on the bed. Allison was leaning against the headboard, remote in hand, blankly staring at the TV. When Marissa laid next to her, she put down the remote and gave her a smile. "You look good in my Hello Kitty tank. I'm kind of surprised your boobs fit in it."

"It's comfy. Thank you." She smiled but saw the severe look in Allie's eyes. Marissa sighed and looked over at the TV.

"You know, there are going to be so many more events and milestones. Your sister has a whole brood of kids. There are birthdays and holidays. And Jared has other friends, though maybe not many," Allison added, unable to resist taking a shot where she could. "And they are going to have their own milestones and celebrations. If this is about Jared .. . you can't shut down every time he's in town." She paused. "I know this isn't what you wanted to do. But you made a choice to let him go, and now you have to actually let him go."

Marissa turned to avoid Allie's eyes but shook her head. "It's just everything," she said quietly, trying to hide her tears. Allison knew the truth about why Marissa had broken it off with Jared and why she had chosen to stay in Port Townsend. She knew everything because, at the urging of Dr. Seaver, Marissa needed someone close that she wouldn't need to lie to. Since she couldn't tell Jared the truth, Allison was a natural choice.

"I know, hon." Allison put her arm around Marissa's shoulder and hugged her close. "Alright, that's enough of me telling you how to live your life. Let's make a sleepover out of this. I've got a Roku with the works in here, so we can stream anything you want. I can also order us some food if you want to eat. What do you think?"

"I'm down." She smiled, wiping the tears from her eyes.

"Good. Because you didn't actually have a choice." Allison looked proud of herself as she settled in and scrolled through their streaming options.

Marissa took a deep breath, feeling herself relax. She didn't know what she would do without Allison to ground her. She leaned her head on Allison's shoulder as Ellie jumped up on the bed to curl up at her feet.

Chapter 4

Marissa spent most of the week with Allison. The first two days at the hotel, then back at her house on Allie's days off. It reminded Marissa of their high school days. It made her feel somewhat normal. And with Allison keeping her in check and relaxed, Marissa's flare-up had eased, giving her a much-needed rest from the pain. So by the following Friday, she was feeling closer to her usual self.

"Why don't you tell me what happened last week that had set you off?" Dr. Seaver tilted her head to the side and feigned a look of interest.

"It was a lot of things," Marissa answered, although she was sure it wasn't going to be an acceptable answer.

"Was it?"

She stared at the blonde woman and let out a long sigh as Dr. Seaver continued.

"Why don't you talk to me about Jared?"

"He came for Bree's birthday," she replied dryly. Her throat felt sore. "He has a new girlfriend. She looks like she's maybe twenty."

Dr. Seaver stared at her expectantly as though she already knew what was coming. When she didn't say anything, Marissa reluctantly continued.

"He introduced me as 'Mel's sister.' It felt like a slap in the face."

"I can imagine." She kept her face neutral, but Marissa felt like none of this was coming as a surprise. "You were together through high school, right? And married pretty early, didn't you?" Marissa just nodded. "And then you divorced. Remind me why?"

"Because I felt like we were too young, and we weren't ready for that kind of commitment."

"Did you both do any dating after that?"

"Yes."

"Did you still talk?"

"We did. We were still good friends. There were no hard feelings." Their first divorce had been smooth. They both agreed it had been too soon for such a commitment.

"And then, four years later, you were married again, right?"

She had no idea why any of this was necessary. Her relationship with Jared had been public knowledge for everyone they knew. "Yes."

"And that marriage lasted about three years?" Marissa nodded. "Tell me about how it ended that time."

"As Jared became more popular on his radio show and started doing live shows, he started drinking a lot. By the end, he was drunk 99 percent of the time. I moved out, hoping he would give it up. But it wasn't until after I filed for divorce that he sought out help and went to rehab."

"And was he angry with you then?"

"For the first few months, yes. But once Jared was sober, he understood."

"And when he was angry with you, how did he treat you when you saw him?"

"He was an ass, but he still acknowledged me. He still talked to me. He answered my calls and texts. He eventually allowed me to help him find a rehab."

"And you both dated during this time apart?"

"We did." She had even liked Jared's girlfriend. The girlfriend's brother had been in rehab with him.

"And you both still decided you wanted to give your relationship another go?"

Just hearing it all out loud was exhausting. Their history was long and exhausting, and this was twenty years of history summed up in a matter of minutes.

"We did." They had agreed not to marry again but moved back in together, planning on giving it a real go.

"And how was your relationship this time?"

"It was nearly perfect," Marissa said sadly. "We were even talking about having a baby. Things had never been so easy before."

"And then everything happened."

"And then everything happened," Marissa repeated sadly.

"Remind me what it was like right after." She leaned forward with mild interest, clicking her pen every few minutes when she wasn't writing.

"Well, Jared stayed with me in the hospital. And then I went home with him, but it was a lot. I couldn't sleep; I would wake up screaming. I even clawed at him during a nightmare." She thought back, remembering his patience. "So I came home, stayed with my mom for a month or so before she moved out and gave me the house. Jared would drive up on Fridays and spend the weekends with me before returning home to work. We did that for about a year."

She sighed. It had been hard, but they had made it work.

"And then what happened?" Marissa hated how she was making her say everything, even though she was already aware.

"I started receiving pictures. Mostly of me but some of Jared and me. And then some of just Jared. It was the MO of the Couple's Killer. The next step, if it is the same person following the same pattern, would have been to take and kill him."

"So what did you do?"

"I told him I wasn't going back to Seattle. It wasn't up for discussion; I had already made all the arrangements I needed to. I told him that we were over. I told him that we were never going to work. We had already tried and failed. We just kept coming back together because we were familiar. I told him I didn't want to try anymore."

"So you let him go."

"Yes."

"And you did it in a way that you knew he would be angry. Why is that?"

"Because that was the only way he was going to accept that we're done."

"And now, six months later, you're upset he's still angry."

"No. I knew Jared would be angry. I knew it wasn't going to go back to normal. I just..." What did she expect? She wasn't sure.

"It doesn't seem fair to either of you. You expect Jared to be able to just be friends after everything the both of you have endured together. And then when you see him, and he's moved on, you take it personally and completely shut down. You can't live your life that way. If you're going to let him go, you need to let him go."

Breathing heavily through her nose, Marissa felt that shooting pain in her chest. It felt heavy.

"Did it make a difference?" Dr. Seaver continued, not noting Marissa's discomfort.

Marissa shifted uncomfortably before nodding. "He's still here."

This was all the proof she had needed. It had been the only thing she could think to do. Her Hail-fucking-Mary.

Dr. Seaver continued without noting her comment. "It's come to my attention that you've fallen into some self-destructive behavior."

Dr. Seaver raised an eyebrow, and Marissa found herself sinking back into the couch. Her face grew hot.

"You've been running yourself ragged, you're not eating, and there was a concern of self-harm."

"Wow. Is that all?" Marissa folded her arms across her chest, anger rising. The anger soothed the pain, at least.

"Am I wrong? Honestly?" Dr. Seaver gave her a wary look.

Allison. It had to be Allison. "You are wrong. You are assuming this is all about him."

"I'm not assuming anything. Why don't you tell me what this is about?"

"I feel like that kind of speaks for itself."

"If you talk to me in riddles, I can easily make a phone call or two and keep you from returning to work. I know the time for your review is coming up."

Marissa felt like a scolded child, and it was not appreciated. "It feels like I can't close my eyes and not end up back there. Every time. Every time I close my eyes," she finally said. "I don't feel sane anymore. I always feel like I'm just on the edge of a panic attack, always amped up. Even if nothing is happening."

What she didn't add was how often she wanted to scream into the air and ask them what they were waiting for. Her heart rate must have been on the rise because Ellie got off the floor, climbed onto the couch, and put her head in Marissa's lap. If she was being honest, she would have admitted that while she was scared, a part of her didn't care. She didn't care about her own safety. She wasn't looking to get herself killed, but she wasn't particularly interested in saving herself either.

"I have no control. The precinct that I worked at for years doesn't believe me. They take my calls to appease me, but they don't believe me. There hasn't been any progress." Marissa petted the top of Ellie's head, looking at the floor as she spoke. "I have no control."

Dr. Seaver seemed to accept her answer and let out a sigh as though she'd been holding her breath. "Are you having any suicidal ideations?"

"No." That was the truth. She had no interest in ending her own life, and maybe that was the narcissist in her. But she also wasn't interested in protecting it anymore.

"Okay. So what I want to do is up your prescription for antidepressants and give you a different sleeping aid to try." Dr. Seaver prattled on with what she should do when she felt out of control, whom she should call, and so on. Marissa zoned out. Her face was still hot and flush with anger. She barely heard anything else Laura Seaver said. As soon as the time was up, she all but bolted out of the little building.

She made the fifteen-minute walk to the Mansera Hotel in half the time, shoving the doors open and storming past Lee, who was trying to tell her the dining room was closed.

"How could you?" Marissa leaned against the bar, staring at Allison, who stared back while she wiped the glasses.

"How could I what?"

"You know exactly what. You called Laura Seaver." It had to be her. She was the only person she had seen in a week. And Allie didn't deny it.

"I'm worried about you, Rissa." She sighed and glanced around the empty dining hall, nodding at Lee to be anywhere else. "I know you're having a hard time, and I just want to make sure you're going to be okay."

"You had no right," Marissa said half-heartedly. She knew deep down Allie was probably right, but it still felt like some kind of betrayal. "Am I not allowed to struggle?"

"You're allowed to struggle, Marissa." Allison paused, trying to temper herself. "I will not apologize for trying to help you. I love you, Marissa. Let me be here for you." Allison put the glass down she had been working on and put her elbows on the bar, looking Marissa directly in the eyes. "You think I didn't see those cuts on your thighs? Do you think I haven't noticed how heavy-handed you are with drinks and pills? And how empty your fridge is?"

"I'm doing my best, Allison. I'm sorry it's not good enough."

"No, you don't get to do the pity party thing. You're not trying at all, Marissa. You're just giving up. That is the whole problem."

"Whatever. I'm going home." Marissa turned to leave, but Allison stepped out from behind the bar and stood beside her.

"You can be as mad as you want. But you better fucking text me later telling me you're okay. Alright?"

"Fine." Marissa let her glare linger before she whistled for Ellie, who had curled up on her dog bed behind the bar. She stretched and trotted to Marissa's side as they headed out.

Marissa walked much slower back, taking her time. They walked along the pier, Marissa leaning against the railing once she made it back downtown. The worst part of it was Marissa knew Allison was right. It didn't make her any less angry, especially when she thought about how she called Laura Seaver. It made her shudder, bringing up the memories from when the two of them had been a couple. She had probably been Marissa's least favorite of Allison's ex-relations. And that was saying a lot.

"Hey, haven't we met somewhere before?"

A familiar voice startled her, causing her to jump where she stood. Turning, she found striking blue eyes. Ellie stood and put herself between Marissa and Jack, surprising Marissa. "Easy girl. Lay down." The shepherd grumbled but did as she was told. "Jack, right?"

"Yes, ma'am. I hope there aren't any hard feelings about the other night; I didn't mean to upset you."

"Not at all." Her cheeks flushed with embarrassment as she remembered nearly taking his arm off. "And I hope I didn't hurt you, did I? It's all a little blurry."

"Not at all." He grinned. "And for what it's worth, it's all a little blurry for me, too." He glanced down at Ellie, who was still staring at him but lying down as she'd been told. "So why does such a beautiful woman such as yourself look so sad?"

Marissa leaned back against the railing, looking out at the water. "Oh, you know. Just having a day." She smiled over at him. "And what brings you out here? And to Port Townsend?"

"Well, I thought I saw a woman standing by herself out here looking sad, and I just can't let that happen." He looked out into the water. "I work up in Alaska on fishing boats, anywhere between six and nine months out of the year. I came through Port Townsend a couple years ago and thought it would be a nice place to spend the next few months off. Won't be leaving till mid-January."

"Oh wow." Now that he mentioned it, he did have the appearance of one who was built to work on a ship. "That sounds exciting."

"Not really. But it gives me flexibility in life that I like. I can do what I want when I want."

"That must be amazing." She meant it. An untethered life looked more and more appealing sometimes.

"It's not too bad." He smiled at her before looking back at the water. "But you didn't answer my question. What are you doing out here looking so sad?"

Marissa sighed. "Like I said, it's just been a day. It's been a couple of years." Wasn't that the truth? "Because specifically today, my best friend thinks she needs to be my mother," Marissa said with bitterness.

"Not to step over the line since we just met and all, but I'm sure it's only because she cares."

"I can't argue with that."

"Why don't you let me buy you lunch?"

She looked at him and, for a moment, seriously considered it.

"Maybe another time? I think I just need to go home right now."

He looked disappointed, but he smiled back at her. "Of course. As I said, I'm in town until January. And I'm just staying up the road at the Tides Inn and Suites."

"Perfect. Thanks."

"Of course. I look forward to lunch."

He flashed her another smile before pushing off the railing and heading back across the street. Marissa watched him leave, letting out a heavy sigh. Once he disappeared up the road, she turned, leaned back on the railing, and looked into the water. Maybe she should have said yes.

Pulling her phone out from her back pocket, she stared at the background. They looked so happy in that photo. She kept meaning to change it, so she wouldn't feel the heartbreak every single time she unlocked it. But she couldn't bring herself to do it.

She hit the phone symbol, scrolled through her contacts, pressed Call, and listened as the phone started to ring.

Unsurprisingly, it went straight to voicemail. Grumbling, Marissa hung up, scrolled through her contacts again, and dialed a different number. It rang a few times before she heard a woman on the other end of the line.

"Seattle Police Department."

"Hey, Nell. It's Marissa Ambrose." She heard the hesitation on the other line.

"Hey, Marissa. What can I do for you?"

"Is Lieutenant Cooper in?"

"Let me see..." She paused.

"We both know he's there, Nell. Please just put him on." She was sick of the roundabout games they seemed to play every week.

"Alright," Nell said, sounding less exacerbated this week and more sympathetic. "Just give me a minute, and I'll put you through."

Marissa waited for a beat, staring out at the waves coming in as she waited. Just as she was considering taking the phone from her ear to see if Nell had hung up, the phone rang again, and a gruff voice answered on the other end.

"This is Lieutenant Cooper; how can I help you?"

"Lieutenant. It's Marissa." She heard him sigh. "I've been calling to check in but haven't been able to get through the last couple of weeks."

"Ah, yes. Marissa." If he was attempting to cover up his annoyance, he was doing a terrible job. "How are you doing?"

"The same." She let her shoulders fall forward and closed her eyes. "Has anything in the case changed at all?"

"No," he said flatly. "There have been no changes. I told you I would call when there is something to tell you." He paused. "Are you still receiving pictures?"

"Yes. Yes, I am."

"And you still believe it's connected to the case?"

"You know I do."

"Do you have any proof?"

Marissa wanted to yell into her phone. Remind him he was supposed to be a detective and that maybe he should do his job. Instead, she just shook her head even though he couldn't see it.

"No, sir. Nothing more than what I've already given you."

"And you're still seeing your therapist?"

"Yes, sir." She sighed, her temper starting to win. "You are welcome to call her and get the details. I'm of sound mind, and I know what happened. I'm not fucking crazy."

"Marissa." He sounded tired on the other end of the line; they'd had this conversation far too many times to count over the last two years. "No one is saying you're crazy. We just can't do anything without any proof. It doesn't fit the profile. Our unsub never spent more than a few weeks sending pictures." He paused again. "Look, I'll call over to the PD there and see if they have seen anything or have anything to offer. But that is the best I can do right now."

"Cool." It was the best she could force out.

"How are you feeling?" He sounded generally concerned, but it didn't give any sense of comfort.

"Like I'm going crazy," she muttered. "I'll call you back next week."

She hung up before he could respond, sucking in air as though she were out of breath. Replacing the phone in her back pocket, Marissa looked out to the water.

"Let's go home, Ellie." She patted her side and started walking, the shepherd trotting alongside her.

Marissa found herself wishing she had taken the damn car this morning instead of walking. Her body ached by the time she made it back to the neighborhood, having to stop several times before she made it home. She could feel her legs quivering beneath her. She imagined it was what it must feel like to have your bones beaten with a lead pipe. Repeatedly. It was baffling how one day she could run five miles, but the next day an easy walk would be the end of her.

She was entertaining the mental image of lead pipe meeting bone as she approached the porch when she stopped, her blood running cold—there, in front of her door, was a large white envelope, plain with no writing on it. But Marissa knew what it was. Sighing heavily, Marissa took one of the poop bags from her pocket and used it to pick up the envelope and bring it inside. She knew there wouldn't be any fingerprints on it but kept them from contamination, nonetheless.

Unlocking her door and shoving it open, she let Ellie in before closing it behind them and heading straight to the kitchen. Carefully, she opened the envelope and emptied the contents onto the counter. Using the dog bag, she spread them out to look over the photographs; there were only three this time. It probably had something to do with the fact that Marissa hadn't really left the house much in the last week. The first picture was Marissa entering Dr. Seaver's office, the next of her walking along the beach up by Fort Warden, and finally, a photo of Marissa sitting at the bar at the Mansera Hotel.

Shaking off the chill that ran through her, she got up and ran to her study, where she grabbed her fingerprinting kit to run the envelope and photographs for prints. This had become such a routine. And like always, no fingerprints had been left. When she first began receiving photos, she took them to the police station, but that would take hours. No one felt like it was much of a priority. Sure, this fell under the definition of voyeurism, but it wasn't considered a real threat. So she just started checking from home. She was trained and knew how to lift prints and efficiently run them through the same database on her laptop as she could at the station. But then, there were never any prints to find.

When she was certain there was nothing on the photographs, she threw the envelope away and put the photos in the lockbox with the rest. Out of sight, out of mind was the hope. She could hear Tom's voice in her head telling her this was no way to handle a case. She wandered to her pantry, then to her fridge, but just continued to walk through her downstairs until she found herself in the bathroom. Digging through the medicine cabinet, she grabbed the pain pills. She popped two before making her way upstairs, Ellie following behind her. Pulling her phone out of her pocket, she yanked her pants off before climbing into bed. Getting herself under the covers, she grabbed her phone and pulled up her texts.

She texted Allison, only to receive a response moments later.

[Marissa: *I'm fucking fine. I'm going to take a nap. I'm still mad at you.*]

[Allison: *I love you too. I'll be there after work.*]

She again scrolled through her contacts, stopping at Lydia. Lydia Disher, her partner's wife. No, Marissa still had to correct herself. Her former partner's widow. She and Lydia talked about as often as they used to; they were friends but not the kind you spoke to regularly. The difference was now, when she spoke to Lydia, she always felt the weight of guilt over Tom's death. Even Lydia didn't blame Marissa, but that didn't make her feel absolved. She still couldn't call. Instead, she sent a quick text.

[Marissa: *Hey Lydia. Just wanted to say hi. Hope you guys are doing well. I hope you're not working too hard.*]

Lydia was definitely working too hard. Now a single mom and an ER nurse. After hitting send, she put the phone on her nightstand and curled up, calling Ellie close. She tried to relax for sleep, but her body was so tense that rest didn't come. She tossed and turned before she finally sat up, grabbed all the pillows on her bed and arranged them behind her back, and reached for her heating pad from her nightstand. There was a familiar pain in the center of her back, one she knew was going to keep her up most of the night.

Chapter 5

Marissa didn't even bother to get out of bed when Allison came by after work. Thankfully, Allie didn't seem to mind, and she brought food. Nothing too heavy but enough to count as putting something in her stomach.

"I'm still mad at you," Marissa reiterated as she pulled out a famous Jack in the Box taco.

"You can be as mad as you want." Allie settled in next to Marissa on the bed, pulling out her box of curly fries. "It's only because I love you, and I don't know what I would do without you."

Marissa twitched her nose, taking another bite of her food before letting out a sigh. Before she could answer, Allie bumped her shoulder. "I guess that's fair," she muttered.

"I'm sorry, I couldn't hear you. What was that?" Allie grinned playfully.

Despite how tired and achy Marissa felt, she couldn't help but smile. "That's fair. I don't know what I would do without you either." She leaned over, resting her head on her friend's shoulder.

"Now that you've eaten, do you need anything? Is there anything I can get you from downstairs?"

Marissa considered for a moment. She did have an unopened bottle of wine downstairs that was just waiting for a girl's night. But if Marissa were being honest, she wasn't really feeling up to it tonight. Everything still hurt.

"No, I'm good. How long are you hanging around for?"

"Oh, I already ran home and fed Wicket. You've got me all night and tomorrow. I was thinking we could do a movie marathon."

"I'm down." Marissa straightened before leaning over to the other side to turn up her heating pad. She took one of the pillows she had shoved behind her and offered it to Allie, leaving the remaining three as is. She spent the next five minutes struggling to find that comfortable spot that didn't send searing pain up her back.

"I was thinking of a ninety's marathon. Like, *American Pie, She's All That, Ten Things I Hate About You...*"

"Oh, I like that," Marissa answered, finally managing some comfort. "Let's start with *Clueless.*"

Chapter 5

"Definitely," Allie enthusiastically agreed, finding the movie among the streaming channels in minutes.

When Saturday afternoon rolled around, Marissa pulled herself out of bed. Looking in the mirror, she studied the reflection that stared back. She felt like a shadow of her former self. Marissa used to take so much pride in her looks, had routines morning and night, and spent a lot of time focused on her hair. Now, she barely bothered to wash her face. Her dark, thick hair was long and full of curls after spending the last forty-eight hours up in a very messy bun. Throwing some cold water on her face, she pulled her hair back up and went into the hallway. Marissa stopped at the top of the stairs, taking a deep breath before looking into her office. From the hallway, she could see half of the whiteboard beside the window. Stepping into the room, she let her eyes fall over the board, studying the same images and words for the hundredth time.

It was almost a carbon copy of the setup they'd had in the SPD room. Pictures of the victims, descriptions, dates, and times written in marker. Above the pictures of the victims, she had stuck two pink post-it notes, numbered 1 and 2. The rest of the board was covered in different colored Post-its: thoughts she'd had, theories they'd been working.

In the corner was a map with pins when they thought maybe it was about the location. Her own picture was at the end of the board, along with Tom Disher's. Hers was the only one that wasn't marked deceased. While she had been able to re-create the board, she had not had much luck adding to it. She hadn't been in much of a position to do any further investigating. All she could do was add her own theories and watch for the pattern, making sure it wasn't happening somewhere else. With a heavy heart, she stepped out of the room and closed the door, heading down the stairs.

She let Ellie out and went straight to the coffee pot. While she waited for the coffee to finish, she flipped through her phone—no new messages. Fuck, she needed to change the wallpaper.

Opening up her texts again, she opened Jared's conversation. It was now full of unanswered pleas and apologies. It had been over two weeks since her last message. "I hope you don't plan on staying mad at me forever." She knew it was more like putting her thoughts out into the void; he wasn't going to answer. It had been months now. Closing her texts, she scrolled through her contacts and stopped at her sister.

It only rang once before her chipper voice rang through. "Hey, Riss, what's up?"

"Hey. Why don't I take the girls for the night? I owe the girls a slumber party, and you and Brian can have a date night."

"Uh…" Melanie was clearly caught off guard, but as her thoughts caught up with her, she heard the bounce in her voice. "Oh my god, yes! That would be amazing!" She paused. "Are you sure you want all four of them?"

Marissa laughed. "Of course I do. Give me a few hours to pick up some supplies for tonight and then drop them off. You guys deserve a night off."

"Okay. I'll get the girls ready!" She could hear her sister giggling with excitement. "Thank you so much!"

Once she hung up, Marissa grabbed her hoodie and called Ellie inside. "Come on, girl. We're gonna go to the store. Buy some food."

Marissa spent the afternoon at the store, circling the isles and coming home with only junk food and sodas. The girls came over in the afternoon, Mel all but tossing them inside and running off after double-checking once again that Marissa was sure. She adored her nieces. Bree was almost a teenager, as she liked to remind everyone often, just in case they forgot. She looked just like Melanie had when she was that age. Long, wild hair with big, bright brown eyes, tall and lanky but starting to hit maturity. She went out of her way to make sure she was being helpful and was always so sweet.

Blaire and Bridget were eight and six, respectively, but looked and acted like twins. They were little troublemakers who liked mayhem and mischief and loved lying around with Ellie. And then there was Baby Bethany, the sweetest of the four, always giving hugs and just wanting to cuddle.

They spent the evening watching Disney movies and eating junk food. When it came time for dinner, Marissa ordered pizza. Allison stopped in just to check up and stuck around to watch *Tangled* before heading home. As hard as she tried, Marissa couldn't really stay mad at Allie.

As the night went on, Marissa turned the pullout couch into a bed. Slowly, all of them were asleep except Bethany. So she cuddled up with the four-year-old and put on *Fantasia*. Marissa had hoped it would help soothe her to sleep, but as the movie came to an end, she still couldn't sleep. Tucking all the girls in, she carefully got up and brought the empty popcorn bowl to the kitchen.

Sitting down at her kitchen island, she thumbed through her phone, staring at her text messages and searching socials. Before she could think better of it, the phone was to her ear, and the other end of the line was ringing.

"Marissa," a growl echoed on the other end of the line.

"I'm sorry. I know it's late." Marissa closed her eyes. Angry or not, the sound of his voice instantly made her heart race.

Chapter 5

"You need to fucking stop. Stop fucking calling me. Stop fucking texting."

There was a long pause, but he didn't hang up.

"I just..." She hadn't really had a plan when she called. She hadn't actually expected him to answer. "I miss my friend."

"Marissa." Jared sighed heavily. "Just fucking stop."

"I know you're angry. I know that I hurt you. But I need—"

"Nope. Not a chance." He grumbled into the phone, keeping his voice low. More than likely because Kirstie was right there sleeping. "I don't fucking care what you need. I stopped caring about what you fucking needed the second you made it clear you didn't care about what I fucking needed."

"I—"

"Nope. You're going to listen to me. The only reason I answered you in the first place is that I need you to fucking understand that you need to fucking stop. You made your bed; now you have to fucking lie in it." He paused, letting out a big sigh. "I don't know if we can go back, Marissa. From where I'm standing right now, I don't see how."

Dropping her head into her hand, she nodded to no one but herself. "Yeah, okay." What else could she say? "I'm sorry," she all but whispered before she hung up.

He wasn't wrong. Marissa knew he wasn't wrong. What else could she do? She needed him to be this angry. But for the first time, she didn't have her best friend. She dropped her arms and buried her head down on her island counter, only to lift it back up at the sound of footsteps.

"Bridge, what are you doing up?"

"I thought I heard something." She rubbed her eyes. "Are you sad?"

"I'm just tired, honey."

"Mommy says you miss Uncle Jared."

"Yeah, I do," she told the six-year-old honestly.

"She also says Auntie Kirstie makes you sad, too."

Marissa raised an eyebrow. "You're calling her Auntie Kirstie already?"

"Yeah. Mommy asked us to call her that when she took us to the aquarium last week." She covered her mouth. "I wasn't supposed to tell you that."

"It's okay, sweetie." She was going to just pretend she hadn't heard it. It may have been childish, but it was absolutely the answer right now. "Are you thirsty?"

"Nope." The little girl grinned at her.

"Okay. I'm going to get myself something to drink, and then how about we watch *Fantasia 2000* and lie back down?"

"Is that the one with the whale?"

"Yes, ma'am, it is."

Bridget giggled and did a little happy dance. "That one is my favorite."

"Perfect. You go lie down and get comfy, and I'll be right there."

Once the six-year-old was out of sight, Marissa pulled the bottle of rum down from her alcohol cabinet, twisted the cap off, and took a large gulp. And then another. Once she put the bottle back, she grabbed a soda from the fridge. She returned to the living room to watch *Fantasia 2000*, Bridget already sleeping soundly into the first song.

Settling in her Lazy Boy chair, she raised the footrest and pulled a blanket over her, patting her leg to invite Ellie all the way up. The shepherd had her head on Marissa's leg, waiting patiently for an invitation. How they both fit so comfortably in the chair was anyone's guess, but the sixty-pound dog believed herself to be a lapdog.

On-screen, the music had changed from "The Pines of Rome" with the whale artistry to "Rhapsody in Blue." She wasn't able to focus on the cartoon, though. Instead, her mind drifted back to the last time Jared had been in the house with her.

It felt like a lifetime ago when they had been sitting on her kitchen floor, each with a spoon in a carton of vanilla ice cream. Jared had come to spend the weekend with her, as he had done for the past year. He would make the two-and-a-half-hour drive in the middle of Friday, trying to beat traffic, and would stay until usually late Sunday night.

It was only Friday night, and after an enthusiastic hello, they'd decided that ice cream sounded better than dinner. Jared had taken a bite and smiled at her, watching her while she nearly gave herself a brain freeze.

"What?" Marissa had laughed.

"Come home," Jared said after a moment passed, putting his spoon down.

Marissa paused and looked down at the ice cream carton. "No," she said softly.

"Please come home."

Marissa had wanted so badly to put this off. "I'm not going back." She closed the carton, rose to her feet, and put it back into the freezer before turning back to him. She remained standing, leaning her hand against the counter for the support she was going to need.

"What the hell do you mean?" He furrowed his brow. "We talked about this. We've been talking about this."

Marissa sighed, fidgeting as she stood there, trying to avoid his eyes. "I know." She lowered her voice, still looking at the floor as he stood in front of her. "Can we just not do this now? Enjoy the weekend?"

"No. You can't do that. You can't avoid answering me." She could feel his eyes boring into her as he stared intently at her.

"I'm not avoiding. I just..." This had all been so much easier in her head. "I just wanted to enjoy the weekend." She took a slow breath, realizing he wasn't going to let this go.

Without looking up, she heard him clench his jaw. "When were you planning on telling me you weren't coming home?"

"I don't know," she admitted.

"God damn—I'm trying here, Rissa. I've been patient. I've been following the plan. Your fucking plan. And now you're telling me you just aren't going to come home?"

"I know. I'm sorry. Plans change." Marissa sighed. "I just ... can't. I'm sorry."

"Why not?" Jared sure as fuck wasn't going to make this easy.

"Please." She closed her eyes. "Don't ask me that."

"Why? Not?" He emphasized each word.

"Because." Taking a deep breath, she straightened her shoulders, slightly lifting her head but still avoiding his eyes. "I'm not going back. I've already made all the arrangements. For the condo. For the work transfer. I'm—I can't go back."

"So ... so you made this decision a while ago. And didn't bother to even fucking include me?! How long were you going to keep up the lie?"

"I've been trying to talk to you for a while now. I just didn't know how. It wasn't a lie." She paused. "I just wasn't ready for this to be over."

He stared at her, confused. "Over? What the fuck does that mean?"

"Because your life is there." Marissa swallowed anxiously before looking up at him. "And mine is here now. I can't go back there. This isn't fair. To either of us."

"Your life was there, too!" Jared gestured into the vague distance. "We have plans, Marissa. Plans that require us to live in the same city, let alone the same fucking house." He paused, the realization washing over his face. "Are … are you leaving me?"

"Jared." Marissa had closed her eyes and looked away. "You know I love you. You are my best friend in the entire world."

"Answer the question."

She kept going. "The last thing I ever want to do is hurt you."

"Answer the question."

"Things have changed. Plans change. People change." She was starting to feel frantic but refused to let the tears surface, fighting back any sign of weakness.

"Answer the fucking question, Marissa!"

"Yes!" She had snapped as she met his gaze again, forcing the words out. "Yes, I am. We have tried this so many times, and it never works. And I do love you. But it's just not enough!"

"Don't give me that fucking bullshit! Never works? Other than you changing our plans without discussing anything with me, what was going wrong?! Give me a real fucking reason and not some fucking lie for your therapist!"

Chapter 5

He knew her so fucking well. Marissa hadn't been sure she was going to be able to go through with this. "How many times have we given this a try? We've been divorced twice, or don't you remember? Something always goes wrong. I just don't want to do this anymore."

"Oh, come off it. You don't want to do this any-more, but you're fucking happy to lead me on every weekend for how long with the empty promises of coming back home? Of starting a damn family!" His face was red with rage, and he clenched his fists.

"I wasn't leading you on. I meant all of it. I just realized." She started stumbling over her words a little, losing her nerve. She had to slow down. "We've spent so much time trying so hard to make this work. It shouldn't be this hard. We've spent the better part of our lives trying to make it work, and I just don't want to keep working so hard to fix us. I almost fucking died, Jared. I'm sorry, but I can't do this anymore."

"I know!" He had snapped right back at her, hit-ting his fist on the counter. "I know you did, and it fucking scared the shit out of me, and I've been by your side every step of the fucking way!! I've done everything you wanted. Everything you've asked. And you just ... just decided this for us? I don't get a fucking say?"

Marissa blinked, looking down at Ellie, who nudged her leg.

"You have been so amazing. And I'm so sorry. I'm so sorry. But no. Because we'll just keep going in circles like we've always done." She sucked in a breath, the pain on his face so much worse than she could have imagined. "We're familiar, but it doesn't mean we're meant for each other."

"No," Jared had said firmly.

"What do you mean no?" She had stared at him in disbelief.

"No," he repeated.

"It's over, Jared."

"No. No! We've been doing great!" Jared took a step toward her. "Give me a real reason."

Marissa paused, swallowing as she looked down at the floor. "Have we? Are you happy right now? Is this what you thought your life would be at this point?" If this kept going, Marissa was going to cave.

"No one's life is what they thought it would be. I deserve the fucking truth, Marissa."

She had sucked in another deep breath and had taken a step back. She didn't have a choice. "I'm telling you the truth. I don't want this anymore." She had shuddered. She'd had to force the words out, and she couldn't even look him in the eyes.

"You're lying."

"No. It's over." Marissa looked back up at him with wide eyes, taking another step back. "Why would I lie?"

"You tell me."

Chapter 5

"I'm not lying, Jared." She had swallowed hard. "I'm just done."

"That's it? That's all I get? You're really not going to give me a reason?"

"I'm sorry," she'd said weakly.

There had been an uncomfortable silence as Marissa shifted her feet beneath her. When the silence continued, she finally looked up to see him just staring at her. She immediately wished she had kept her eyes down. "I never meant to hurt you."

"Don't!" he snapped, his voice low and quivering, causing her to jump. He turned, grabbing his jacket before turning back to her one last time. "Goodbye, Marissa."

She hadn't started breathing again until she heard the door slam behind him. Crumpling to the floor, she broke down sobbing, unable to catch her breath.

Just the memory of that day brought her to tears. She hadn't meant a single word. There were so many moments she almost backed out, losing her nerve.

Marissa wasn't truly shocked that he was still so angry. Chances were he would never forgive her. Now in her chair, shaking her head, she bit down on her lip hard enough to make it bleed, the metallic

73

taste causing her to shudder. Ellie whined and nosed Marissa's neck, doing her best to be comforting. Scratching the shepherd behind her ear, she glanced over at the girls again before turning back to the movie.

Chapter 6

The next couple of weeks felt like they dragged by. September turned to October, and the leaves started to fall, the streets and sidewalks full of autumn colors. No news came from the SPD.

For Marissa, these weeks were full of various ups and downs, some due to med adjustments, and she still had not been cleared for active duty. Things felt stagnant.

She had been asked to act as an extra set of eyes on some local cold cases—but nothing official. She had actually canceled a few sessions with Dr. Seaver before Herbert Jackson, the head of the Port Townsend Police, knocked on her door with the cold case assignments, reminding her that she wasn't allowed to work unless she saw someone who would give her the green light. The PTPD had been understaffed for as long as Marissa could remember, and Jackson continued to advocate for Marissa to go back to work and join the force, but she couldn't do it without being given the green light. The fact that she had to rely on Dr. Laura-fucking-Seaver felt like some kind of sick joke from the universe.

After a few weeks off, Dr. Seaver's office felt smaller than it previously had. As Marissa shifted to get comfortable on the couch, Ellie laid down at her feet. Dr. Seaver was curled up in her big gray chair, pen in hand, notebook on her lap. She gave Marissa a tight smile, her hair was always pulled back in a neat blonde bun that made her face look pinched.

"So, it has been about three weeks since your last visit."

If it were up to her, she wouldn't be there. She wasn't sure there was a question there, but the long pause made Marissa nervous. "Yes."

"Well, I'm glad you've come back." Something about her voice made Marissa think she didn't really mean it. "Why don't you tell me how the last few weeks have been?"

"Pretty uneventful," she said honestly. If anything, it had almost been boring.

"Nothing of note?"

"I did go on a lunch date." Marissa rolled back her shoulders, not really wanting to talk about it, but there they were. "You remember I told you about Jack, the guy I met at the Mansera?"

76

"Yes," She leaned forward, feigning interest.

"He took me to Doc's Marina Grill. We had delicious seafood, no alcohol. And then walked along the pier."

"That sounds like a successful lunch date."

"It was. Until he tried to put his arm around me." She sighed at the memory, still frustrated with herself. "I once again freaked out. And this time, I couldn't even blame alcohol."

"How did he take it?"

She shrugged her shoulders. "I was honest, although I left out all the details. I just told him I'm still working through some trauma." Marissa hated saying it out loud. It felt like she was openly admitting she was a victim. She was sick and tired of feeling like a victim. "He was actually really understanding."

There was a long pause before Dr. Seaver broke the silence. "But...?"

"But it's not exactly like I see myself dating anyone in the future if I can't be touched."

"Do you want to date?"

"I don't want to be alone," she admitted. "I don't necessarily want to date anyone or be in a relationship. But I would like to think that one day maybe I could accept a hug without freaking out."

"So let's take a closer look at that. Is it a certain kind of touch or a particular placement?"

Marissa thought hard about it. It was a fair question, but ultimately, she couldn't be sure. "I don't know."

"Is it from everybody or just men?"

Marissa thought again. "Well, it's not everybody."

Mel could give her a hug. Jared had been able to, as well. Shrugging, she sat back and folded her arms across her chest.

"I think that not wanting to be alone is perfectly reasonable. And I think it is something that you can accomplish."

Marissa wasn't feeling exceptionally optimistic.

"What happens when you're touched and you have this reaction?"

Marissa was quiet for a long moment, trying to put it into words. "It's like a sudden sharp shock. It hits me all over, all at once. And I want to vomit and scream and escape all at once. I feel like I can't breathe. Like all the air is being squeezed out of me, and I can't inhale. Every inch of my body feels like it's on fire, and I literally want to crawl out of my own skin."

Dr. Seaver nodded in that annoying way she did and wrote something down before looking back at Marissa. "And after this happens and you've been able to remove yourself from the situation, a little time has passed…" She leaned forward with interest. "What happens then? How do you feel? How long do those feelings last?"

Marissa sighed, shifting uncomfortably again. "That feeling of wanting to get out of my skin lasts a while." She thought back to the lunch date and how much she had just wanted to leave after. "I just want to be alone. I sit in the shower for as long as I have hot water; I turn my phone off. I shut down." She shrugged her shoulders. "I feel at a loss. Rage and grief, for anywhere from a few hours to a couple of days." There was something about saying the words out loud, letting them roll off her tongue, that made her shudder.

Dr. Seaver talked about a safe space, making it in her mind and talking herself down. In theory, she was sure there was merit to her methods, but it wasn't resonating with her at the moment. She watched the clock until the time ran out, nodding her head every so often.

Marissa stepped outside, dropping her sunglasses off the top of her head to her eyes, the sun much brighter than she was prepared for. Pulling her phone out of her pocket, she turned it back on. Instantly, there was a new message from Allie.

[Allie: *Where are you at? It's my day off, and I want to take you to lunch.*]

Hitting the call button, it only rang once before Allie picked up. "Hey!"

"Hey," Marissa said with slightly less enthusiasm. "What's up?"

"I want to take you to lunch!" she said in the exact same tone Marissa had read in her text.

"Why?"

"You don't always have to be so suspicious, you know," Allison sighed. "Can't I just hang out with my best friend?"

"I suppose." She still wasn't buying it. Considering they hung out most days, it felt like there was more meaning behind this.

"Let's go to the sushi bar!" The Ichikawa Sushi Bar was their place for sushi and sake.

"Alright. I'm just getting out of Seaver's office."

"Perfect! I'll meet you there in fifteen minutes!"

Marissa hung up and made a face. She didn't particularly feel up to being social, but Allie would just show up at her door if Marissa canceled on her. So patting her leg, she motioned at Ellie to follow and headed down the street, shoving her hands into her pockets. It was only a five-minute walk down the lane and up a hill.

As she arrived, she leaned against the wall, waiting. Ellie sat at her feet and looked around, ears perked forward. Glancing down at her phone as it buzzed, she let out a heavy sigh as messages came through from her mom. She had given up on phone calls, for the most part, and was now spamming her phone with text messages on a daily basis.

80

Chapter 6

[Mom: *Hi Sweetie, I just wanted to check in and see how you were doing. We haven't talked recently, and I just want to make sure you're doing okay.*]

Moments later, another text.

[Mom: *Didn't you tell me you were going on a date? How did it go? I want to hear all about it.*]

Thankfully, Allison arrived seconds later, a big grin on her face. She pushed her sunglasses up, holding her long, dark hair back from her face, and pulled Marissa into a hug. She also took an extra moment to greet Ellie before opening the door. "Let's go. I'm starving!"

Marissa followed her in, still feeling suspicious of the impromptu lunch. As they sat down, Allie wiggled in her seat, unable to stop smiling, although as she watched Marissa, she was clearly making an effort to stop.

"So, what's up?" She raised an eyebrow.

Allie just smiled and shrugged her shoulders. "Let's order first."

"Well, now I'm really curious." She folded her arms on the table and leaned on her elbows. "Besides, I'm pretty sure they are already on their way with our order." They were regulars, so much so that when the staff saw them come in, they usually just went to make the order. "Spill it."

Allie huffed and ran her hand through her hair, putting her sunglasses on the table. "So, a couple of months ago, I started talking to Natalie again."

81

Natalie. Natalie had been Allison's Jared, for lack of a better comparison. They had started dating in high school and had been together on and off forever, although their last breakup had been explosive. Marissa hadn't been sure if they even talked anymore. Obviously, the answer was yes. Marissa kept her expression still and leaned forward as she listened intently.

"We obviously needed to work through some things, but we've decided to give our relationship another try." Allie was all but bouncing in her seat. Marissa waited, expecting something else. She didn't have to wait long. "But to give it a real try, I'm going to move to Seattle."

Marissa didn't know how to react. She could see how excited Allie was, but she felt her heart sink regardless. Here, Marissa had finally moved back to their hometown after over a decade, and now Allie was going to escape it. And for someone who had left Allison in pieces. That breakup had nearly destroyed her. "That's ... not what I expected," she managed honestly.

Allison let out a sigh. "I know. And I know what you're going to say—"

"Do you?" Marissa leaned forward on her elbows, watching her friend's expression drop. "Don't get me wrong, Al, I want you to be happy. But do you remember your last breakup?"

The solemn expression on Allison's face told her that she did remember. If Jared and Marissa's relationship was considered turbulent, then Allie and Natalie's was a damned dumpster fire.

"It wasn't great," she admitted.

"Allie, I think you're understating it a bit. You were so unhappy, you started cheating on her."

Allison took a deep breath through her nose and folded her arms in front of her on the table. She went to say something as the staff came over with their food. Smiling up at the waitress, Marissa thanked her before sighing back at Allison's defeated expression.

"I'm sorry. I just want to make sure you've thought this through. That's all."

"I have. We've been talking for months…"

Marissa blinked. She had been so wrapped up in the despair of her own life, she hadn't even noticed a change in Allison. As she thought back, she could see it clear as day. Some fucking detective she was.

"For months. We are in a really good place, both of us. And we've been talking about my moving to Seattle for a while now." Allie started moving her food around with her chopsticks, no longer meeting Marissa's gaze. It only took her a second to understand why.

"But you've been putting it off," Marissa said softly.

"I've been putting it off." Allison nodded, lifting her eyes back up to meet Marissa's. "I wanted to make sure you were going to be okay."

Now Marissa looked down at her food, though she wasn't feeling particularly hungry anymore. She couldn't be the reason anyone put their life on hold. She may not have felt great about Natalie, but she wasn't going to let anyone, especially Allison, miss out on a chance to live her life because of her.

"Allie," Marissa started, trying to pick her words carefully. "If you're sure this is what you really want. If this is what is going to make you happy, then I fully support you. Don't you dare put your life on hold because of me."

She shot a finger up as Allison went to say something.

"I am a big girl. I will be okay. Besides, Seattle is not that far. It didn't come between us while I lived there, and nothing is going to change with you there.

Allie smiled with relief, reaching over to put a hand over Marissa's. "Thank you. I'm really happy, Riss."

"Then I'm happy for you." And even though she still wasn't sure about Natalie, the glow that surrounded her friend did make her smile. Allison deserved to be happy.

"Hey, how was your lunch date with what's his name? Is it Jack?"

"Yeah." She gave her friend a smile. She almost retold how the lunch date went, just like she had told Seaver. But instead, she just gave her a shy shrug. "It was really nice. He's sweet."

"Are you going to go out on a real date with him next?" Allie was still vibrating with excitement, and Marissa didn't want to take away from that.

"Maybe." It was unlikely, but for her friend's sake, she would make it seem possible. "So. When are you planning on making the move?"

Allison shifted in her chair. Marissa could tell she wasn't going to like the answer. "In a couple of weeks." She gave Marissa a sheepish smile. "I've been trying to find a way to bring it up now for a while."

"What's a while?" She raised her eyebrow, taking a sip of her water.

"About a month. Month and a half."

Marissa made a face, unable to stop herself. She wondered if this was how Allie felt when Marissa left Port Townsend. It was so long ago. She could still remember the excitement of moving out to the big city and starting her life with the man she loved. They were married right after that. Of course, that had been over a decade ago and hadn't worked out. She hoped it would be different for Allie and Nat.

"What's the plan for the house?"

Allison seemed relieved and wiggled more with excitement as she relayed all the plans to Marissa. "I'm going to list the house on Airbnb. That way, it's there whenever I'm in town but can pay for itself."

"Your house is pretty much built to be an Airbnb." Allison owned a small one-bedroom house, conveniently nestled the perfect distance away from downtown, uptown, and Fort Warden.

"Agreed. I'm pretty excited."

They stuck around the restaurant for a couple of hours, talking about all of Allison's plans. Marissa wanted to be supportive but still could not stop her brain from recounting that last, explosive breakup. But maybe if Natalie and Allison could get past their issues and still come together, perhaps there was some hope that she and Jared could at least find some common ground again.

Allison was all but glowing as she shared her plans. Marissa listened intently, trying her best to ignore the voice in the back of her head that kept pointing out all the little things she had missed over the last couple of months. She had been too involved with herself to put any of it together. She looked at the pictures of the apartment Allie was moving to, which she had found with Natalie. It was a beautiful place in a nice location. Things had been paid for, and everything was already in motion. Marissa still wasn't sold on if it was going to work or not, but it was clear that Allison was ready to make the leap.

Marissa did her best to be helpful while Allie got ready over the next few weeks. She helped her pack boxes and went to the thrift shop to donate a few things that no longer had a place. She helped her clean the house, not that it was a big feat; it was a small house. Marissa told her about all the hotspots she would need to visit and the best places to eat, giving her the grand Seattle tour without actually taking her around from place to place. The internet was great for that. Fuck, she was going to miss her.

Before they knew it, the night of her going away bash was upon them, and Allison was set to leave the next day. Marissa had planned everything down to the very last detail, with a little help from Melanie. The sun was barely in the sky when both Melanie and Marissa arrived on Allie's doorstep, still dressed in their pajamas, and knocked on the door. When a groggy Allison answered, they allowed her to put her shoes on and then shoved her into Mel's car. Mel had closed her bakery to the public for the day, cooked some delicious pastries for breakfast, and set up the TV in the dining room so they could comfortably spend the morning watching classic films, such as *Breakfast at Tiffany's* and *Casablanca*—two of Allie's favorites; she favored herself to be a more modern version of Scarlett O'Hara.

As the afternoon rolled around, they piled back into Mel's car, still in their pajamas, and drove down toward the Fort and the beach. It wasn't exactly beach weather, but they got in the icy water like giggling girls anyway and splashed around. Ellie, not a huge fan of water, watched from a safe distance. It was something they had done often during their school days, especially when they were skipping classes.

"God, nothing beats the beach in October." Marissa breathed in the salt air as she sat down on a rock, her bare feet in the water.

"Agreed." Allie grinned, sitting next to her and looking out into the Sound.

"There is something wrong with the two of you because it's freezing out here." Melanie dramatically pulled her arms into her oversized hoodie.

"No, it feels just right." Marissa closed her eyes, feeling the breeze. "I'm going to fucking miss you."

"I'm going to miss you, too." Allie sighed. "But like you told me all those years ago, Seattle isn't that far."

"I know." Now it was Marissa's turn to sigh. Taking another deep breath, she opened her eyes as she exhaled, looking over at Allie. "You are going to love it so much, Al." Marissa smiled, thinking back to the excitement of moving back to the big city. "And you guys are in the center of it all."

They hung around the empty beach, taking in the brisk, cool air for a bit longer.

After stops at Allie's and Mel's to allow each to get ready for the night, they ended up at Marissa's, where she also changed into evening-appropriate clothes and took some precautionary medication, hoping to stave off the aches till the next day. She just wanted to enjoy this night to the fullest.

They met up with some other friends of Allie's, acquaintances Marissa knew and was friendly with, but nothing beyond that. They started at Sirens, a bar on the pier. The women munched on appetizers and enjoyed fancy cocktails.

"I'm so excited for you!" Mandy, the sandy blonde-haired girl exclaimed, taking tiny sips off her drink.

Marissa did her best to mingle with the rest of the group, but something about being with more people made her feel more isolated. She did, however, make sure to keep up with the drinks. And the more drinks she consumed, the easier it became to be social.

By the time they made it to the Mansera, the world was wobbling beneath Marissa's feet. Ellie was leaning hard against her legs, and she realized more than once that she was leaning down to use the shepherd to regain her balance. It was loud and crowded, and everyone else was paying for their drinks. She vaguely remembered seeing Jack and his charming smile; thankfully, he kept his hands to himself.

It felt like no time had passed at all when Marissa was hugging Allison close, standing on the tips of her toes as she squished her best friend. "Fuck, I'm going to miss you."

"I'm just going to be a ferry ride away," Allison said with a grin as she pulled back.

"You better call me when you get there."

"I'll call, but that hangover is going to be a bitch," Allison laughed.

Mel took Marissa's arm and led her toward their ride. "Why do you have my shoes?" Marissa asked Mel when she spotted them in her sister's hands.

"I'll tell you tomorrow," Melanie said with amusement as she got Marissa into the back seat of the car. Ellie jumped in beside her before Mel got in.

Marissa felt like she had just closed her eyes when Mel shook her shoulder and led her out of the car. "Did we get an Uber? Because it's like a two-minute walk," Marissa observed, proud that she wasn't stumbling over her words, as it took effort.

"Walking implies that you wear your shoes," Melanie said as she pulled Marissa's house keys from her purse and unlocked Marissa's door, first letting Ellie in and then leading Marissa in.

"Do you want some food?" Mel offered, attempting to lead her to the kitchen.

"No," Marissa said quickly. Even in her drunken stupor, she didn't need Melanie to see how little she actually had in the kitchen. Although, the ice cream in the freezer would be amazing.

"Do you want to go up to bed?"

"Um..." Marissa did not. She wasn't even sure why she was already home. Wasn't it too early? "Nah. You wanna stick around and watch some TV with me?"

"No, hon, I need to go home," Melanie said with a smile, plopping Marissa down on the couch. "But we'll hang out soon."

"You're my favorite sister," she announced.

"Well, being on the same continent makes that easier."

If Marissa didn't know any better, she would have thought the expression that flashed on her sister's face was sad. "What's up, buttercup?" She had meant to sound more serious than it came out.

"Nothing," Mel said with a smile Marissa did not find convincing. "Do you need help getting upstairs?"

"No, I'll be good right here." She pulled Mel in for a hug, holding her sister close for a long moment.

"Alright. We'll talk tomorrow, okay."

"Okay, little sis. I love you!"

"Love you too, Riss."

Marissa collapsed on the couch as she heard the door close behind Melanie. She struggled to ignore the feeling of sadness as she stared at her ceiling. She knew if she closed her eyes, dreams would follow, and if she lay there continuing to stare at the ceiling, her mind would wander to places she would rather not go. Fumbling around the couch, she felt around for the remote. She was sure there was something on that would eat up the time until she could pass out.

Chapter 7

Marissa groaned at the harshness of the light, pulling her sunglasses up on top of her head. The sun was only beginning to come up, the orange and pink hues of sunrise still in the sky. "What's going on, Jackson?" It wasn't like this was routine. Marissa was still technically benched from working at the moment. Still, on the phone, Jackson had explained that in all his years as sheriff, he had only seen three homicide cases, and none of his current staff had any experience.

Marissa glanced around the empty street. It was still too early for most of the shops to even be open. On the corner of the main road, stairs led to a candle shop and an insurance company. But more relevant to the moment, they also led Port Townsend's questionable Shanghai tunnels.

"Come on. She's down here." Jackson led her down the stone stairs, waiting for her to follow. As she hit the last step, he sighed and stopped her. "When I called you in, I didn't know." The older man placed a hand on her shoulder, causing Marissa to pause before allowing her to move further. As she met his eyes, all the air left her lungs. Panic rose and lodged in her throat as every worst-case scenario ran through her mind.

"Who?" But she didn't wait for him to answer, removing his hand from her shoulder and turning to the spot beneath the stairs. There, past the gate, was a woman's body. She reached out for the wall to brace herself as she walked closer and then stopped, immediately identifying the lifeless body sprawled on the ground.

Allison.

She was on her back, her eyes still open and looking off to the right. She was still wearing the clothes Marissa had seen her in less than ten hours earlier.

Realizing Ellie was following right behind, she turned to the service dog. "Down. Stay." Ellie immediately lay down, staying put, as Marissa approached the body.

Taking in a deep breath, she slowed her breathing and tried to focus. There was noticeable bruising around her neck and around her wrists. Based on the dark patches she could see, the blood had pooled on her back, but it was still blotchy. Meaning the time of death was somewhere between six and eight hours earlier.

Before she could say anything, Herbert came up alongside her, wiping the sweat off his forehead with one hand. "Mr. Davenport is on his way."

Marissa nearly coughed at the mention of the medical examiner's name. The man had been working on retiring for the past decade but could never bring himself to do it.

"She's been here somewhere between six and eight hours, based on lividity. She's still dressed in the same clothes I saw her in last night. She's going to have alcohol in her bloodstream because we were out drinking for most of the night." She came along the body and squatted down, looking over her friend. "Strangulation was most likely the cause of death."

"You don't need to do this. Not right now."

Realistically, she shouldn't have been there. But they had called her in. And it was Allison.

"It's fine." She managed in a strained voice. "All of this needs to be bagged up." She pulled herself back up to her feet, looking around. "Where is her phone?"

Herbert shook his head. "We haven't come across it yet."

"And who called it in?"

Before he could answer, she was already making her way back to the stairs and up to street level. Thankfully, Herbert kept up with her.

"We received two calls: one from the ghost tour guide, Simon Adams, and second from Mr. Lawson, owner of the insurance company down here. I've got Stilinski taking their statements."

Marissa nodded. "Okay. I need some air."

She didn't give him a chance to respond to her and all but ran up the rest of the stairs. Using the stone pillar at the top of the stairs, she took several deep breaths, trying to get something under control. Her thoughts, her breathing. Anything. Ellie yipped at her, trying to get her to sit down, but Marissa barely paid her any mind.

Looking down the street, she could see people were beginning to open up the town, just like any other Saturday morning.

"Oh my god," she whispered to herself, her knees shaking.

She had seen her fewer than eight hours ago. Celebrated her big move. She was finally getting out of this stupid little town, ready to make a commitment she had been dangling in the wings for years. And now it was all gone. Marissa rushed over to the garbage can on the corner as bile forced its way out. She heaved over the can until she was sure she had dislodged a rib bone, dropping to the ground.

Marissa's mind was racing. She needed to call Tyler, Allison's brother. Their parents had died years ago, and now it was only the two of them. No, now it was only him. She would need to call Natalie. Natalie would be expecting Allie this afternoon.

Marissa forced herself to stand up and move back, sitting on that top step leading back down to the tunnel. She stared at her phone in her shaking hand. Marissa needed to call someone. She couldn't go back down there. She couldn't compartmentalize yet. That was Allison, not a body. Opening the contacts on her phone, she read through the same names for several minutes before finally pressing "Call" on a name.

"Mel?" her voice shook, quieter than she had intended.

"Marissa?" Melanie was immediately concerned.

"I need you. Main and Taylor Street. The Shanghai tunnels."

"What's wrong?"

"It's Allison." She lost any composure she had left, sobbing openly.

Veronica, who had been stationed by the stairs to make sure no one contaminated the crime scene, approached her, leaned down, put an arm around her shoulders, and assured Marissa she'd stay with her until Melanie got there.

She felt like she was watching the scene unfold, an out-of-body experience. With her knees pulled to her chest, she was trying to take up as little physical space as she could. By the time Melanie arrived, she was in a full-blown panic. Her hands were frozen, and her whole body shook violently, her breathing rapid and unsteady. Veronica filled Melanie in, as Marissa was unable to form words.

Melanie tried to ask her things, but Marissa could hear the blood pumping in her ears, unable to focus on any words around her. Ellie all but curled into her lap, resting her nose against Marissa's neck.

They sat there on the curb for a long time like that. The corner was cordoned off as a crime scene as the street started to get busy, the tourist town beginning to wake up. Marissa hadn't noticed Mel calling Brian, but he arrived nonetheless just as she started pulling herself together.

She stood, though her hands were still frozen in tight fists. "I want updates. Right away." She had to spit the words out to Jackson, who solemnly nodded. "I'm on this case. I just need a minute." No one argued.

The truth was if she had still been with the SPD, she wouldn't have been allowed to be on this case. It was a conflict of interest. But the small town had limited resources, and they wouldn't ignore the advantage of having her on the team. The entire reason she had been called in was because of her homicide experience.

Her sister and brother-in-law helped her home, and Melanie stayed with her, sitting at her kitchen island and making them tea.

What Marissa really wanted was a Xanax, but for some reason, she felt a sense of shame at the idea of Melanie seeing how many meds filled her medicine box.

"Someone needs to call Tyler. And Natalie."

"Of course. I will call them both," Melanie volunteered, passing her a mug of hot tea. "What can I do for you?"

"Nothing. I just—" Marissa paused, staring at the liquid in her cup. "I just need a minute to compartmentalize."

"You know you don't have to work on this case." It was a half-hearted statement because Melanie knew her better than that.

"Yes. I do," her sister said quietly.

"Have you eaten anything?" Marissa just shook her head as Melanie opened her fridge. If Marissa had been more alert, she would have stopped her to avoid the lecture she knew would follow. "Have you been eating at all?" Melanie sounded horrified.

"Of course. I just haven't gone shopping yet," she said casually, hoping Mel would believe her. Whether she did or not, she let it go, but not before giving Marissa a disapproving mom look.

"I need to lie down," Marissa said after drinking most of her tea. She wasn't even sure she had tasted it. All of her just felt numb.

"Okay, let's get you upstairs then."

"No, I know you've got to get to work. And I'm a big girl. I can take care of myself." Sometimes she wondered if Melanie remembered who the big sister and the baby sister were in this relationship.

"Nonsense." Mel hooked her arm in Marissa's and started leading her up the stairs. "I already had Brian run down and close up for me today on his way to the paper." She turned to Marissa when they got to the top of the stairs. "I'm not staying because you can't take care of yourself; I'm staying because you shouldn't have to be alone right now."

With a sigh, Marissa nodded. "Okay." She patted her leg for Ellie to come to join them. "My room is a disaster, though. Don't judge me."

Melanie waved her off, tossing Marissa's clothes from the night before off her bed, and pulled the covers down. "Come on." She got her into bed before climbing up beside her, apparently unable to resist her mothering tendencies. Ellie hopped up once they were both settled and whined as she put her head on Marissa's legs. Melanie started scrolling through Netflix, looking for something to keep in the background.

Marissa fell asleep almost immediately. She was in and out all day. She heard the TV on occasion, although she had no idea what her sister was watching. She heard Melanie on the phone, too.

"Natalie, I'm so sorry—"

Marissa rolled over and tuned her out. She couldn't listen. It was so hard to comprehend. Last night, they had been laughing and drinking together. Things Allison would never do again. She drifted back off to sleep.

Marissa felt Melanie shaking her once, trying to wake her up. She must have had a nightmare. Her sister wanted to assure her she was okay. She just rolled over the other way.

A few hours later, Marissa woke up to her sister sounding stern. She noted the room already getting dark and Melanie had turned on the lights.

"Look, I thought you would want to know," she paused. "Well, how do you think she's doing?"

There was a long stretch of silence.

"She's asleep right now. I'm staying with her tonight."

Another period of silence. She assumed it must have been Jared. Marissa stayed perfectly still, feigning sleep, but she was aware of her sister standing in front of the window, looking out at the darkening sky, occasionally glancing back in Marissa's direction.

Melanie lowered her voice, "You know, Jared, it would probably mean a lot to her to hear from you."

Marissa could only imagine the things he was saying on the other end of the phone. Regardless, the last thing he was going to want to do was to talk to her.

Allison and Jared: Marissa's two best friends in the entire world. Despite her sister's presence, she had never felt so alone. Rolling back over, she pulled the blankets up close and tried to block out everything as she prayed to find sleep again.

Chapter 8

Marissa stared at the doorknob for a long minute, still unable to believe she was standing there. She had just been there, helping Allie get the last of her stuff boxed up to send to Seattle. The boxes were still stacked up in her car parked out front along the curb. A couple of boxes were still on the front porch.

Using her own key, she unlocked Allison's front door and pushed it open. The sun shone through the front windows, lighting up the small living room. Ellie followed her in and curled up in the sunlight; the house was small enough that she was able to keep track of Marissa wherever she went from right there. It was exactly as Marissa, Mel, and Allie had left it the two days before: clean, bright, and cozy. Precisely as it was described on the Airbnb website.

But Allison had planned on spending one more night there, so maybe there was still something. Marissa went straight to the bedroom, a small room with a bed in the middle, end tables on both its sides, and a window above the bed. In the center of the perfectly made bed lay a large gray cat who lazily stretched out and yawned, reaching for Marissa as she came into the room.

"Oh, Wicket..." She almost cried again, although she wasn't sure she had any tears left. Reaching out, she gave the cat belly rubs and wondered if she knew anything was wrong. Stepping away from the cat, she wandered over to the end tables and opened the drawers. They were all bare. Allie had packed up everything.

She spent the next couple hours searching every nook and cranny she could, but she found nothing. She checked the time on her phone. Tyler was driving in from California. She didn't know if he would want to stay there, but she knew she needed to get everything back inside. With a heavy sigh, she glanced around once more, but she was convinced that Allie had left nothing behind to be found.

Marissa moved to the porch and started taking the boxes back inside—boxes from the porch, the car, and the trailer she had rented to get her things to Seattle. By the time she got everything back inside, the sun was beginning to set. She called U-Haul and asked them to come pick up the trailer considering the circumstances. Thankfully, they were accommodating. She had just sat down at the kitchen table with a glass of water when she heard the knock at the door.

As she got to her feet, she heard the door open and smiled as she saw Tyler's familiar slim figure walk into the living room. "Hey, Riss," he said softly. He looked just like Marissa remembered him: tall and slender with a dark mop of hair that fell in front of his blue eyes.

"Hey, Ty." She had promised herself she wasn't going to cry, but with the sight of him standing there, she couldn't stop the tears forming in her eyes.

Without a word, Tyler stepped forward and pulled her into a hug, and any ability to hold those tears at bay just fell away. He held her close, tears of his own falling down his face and onto her neck. He might as well have been her younger brother, even though he stood nearly a foot taller than her. They had all grown up together.

Eventually, they both pulled back, wiped away their tears, and sat down on either end of the couch, looking at all the boxes in front of them.

"I can't believe she's gone," Tyler finally said.

Marissa looked down at her hands as she fiddled with the cuticle on her thumbnail. "I know. We were just celebrating. I just helped her pack all of this up."

"I suppose we have to go through all of this," he said after a long moment.

"We don't need to do that right now," Marissa said gently. "How long are you here?"

"At least the week. To help make the funeral arrangements and everything." He let out a heavy breath. "Figure out what to do next. But then I have to get back."

"Of course." Now it was Marissa's turn to sigh. "Is there anything I can do? Is there anything you need?"

"You've already done more than enough." He gave her a smile. "Just catch the son of a bitch who did this."

A soft mew came from the kitchen as Wicket made her way out to them in the living room. She rubbed up against Ellie before jumping onto the couch, impatiently seeking attention. Marissa smiled at the cat, giving her the pets she was searching for.

Tyler rubbed his face and took a deep breath before pushing the hair from his eyes. "Poor girl, she has no idea what's going on."

Marissa had to bite her lip to keep herself from crying again, focusing her attention on the gray cat. Tyler got to his feet, motioning for her to stay.

"We can't just sit here and be sad," he said finally. "We need to drink. Stay here; I've got stuff in the car."

"Sounds good to me." A drink was exactly what she needed. Ellie was with her, and she had no one to answer to. There was nowhere else she needed to be.

Moments later, Tyler reemerged with two bottles of Glenfiddich Whiskey in his hands. "Dude. That is not cheap shit."

"No, ma'am, it is not." He gave her a sly smile.

"What do you do again?"

He laughed. "I'm a—" he started, but Marissa threw up her hand.

"Never mind. You know what, I'm gonna stop you right there. Just go get us some glasses, and let's get drinking."

He nodded, heading to the kitchen. Marissa looked around for the remote to the little TV in the corner of the room. She let Netflix pick for her, turning on the first episode of *New Girl*.

"How appropriate," she muttered as Wicket crawled all the way into her lap. A moment later, Tyler returned, two full glasses of whiskey and the bottle all in hand.

"Oh, Allie loved this show."

"Yeah, she did." Marissa took her glass from him and raised it slightly. "To Allie."

Tears fell as Tyler raised his glass, and then both shot back large gulps of their drinks. It burned her throat but warmed her stomach. She welcomed the feeling.

Sitting back, Marissa allowed herself to get comfortable on the couch, taking her time and sipping the rest of her whiskey. She planned on savoring it and enjoying the laughs from the mindless sitcom.

The next thing she knew, she was slipping off the couch in her sleep.

"Fuck," she mumbled, sitting up. On the table in front of her sat two empty glasses and two empty whiskey bottles. At the other end of the couch wasn't Tyler, but Ellie, sprawled out on her back and perfectly content and asleep.

Without getting up, she looked around to see where Tyler had gone. She just barely had eyes on him curled up on Allie's bed, Wicket at his feet. Sighing, Marissa put her feet on the ground, pulling herself upright. Her head was pounding like a fucking gong going off. That was a lot of whiskey. Top fucking shelf whiskey.

"Phone," she mumbled half coherently to herself while trying to remember anything after the second glass. Looking over at the TV, Netflix was in judgment mode, asking if they were still watching but already into season two. Where the fuck was her phone?

As though a sign, she heard her phone's "Whistle Stop" from *Robin Hood* ringtone going off, although it took her a minute to find it deep between the cushions. She dug her phone out to see it was Herbert Jackson calling.

"Fuck," she muttered before answering. "Hello?"

It was like the man had a radar for when she was hungover.

"Yeah, I've been trying to get a hold of you. Where have you been?" He didn't sound too annoyed or too surprised. Marissa didn't know if that annoyed her or not.

"Sorry. Tyler Drake got in last night...."

"Oh. Right." Jackson was uncomfortably silent for a moment. "Well, are you available? I know you technically haven't been cleared to work, but we've got another body."

"Of course. Who? Where?" Marissa's head started to clear.

"We're down by the fountain where that ghost tour starts. It's Old Lady Cindy."

The homeless woman that everyone in the small town knew. Marissa blinked, glancing over into the bedroom.

"Okay, let me just get someone over here for Ty, and I'll be there. Give me fifteen, twenty minutes tops." She was being generous, but it seemed to pacify the more senior sheriff.

Jesus fucking Christ, it was only 4:23 a.m.

She frowned as she hung up the phone. Tyler didn't need a babysitter by any means, but that didn't mean he needed to be alone right now. Scrolling through her phone, she landed on the only person she could think of.

"Hey Mel, I know it is insanely early, but I need a huge favor..."

It was a big ask, she knew, but Mel and Tyler had grown up close, so it wasn't a huge stretch. They were friends, and that was what Tyler needed right now.

Secrets & Photographs

Once Melanie arrived, Marissa all but ran out the door. Allie's place was close to the most recent crime scene, only taking her moments to walk to the fountain just off the main street. It was a giant, gaudy fountain at the bottom of the hill separating downtown from uptown. Crossing the crime scene line, she walked over to Jackson, who she was surprised to still see on the scene.

"We're still waiting on Davenport; he was even harder to get a hold of than you. And that assistant of his was spending the week in Seattle for some kind of conference."

Marissa knelt beside the body of what used to be Cindy, putting on gloves to not disrupt the scene. Cindy was an older woman, probably somewhere in her sixties or seventies. She had been panhandling around Port Townsend for as long as Marissa could remember, from when she was a little girl. Many stories had circulated all these years about what had landed her in the lifestyle Cindy had seemingly chosen for herself. The one that had been told to Marissa was that Cindy's husband, the love of her life, had died in a war, and she just left her house one day and never went back. Cindy had left her home, her family, and most said, a lot of money. She just never went home. Marissa brushed the hair out of Cindy's pale face and hoped that maybe she had found some peace.

"The blood has barely begun to pool; she's probably been there less than six hours. Maybe less than

108

four." She looked at the bruising along the neck, taking a breath through her nose. "Again, I would say strangulation is the probable cause of death."

Looking her over carefully, Marissa frowned.

"Though, she has blunt force trauma to the back of the skull, so you'll need to wait for the autopsy for the official cause of death." Getting back on her feet, she took the gloves off. "Was there anything from this crime scene connected to the Drake case?"

It felt weird to refer to Allie as "the Drake case," but she needed to prove she could compartmentalize.

Jackson shook his head. "Strangulation and found along a ghost tour. Other than the fact that our crime rate is so low, there isn't much reason to think they are connected."

Marissa twitched her nose, displeased at the dismissal. It was too much of a consequence considering murder wasn't something their small town dealt with often. "Who called it in?"

Jackson had to look through his notes. "Simon Adams."

Marissa frowned. His name sounded familiar. "Wait a minute. Isn't that the ghost tour guide who called in Allison?" She didn't raise her eyes from Cindy's body. She knew she was right as Herbert Jackson flipped through his notebook.

"As a matter of fact, it is."

"I assume someone is taking his statement?"

"Colbert is getting his statement and info now." He huffed and shuffled his feet. "You don't think we're dealing with some kind of serial killer here, do you?"

His disbelief wasn't wholly unwarranted. The small town hadn't experienced anything like this in decades. Facts spoke for themselves, though, and coincidences were unlikely.

"I don't know. And until we have more, let's keep this one quiet. We don't need people to panic," she said finally, getting back to her feet. "Does she have any family we can get in touch with?"

"I think she has a granddaughter down in Olympia. I will see about getting in touch with her."

Marissa nodded, looking back down at Cindy again. Sometimes this job really just sucked. With a heavy sigh, she rubbed her temples, the hangover from very expensive alcohol lingering. She walked over to the fountain and circled it slowly, twice. Ellie was sniffing around the fountain with great curiosity, too. Frowning, she put on another pair of gloves and called Jackson over. "Look at this."

On the inside of the fountain were dark specs of blood. "This is probably the cause of the blunt force trauma. They might have tried to drown her first. Have them check her lungs."

"Damn. How did you even see that?" Jackson squinted.

Marissa chose not to answer because it would have sounded something like her calling him old. Looking back at the fountain, she huffed. Too many people came in contact with it daily to search anything for prints. Looking around, she noted the surrounding park had no cameras anywhere.

"What time did Simon call in?"

"He called it in around 3:30 for the second tour of the night."

Marissa frowned. "What day is it?"

"Well, it's Monday now."

"Why the hell was there a second ghost tour going on a Sunday to Monday night?"

"Because it's October, Marissa. We're getting ready for Halloween," he stated, as though it was the most normal thing in the world.

Blinking at him, she had to take a minute to process. God, she hated this small town.

Fighting the urge to roll her eyes, she just shook her head. "I'm going to go back home and get some sleep. But I'll be in this afternoon to grab the copies of the reports and take a look."

"You know I could just have Veronica run them by if that's easier?"

She let out a breath of relief.

"That would be great." She turned but stopped. "Before I go . . ." She turned back to Jackson. "Do you know if the autopsy has been done yet for Allison Drake? Tyler wants to make the funeral arrangements."

"Later today. So, he can make the arrangements as needed. It was pretty open and shut; you know, we just had to be sure." He gave her a look of sympathy that made her stomach turn.

Marissa nodded and gave him a weak smile. "Thanks. I'll let him know."

Patting her leg for Ellie to come, she crossed the crime scene line and started walking.

She should have gone back to Allie's place, let Mel go home, and stuck around for Tyler. Folding her arms to shield herself from the breeze coming in from the sea, she tugged out her phone, pulling up Mel's number.

"Hey, it's me. How is it going?"

"He's sleeping like a baby, and I'm just watching season two of *New Girl*. How are you?"

"Hungover and tired," she admitted. "Would you hate me if I asked if you could stay with Tyler for today? I need to get some sleep before I go back to work in a few hours. And I just kind of want my bed."

"It's not a problem, Riss. Take care of yourself. I'll call Brian to let him know."

"Thank you so much, Mel. You are a literal life-saver." She paused. "And when he wakes up, you can let him know he can start planning when he's ready. There won't be any holdup."

"That's good to know," Mel said softly. There was a silence, and Marissa heard Wicket purring on the other end. "Just take care of yourself, sis."

"Always." She smiled, tightening her grip around herself. "Love you, baby sis."

"Love you, big sis."

Once they hung up, she shoved the phone back into her pocket and gave Ellie a pet before she began walking again. "Let's go home."

Marissa dragged her feet up her porch steps and came to an abrupt halt at the sight of a white envelope lying in front of her door. With a heavy sigh, she used the sleeve of her jacket to pick it up, entirely out of gloves and bags.

"It's too early for this fucking shit," she muttered to no one.

Unlocking her door, she let Ellie in before closing it behind them and heading to the kitchen. She dropped the envelope on the counter and stared at Ellie for a moment.

"You're probably hungry, huh?"

She poured some food into the dog bowl and did the rounds around the house, locking the doors and checking the windows. When she made it back to the counter, she pulled the Ring app up on her phone to check if she could see a sign of anyone dropping off the envelope. But as always, whoever left it managed to remain unseen, just off the camera. Early on, Marissa had asked her neighbors if they had any security cameras that might show something. But being the small, quaint town it was, no one felt the need to have security cameras.

Grumbling, she opened the envelope and emptied the contents onto the counter. There was only one photo this time, which was odd. This was only two nights ago, at Allison's going away party. Hours before she had been found dead. It was a little off-center. Allie was whispering something in her ear, and Marissa was laughing. They looked like they were already well into the night. Rubbing her eyes and hoping to push the tears back, she put the photograph with the rest of them, locking it away. She couldn't look at it right now. She ran through what would have been her regular nightly routine, even though the sun was beginning to rise.

It wasn't until she was sitting on her bed, her feet still on the ground, that she let out a heavy sob. She wrapped her arms around her as Ellie tried pushing her nose through, lying across her lap, keeping her from pulling up her knees. It felt like all the air had been removed from her lungs as she kept gasping for it through sobs and tears. Ellie made sure to keep herself between Marissa's arms and her head, whining and licking as she tried to calm her down. Grinding down on her teeth, she dug her nails into her arms, hard enough that she was sure she was breaking the skin and bleeding, but she didn't care. The sudden pain that seared through her arms seemed to dull the rest of her body, easing the painful sobs. Letting go of her arms, she pulled Ellie in close and curled up on her pillow, closing her eyes as the sunlight started to invade the room.

Chapter 9

The next few days were a blur. Marissa didn't have a lot of time for much outside of sleep or work. She reviewed every piece of evidence from both crime scenes and memorized each file as though maybe the next time she read through them, she would find something she had missed in the first hundred read-throughs. In reality, Marissa was avoiding socializing. She checked in with Tyler to ensure he had everything he needed to make the arrangements, but for the most part, she just tried to stay out of the way. Natalie arrived shortly after. She and Tyler had begun going through the packed-up boxes, trying to decide what to do with Allison's things.

It was an adjustment for Marissa to suddenly be back on the job. Jackson had given her a desk and tiny office, a room she was pretty sure had been storage previously. But there was a window, at least. She looked through the crime scene photos, comparing both. Despite the fact there were two murders now, Marissa had interviewed the Mansera staff and had asked about disgruntled customers. They weren't a whole lot of help. Rachel had the best memory of the regulars who had brought trouble and a few tourists who had lodged complaints with management against Allie. Although they were about the same age, Marissa and Rachel didn't really know each other outside of the hotel. She was nice enough for a petite, busty redhead with a temper. Rachel had started working at the Mansera around the same time as Allie, eons ago as far as Marissa was concerned. Marissa decided to narrow in on the tourists since the local drunks all had solid alibis.

"So, like I said, it was a man and a woman. They were staying Thursday through Sunday, I think?" Rachel seemed to be questioning her own memory.

"I can get management to get me the records. Just tell me about the incident."

Rachel nodded. "It was just a few days before Allie's last day at work. So maybe a week ago? It was a couple. They sat at the bar. Ordered food. She got the halibut, and he got the sloppy ham sandwich."

She must have seen Marissa's eyebrow raise as she explained: "They were kind of on our radar upon arrival. The hotel staff had heard him pitching a fit over something earlier in the day, and he was just kind of a douchebag. He ordered her drink and food without asking her about it and then spent a good chunk of the time on the phone. It was while he was on the phone that Emma tripped coming back towards the bar and accidentally spilt a drink all over the girl. The girl was super chill and understanding, but the guy got off the phone and just went off on Emma. Allie came to Emma's rescue and ended up kicking them out. He's our newest one-star yelp review."

"Thanks, Rachel. I'll let you know if I've got any follow-up questions."

"Of course. Don't be a stranger."

After getting the couple's information from the front desk, Marissa wandered the castle-like hotel until she reached Allie's on-call room. She had packed up all her things, ready to head for Seattle, so Marissa didn't expect to find anything. Sure enough, the closets were bare, drawers were empty. Ellie huffed gently at her side, nudging her leg gently. The room had already been cleaned and was ready for new guests. With a heavy sigh, she closed the door and left the hotel. Being there without Allie just felt wrong. She would never be able to look at that building and not feel the weight of her loss.

Back at the station, it was time to meet with Simon Adams.

He was nothing more than a kid in his very early twenties. Marissa actually knew his family. Poor kid.

This was his first job, a tour guide for the local ghost hunt. A job he had only started this season while he picked up some classes at the community college. He shook in his chair, sweating buckets, while Marissa asked him simple questions about how he got started with the ghost tour company.

"So, what can you tell me about the night you found Allison Drake?"

"Not much, ma'am."

Marissa tried not to twitch as he called her ma'am, so she just nodded.

"Everything was going just fine. We had just left the Palace Hotel, and we were at the corner. I was talking about the Shanghai tunnels. And one of the men on the tour noticed her shoes. I called the police right away."

Marissa sighed, seeing his story matched his statement from that night. And held nothing of real value. "Okay, then what?"

"Well, we took that Saturday off, and Grimes, our boss, was so pissed because—" He paused for emphasis as though it were necessary. "It's Halloween, you know. But the cops didn't want us coming in and out of their crime scene."

"Right." She blinked, watching him awkwardly messing with his hair repeatedly as he leaned forward on the table.

"Well, it was the second tour of the night. The first one was uneventful. Everything was completely normal." He shuddered where he sat. "But as people started to gather for the last one, I was sitting on the front of the fountain, waiting like I always do. But as folks started gathering, a woman was circling the fountain and just let out this unreal scream. I've never heard anyone scream like that before. Cindy was just lying there."

"Just lying there." Marissa sighed.

"With her eyes wide open, not moving."

Marissa nodded. There was nothing about the crime scenes that really matched, with the exception of both spots being along the ghost tour. It seemed too big to be a coincidence, but then, even the cause of death may not have matched. They were still waiting on Cindy's autopsy to come through.

For the most part, Cindy's death had been kept under wraps for the moment. The people who were on the tour, except for Simon, were all tourists. Since it had been in the early morning hours before the town had awoken, it had been easier to keep quiet. The hope was to keep the townspeople at ease, but Allison's death on its own had made people nervous. They had multiple calls a day regarding suspicious behavior and tips people thought might be relevant. The tension was hard to miss. Marissa didn't bother attending the first press conference Jackson had held. She hated those things. And it only served to feed the unrest that was already brewing.

Allie's funeral was set for a Friday. It was a much bigger event for a small town than most people were prepared for, but Allison had made a lot of friends in her short lifetime. Marissa sat up front with Tyler and Natalie, both staying close to support him. She felt like she watched the entire experience from somewhere else, almost like watching a movie rather than living it. Tyler made it through his eulogy. Natalie couldn't go through with getting up in front of everybody, and Marissa cut her own short, overwhelmed with grief. Seeing how many people showed up, loved her, was too intense for Marissa.

At the cemetery, Melanie took care of Tyler with Brian's help, allowing Marissa and Natalie to have a moment to themselves. Marissa stood far off to the side, trying to stay out of the way, allowing everyone to give their condolences. She didn't want to overstep what Tyler and Natalie needed, and she also needed some space.

Leaning up against the tree, she watched as people said their final goodbyes with Ellie right by her side. There was a good chance Allison's killer was someone who knew her. From her spot against the tree, Marissa had a good view of all in attendance. Her eyes scanned the crowd, looking for anyone she didn't recognize. She landed on her own family. Her mom stood with Mel, Brian, and Tyler; Brian's parents had been kind enough to take the girls for the day. It was going to be too much and too long for them. Jared was standing by them, his new girlfriend on his arm. He must have felt her watching because he looked over in her direction, their eyes locking in a moment. Swallowing, she continued scanning through the group. Natalie was clustered with her own family and her own friends. She was tall, standing over most of her friends, and stunning even in grief, dark-skinned with dark black hair beneath a hat. Tightening her grip on her arms, she shifted her feet and looked down at the ground.

Once the cemetery cleared, Marissa walked to the place where her friend was laid to rest. "I'm sorry, Allie," she whispered. The last few days, she had been plagued with thoughts of what Allison's final moments must have been like. She was in the rare position where she could imagine the kind of fear Allie must have felt. Every time this week she had tried to think of Allison, it was the first place her mind went to. Covering her face, she let go of the tears that she had been keeping to herself throughout the day. Ellie leaned against her, nudging her gently with her nose.

She wasn't sure how much time had passed before she left the cemetery, but Marissa made sure to finish her flask before she joined everyone in the hall. She didn't plan to stick around, but she wanted to check in and make sure Tyler was doing okay. As she walked through the doors, though, Natalie tapped her on the shoulder.

"Hey, can I just talk to you for a quick minute?"

"Of course." Marissa rubbed her eye, hoping she had managed to regain some bit of composure.

"I was wondering..." Natalie glanced around anxiously before looking Marissa in the eyes. The fear in Natalie's eyes immediately sobered her up. "Do you think you could come out next weekend? There is something I'd really love to talk to you about. But I don't want to do it here. And I'm spending the week in Portland with my sister to just get away."

Marissa blinked and went to answer, but Natalie gave her a hug. Even with everything going on, Marissa wasn't sure she would have considered them close enough to hug. She hadn't been Marissa's least favorite of Allison's exes, but they had never been friends either. Still, as Natalie whispered in her ear, she understood. "I think we're being watched here."

Nodding, she hugged her back. "Of course. Does Saturday work?"

Natalie nodded. "Thank you so much. For everything."

"Of course." Marissa gave her a small smile. "I'm going to go check in on Tyler, then I think I'm going to head home. But I'll see you next weekend."

"Okay." Natalie gave her a smile before someone walked up to offer their condolences to her.

Marissa looked around, an involuntary shudder coursing through her. She knew for a fact *she* was being watched. But Marissa knew that wasn't what Natalie was referring to. She found Tyler easy enough and was able to keep almost six feet between her and Jared as she gave Tyler a hug.

"Thank you for everything, Marissa. I couldn't have gotten through this without you and Mel and Nat." They stood together for a moment, looking out at everyone sharing stories and memories together.

"When do you have to leave?"

"Later today. I need to get back down for work." He sighed heavily, and she shook her head.

Marissa gave him a small smile. "You'll have to come to visit again. Please. Don't be a stranger."

"Of course not." He paused, looking down at his water. "I have one more favor to ask of you."

Marissa turned to look at him. "Anything."

"I can't have pets in my apartment. I talked to Natalie about taking Wicket, but she's already seven years old. She doesn't really know Natalie. Would you consider taking her?"

She was surprised by the tears that welled back up in her eyes. "Of course." She needed to leave, or she was going to entirely fall apart. She gave him a big hug as they said their goodbyes, and she all but ran home.

It wasn't until she was behind her door with it locked behind her that she fell to the floor and openly sobbed, letting herself be vulnerable. She had begun to feel less and less safe falling apart outside these walls. She made her way to the couch, setting her phone to wake her up before it got too late so she could go get Wicket. She just needed to sleep first.

She didn't get to sleep as long as she'd hoped, though. Her phone startled her awake as Melanie called.

"Hey. I just wanted to make sure you're okay. You left pretty early. Mom was really worried."

"Yeah." Marissa rubbed her eyes without bothering to sit up. "I just ... I just needed some space."

Mel was quiet for a moment on the other line. "Did you want to come over for dinner? You really shouldn't have to be alone right now."

Sighing, she shook her head to no one in the darkness of her living room. "No but thank you. I really do appreciate it. I think I'm just going to call it an early night."

"Are you sure?" She heard her sister's concern, and for a moment, she almost changed her mind. Then she remembered her ex-husband and his new girlfriend were also probably there. Today had been plenty without needing to add any of that drama. "I'm positive. But we'll have lunch soon. Promise."

"Okay." Mel sounded defeated, but she accepted it nonetheless. "I love you, big sis."

"Love you too, baby sis."

Once she hung up with Mel, she sat in the dark for at least another fifteen minutes, leaning on the back of her couch, trying to convince herself this was real life. She had never considered what life would be without Allison. There was an emptiness that ached so bad that she felt it from her toes to her fingers. Marissa knew she needed to stay grounded, digging her index fingers into her thumbnails with as much force as she could muster.

She changed from her funeral clothes into pajamas, throwing her hair up to keep it out of her face. She didn't even bother leashing up Ellie and just had the shepherd meet her at the car. Since moving back home, she barely drove her mini anywhere. It wasn't even necessary now, but she figured she could grab all of Wicket's stuff in one go.

It didn't take long to get the cat's stuff together; Tyler had packed it all up and got it ready for Marissa to grab. All she had to do was put Wicket in the carrier. The cat voiced her complaints from the moment the carrier door closed to the moment Marissa got home. Marissa left most of the stuff in the car, grabbing the cat bed and food for the night. She would get the rest in the morning. Although the big gray cat seemed unsure about her new surroundings, she settled on the bed next to Marissa's head while Ellie slept along her legs. At least they all had each other.

Chapter 10

Marissa worked hard all through the next week, doing her best to keep herself distracted. During the day, she was in the precinct going over the same evidence. Nothing new came from it. The determined cause of death for Cindy had come back as strangulation, the blunt force trauma coming shortly before expiring. Jackson held another press conference, covering both as homicides. The unease in the street was hard to ignore. Despite Halloween being right around the corner, they canceled all their normal festivities, which usually paid for most of the town through Christmas time. The ghost tour company's events came to a complete stop. It felt like a gray cloud had fallen over the whole town, and everyone felt it. They were also feeling panicked. Whispers about a serial killer had already begun to circulate.

After the press conference and a very lengthy Q&A about the force's plans to keep the community safe, a vigil was held for the two women who had been staples in their small town. The event was big enough to close down the main road as the people poured in, candles in hand. Officers were scattered throughout, directing traffic and watching the crowd.

Marissa picked a spot near the dock to just take it in and watch. Natalie and her family had been a big part of putting the event together. Cindy's granddaughter had come with her family from Olympia, and she began telling stories of what she remembered of her eccentric grandmother. Many people got on stage to tell stories that involved Cindy. She was always such a friendly face. Sometimes she was selling flowers, other times, bracelets she had made from shells. She loved Port Townsend.

Marissa had been invited to get up and speak about Allison, but she couldn't bring herself to do it. She had a poem about grief she had planned to read at the funeral but couldn't do it then either. Instead, she stayed off to the side, isolating herself from the crowd, watching. Natalie spoke of Allison and her love for Port Townsend. How she found joy in everything she did. She had also managed to get Tyler on video to speak of his sister. Many more friends got up to speak. Even Laura Seaver got up on the stage and spoke of Allie's love of nature and how they had explored so much of the surrounding forests together.

Marissa scanned the crowd, hoping something would catch her eye. But there was nothing. She knew all of these people, and it was hard to imagine any of them taking another person's life.

Her eyes landed on her own family, both immediate and ex-in-laws. Mel tried to wave her over, but she just shook her head, silently hoping they understood she was working. It was easier this way. She was a detective looking for a murderer, playing security as the town came together. It was so much easier than being the best friend of a victim. She may have been both, but she couldn't let herself feel it. Just like she had been doing with so much of herself in the last few years, she shoved that piece of her into a box and set it adrift. She needed to stay focused, and the only way to do that was to keep herself numb.

When she was at home, Marissa continued working hard on feeling as little as possible, using sleep, medication, and alcohol, as needed. Aside from going into the precinct, she mostly stayed home. In her office, Marissa had flipped over the whiteboard. She pinned pictures of Allison and Cindy and wrote the facts below them. She circled the coincidences. The ghost tour locations. The close proximity in time. But it wasn't enough to convince even her that there was a connection.

Were they just random acts of violence? She wrote the question out on a post-it note and stuck it in the middle of the board. Other than the fact that crime never happened here, let alone murder, two murders in two nights were just unfathomable.

Staring at Allison's picture, Marissa didn't notice as tears welled in her eyes. She could still feel her friend's piercing blue eyes and hear her voice reassuring her that it was all going to be okay.

As Friday rolled around, a week after Allison's funeral, she decided to skip her appointment with Laura Seaver. What was the point of even going in this week? This was the only thing that was on Marissa's mind. That, and occasionally how lonely the house felt even with the addition of Wicket. She started mentally preparing herself for a visit to Seattle, spending nearly an hour in the shower, just lost in the thought.

It was mid-afternoon when she finally found her way downstairs. She heard the alarm from her phone before the knock on her door. Ellie whined excitedly at the prospect of seeing another human as Marissa got up from the couch and glanced out the window. Jack was standing on her porch, leaning against the railing. He obviously had remembered which house was hers after walking her home a few weeks ago from their lunch date.

As Marissa opened the door, Ellie cried excitedly as Marissa slid through the front door past the giant dog. "Hey. How are you?" She was trying to remember if they had made plans that she had spaced on. It would not have been unlike her at this point.

"Hi," he grinned at her. He had such a friendly smile. "I was wondering if you wanted to head to the Fort today. I heard people had spotted some whales off the coast, and I thought you could use a pick-me-up?"

A small part of Marissa actually wanted to go. Still, just as she was running through the excuses in her mind of why she wasn't feeling up to being social, she noticed her brother-in-law coming toward her house, as well.

Marissa smiled at Jack and just shook her head. "Rain check?" she offered as she watched Brian duck into her backyard, unnoticed by the handsome man in front of her.

Despite his grin, he looked disappointed.

"It's just been a really long week."

"Of course. I'm sorry, I should have realized." He gave her a sympathetic smile. Just what she hadn't wanted to see. But he did have that friendly smile. "But I will definitely take a rain check. I look forward to it." He brought his hand forward from behind his back and handed her a single yellow daisy. "This is for you. I will see you around." He turned, shoving his hands in his pocket, and walked down the street.

Marissa watched from the porch until he turned the corner and let out a sigh, glancing at the flower. Shrugging it off, she turned and walked through the house, leaving the daisy on the counter as she went to the back porch.

When she arrived, she found Brian already seated in one of the chairs, a bottle of whiskey at his feet. Ellie was all but crawling into his lap, her tail wagging with excitement.

"Some guard dog," Marissa commented, sighing when the shepherd paid her no mind. Flopping into the chair beside him, she flicked off her sandals. She looked over at her brother-in-law suspiciously before eyeing the bottle of whiskey. "Don't tell me you knocked my sister up again."

But she already knew. This was the tradition. Brian always told her before Melanie did, and always with a bottle of liquor. Even before Marissa and Jared's first marriage, she and Brian were close friends. It used to be in celebration. Now Marissa wondered if maybe it was a little less of a celebration than it used to be. They already had four kids. And all girls.

"I can't tell you that."

Marissa nodded her head. "Well, that answers my next question. We're drinking this now." She got up and grabbed glasses.

They spent the better part of an hour talking about his kids and plotting to convince Mel that five was more than enough. It was exciting news, but she definitely felt for him. Hopefully, they would have a boy this time.

"Unfortunately, I don't have much news for you." One of the perks of having a sister-in-law who worked on local cases was that Marissa was always willing to give him the news when she could. He was a good reporter. "I will be heading into Seattle tomorrow to talk to Nat. She had something she wanted to tell me but was uncomfortable doing so here."

Marissa made a face before downing her third glass of whiskey. She hadn't been counting how many Brian had already had, but she was pretty sure she was drinking faster than he was.

"Let's talk about something else."

"How about whale watching?" Brian smirked at her, mimicking Jack's southern drawl.

Marissa frowned. "It was a nice offer. He's a really nice guy." She filled her glass again and swallowed without taking much of a breath in between.

"Nice?" Brian pointed out how nice sounded like fine. She shrugged and shook her head.

"I'm not really looking for anything right now." Then there was that uncomfortable silence. Maybe they should have kept talking about murder. But before she could stop herself, words came falling out of her mouth. "You know Jared didn't say anything to me during the funeral?" The bitterness was sharp.

Glancing over, she saw Brian's face as he was trying to think of something to say. But what could he say? All he knew was that Marissa had decided to stay in Port Townsend and that Jared was just done. With a heavy sigh, she stood before she could think better of it, hanging on tight to what was left of the whiskey.

"Come with me. I need to show you something." She took the last pull off the bottle and put it on the island counter beside the yellow daisy before she made her way over to the opposite end of the kitchen. She hopped onto the counter, wincing as her body protested, and stood, grabbing a gray lock box hidden all the way to the back. Very carefully, she got back down and put it beside the empty bottle of whiskey, then went into her dining room to pull out a key she had hidden in a glass in her hutch. She returned to the kitchen and started to unlock the box.

"I owe you a bottle of whiskey," she announced as she opened the box and dumped the contents onto the island. Dozens and dozens of candid photos spilled over the counter.

Most of them focused on Marissa, some of both Marissa and Jared, but few concentrated on just Jared.

"These kept being delivered." She backed up to a counter, hopping up to sit, leaning her hands on the edge. "Are being delivered," she corrected herself. "I don't know how much you know about my last case in Seattle, but this was always how it started. And then the significant other would end up dead."

Marissa never spoke about that case or the things she endured, but she was sure someone had given him Cliff's Notes at some point. "I stopped getting photos of Jared when we broke up." She hated herself for it, but she would have done it all over again.

Brian thumbed through the photos, running his fingers over them as he spread them further onto the counter, his eyes looking frantic.

"Your case..." Marissa watched quietly as Brian caught up to everything she was saying. She knew it was a lot. "You were a target. No, wait ... you are a target. You made him break up with you to keep him safe. You lied because you didn't want him to end up dead."

The more he said out loud, the more she wanted to slap herself for telling him. It was a lot to process. And it was dangerous information to have.

"Fuck, Marissa. This isn't something you just keep locked up in a box!"

"I promise, I'm taking care of it. The local PD knows. The SPD knows." Not that anyone was doing much, but she didn't need to give him those details. "There are local police across the street for surveillance. I promise I'm not just ignoring it." It did fall lower on her priority list now, though.

Now came the challenging part. "You can't tell anyone. And I mean anyone."

Immediately, she regretted saying anything at all, even though she had gotten a moment's relief.

There was someone out there who knew her and knew she wasn't just a terrible person.

He wasn't pleased. At all. His lips had disappeared in a thin frown as he narrowed his eyes at her. He gritted his teeth, and she could see a vein in his neck.

"I know it's a lot. But I promise I've got this under control."

He continued to just stare at her.

"I'm sorry I told you, I just—" She paused. She wasn't really sure why she had told him. "I shouldn't have told you. But the fewer the people who know, the safer everyone is. I promise I will keep you informed."

"Marissa. This isn't just about you. My girls are in the background of some of these pictures!" he snapped.

"I know."

"Why did you even bother telling me, Marissa?"

"Because I just needed someone to know the truth. I needed someone to know that I'm not a fucking heartless bitch."

At that Brian sighed, silent for a moment. "Explain it to me," he said, folding his arms. "I need to understand."

Marissa took a deep breath. "This was my case two years ago. I don't know how much you know, but the killer targeted couples. He would first send photos of his intended victim, the woman. Just your basic stalker photos, like those." Marissa gestured.

"Then, would come the photos of the significant other; the boyfriend, the husband, whatever. And usually, anywhere between two and four weeks later, he would end up dead. And then so would she. When I started getting photos of Jared, I shoved him away and forced him out of the picture, literally. We're both still here. Six months later."

She shook her head. "I've got police surveilling the house, and I'm taking all the precautions. I've been printing all the photos that come in to make sure there aren't any fingerprints or residue. They are always clean. I'm in constant contact with the Seattle police. I've got extra locks on the doors; I've got the Ring security system."

Now she was stretching it. She barely remembered to bother locking her door. Now that it was just her, her level of caring wavered. But Brian didn't need that information.

When Brian finally left, he wasn't wholly convinced or completely thrilled but seemed to at least take her at her word. Despite the regret she felt for spilling her own secret, it did mean something to her that someone knew. That someone believed her. Dr. Seaver was just like the rest of the Seattle Police Department; she appeased Marissa, but she very often questioned Marissa's memory and whether or not there was a real connection between both cases. This was probably just a case of average voyeurism, which, while classified under stalking, was not nearly as severe as murder. If it was the same guy, why hadn't he come for her yet? He had never spent so much time just taking pictures before. Unsettling? Sure. But dangerous? Maybe not so much.

After Brian left, she returned all the photos to their box, shuddering at the sight of them. She didn't even feel fear anymore, not really. Now she felt angry. Resentful. Frustrated. There was still some fear in there, too, but buried well beneath the others. She fed Ellie and stared at the flower left on her counter. After looking through all those photographs, Marissa was comfortable keeping someone as lovely as Jack at arm's length. He was too nice to get mixed up with her. She considered tossing the daisy away, but instead, she grabbed a small glass, put some water in it, and placed the daisy in the water. She couldn't remember the last time she had gotten flowers.

Chapter 11

Marissa stepped onto the pier with a huff, holding Ellie close. The ferry ride had been quick, maybe too quick. It felt weird to be back in the city. She had come for a few follow-up doctor's appointments that first year, but now it had been a minute. She still had forty minutes before she was supposed to meet Natalie, and after that, she could catch the evening ferry to head back. She had no intentions of being there longer than she had to. Ellie had her nose in the air, tail wagging slowly, excited at all the new sights and smells. Marissa couldn't help but smile. She hadn't spent a lot of time in Seattle, but Ellie was amazing in public.

They spent the first half-hour walking around the marketplace. This was something Marissa really missed. The market in the morning was one of her favorite places, with fresh flowers and art-work and, most importantly, the fantastic food. It took no time at all before she ended up at Mee Sum Pastry for some crab rangoons before heading to Steinbrueck Park north of the market. She sat in front of the art installation, Ellie lying down at her feet, and waited. They were still ten minutes early. The breeze coming in from the Sound felt good against her face, with the sun peeking out from behind gray clouds. Closing her eyes, she focused on her breathing, feeling much more relaxed than she thought she would.

"You're early." A voice broke through her moment of quiet, and Marissa let out a loud sigh. "Sorry to interrupt your moment or whatever."

Marissa opened her eyes to see Natalie staring down at her, though it was bright enough that she had to squint. Natalie was looking around ner-vously, making Marissa very aware that the constant feeling of being watched wasn't supposed to be a normal one. All of the woman's anxiety was only in her eyes, though, as she stood tall with the kind of presence that demanded importance, whether she meant to or not. Natalie had been like that in high school, too. A beauty queen who managed straight A's and loved being the smartest person in the room.

"Good morning to you too, Natalie." She sat forward and leaned her elbows onto her knees. "Are you doing any better?" Natalie just shook her head with a heavy sigh. They hadn't been small talk people when Allison was alive; they certainly weren't going to start now. "You said you had something you wanted to talk about."

"A little." Natalie looked almost relieved if her serious expression gave anything away. "I did. And I appreciate you coming." She sat down beside Marissa and looked at her hands in her lap. Her expression did change. She looked heartbroken. "I always thought it would be Allison and me, you know?" She looked up at Marissa with tears in her eyes before looking down at her hands again.

Marissa struggled to keep her expression neutral. She hadn't been Natalie's biggest fan, although she liked her more than she ever cared for Laura Seaver. But Allison was a huge loss they all shared. She sighed softly and gave Ellie's ear a scratch while Natalie took her own moment, still trying to find the right thing to say.

"She was really excited to start things again," Marissa offered.

Natalie smiled as tears fell down her cheeks without looking up and nodded her head. "I'm sorry. I promised myself I wouldn't do this." She swallowed and raised her head to meet her gaze. "When Allison first called me a few months ago, it was so out of the blue. Our breakup," she paused, glancing at Marissa. "Well, you know. It wasn't great."

Marissa resisted the urge to nod. "Wasn't great" was an understatement. Marissa could still remember the late-night conversations with Allie during that time, always talking her off a ledge. Everything they did made the other unhappy or suspicious. Allison had called Marissa the day after hooking up with someone else, though Allie had never told her who. That was what Marissa had always considered the real beginning of the end for their relationship. Everything after that point just became toxic.

"But she said she wanted to talk. She apologized for her part in everything that happened in those last few months that led to our breakup." Natalie looked at Marissa almost nervously. "I'm not sure what she told you about it."

Marissa sighed. "She said you were both miserable. You maxed out her credit cards; she cheated on you; you cheated on her. She said it was explosive."

Natalie nodded, looking at her hands again. "She was unhappy, and she restarted an affair that made her the worst version of herself." Natalie hesitated. When she stopped, Ellie stood and put her head on Natalie's knee, wagging her tail. Marissa couldn't help but smile at her dog's efforts, and a smile appeared on Natalie's lips. "When she called me up, she said that it was finally over. After all these years. She told me that this relationship had made her do questionable things and that ... this person put her in a compromising position. For a long time."

Marissa listened and absorbed. She blinked but tried to hide her surprise. She had known Allison had been having an affair when she and Natalie broke up, but Marissa didn't know that she had been still seeing the same person all this time. It had been six and a half years.

"Compromising how?"

"I didn't get many details. Just that this person made her feel like she couldn't get out of it. She was getting ready to start going to therapy, to work through it." Natalie sighed heavily. "I wish I had done something more."

"Don't do that to yourself." Marissa put a hand over hers and waited for her to continue.

"She called me when she was getting ready to head home from the Mansera. Said that she had gotten a call from whoever this person is. She sounded frustrated but said she was going to take care of it. She didn't say any more than that."

Marissa sighed heavily, feeling like the floor had been pulled from beneath her. She must have gotten the call after Mel had taken her home.

"I don't know if they were there the day of her funeral, but I didn't know how much you knew."

"No, I appreciate it. This is huge." Marissa had already taken several looks at Allie's phone records. She couldn't remember anything standing out, at least not that seemed out of the ordinary. Maybe there was a second phone.

"I hope it helps somehow," Natalie said without looking away from Ellie. Her voice snapped Marissa back into the present.

"It definitely will. Thank you, Natalie." Marissa paused. "After the funeral, you mentioned that you thought you were being watched—" She could get the SPD to help, at least keep tabs if need be. But before Marissa could finish, Natalie shook her head.

"I really appreciate that, but I think I'm okay. There was just something about that day, during the funeral."

Marissa nodded. She would have to mentally run through that day again and try to remember if anyone seemed out of place or odd.

Natalie gave her a small smile, hesitating. "I know you and I were never close or anything, but it might be nice to hang out once in a blue moon. Remember Allie together."

Marissa nodded, a genuine smile creeping up on her lips. "I would like that."

"Alright. I have to get to work. Thank you so much for meeting me." She got to her feet, as did Marissa, and they caught each other in an awkward half-hug.

"I'll be in touch," Marissa promised as Natalie headed out.

Once she had disappeared from view, Marissa sat back down with a heavy sigh. Clearly, Marissa had missed a lot. There must have been signs, and she had clearly missed them all. Too involved with her own issues to notice if there had been any red flags. And this went back further than the kidnapping. This was six years long, while Marissa worked on advancing her career and life here in Seattle. She wasn't sure what made her feel worse: the fact that she was supposed to be Allie's best friend or the fact that she was supposed to be a god damned detective. It was so much to miss.

Ellie rested her head in Marissa's lap, once again returning her to the present. She glanced off in the direction of the ferry before looking at her phone. They had another two hours to kill before the next ferry would head out. Her stomach felt full for the first time in at least a week, and all she had eaten were those rangoons. She couldn't even entertain the idea of more food. Scratching Ellie between the ears, she sighed. "We could go for a walk?"

The shepherd seemed to perk up at the word, so Marissa got back to her feet. "We aren't going to overdo it, though. We are going to take a nice, easy-paced walk. No running," she said, more for her own benefit than Ellie's, who just tilted her head from one side to the other until Marissa chose a direction to start walking in.

They walked without a destination in mind, Marissa shoving her hands in her pockets, keeping her head slightly down to battle the chill from the breeze off the Sound. It wasn't until she nearly tripped over her own feet that she took a good look around and realized where it was she had ended up. Marissa was standing just on Fifth Ave, right in front of the radio station her ex-husband worked at. She hadn't meant to be there, but her feet seemed to be on autopilot. It was even around Jared's lunch-time. As that realization floated across her mind, she made a sharp turn to head in the other direction when she bumped shoulders with a familiar blonde.

"I'm SO sorry," the blonde said, exaggerating with her hands as she apologized profusely. Marissa was actually pretty sure if anyone was at fault for the collision; it was her. But she was content to let Kirstie feel bad.

"Sorry," she mumbled, hoping that there wouldn't be a sign of recognition. The expression that flashed on that perfect round face told her that was unlikely, even before the girl squealed.

"You're Melanie's sister, Marissa, right? Jared's ex-wife?" Ellie sat down at Marissa's feet as she fumbled over appropriate words in her mind, but none came out. Instead, she just nodded her head. "I don't know if you remember me; I don't think we've ever been formally introduced, but I'm Kirstie, Jared's girlfriend."

"Right." Like she could forget. "It's lovely to meet you. I should let you go; I've got to—" But Kirstie's hands were once again flying around as the blonde started speaking.

"I can't believe how lucky this is!"

Lucky was not the term Marissa would have used, but she tried to keep her thoughts off her expression while waiting for the girl to continue.

"I would actually love to talk to you if you're able?"

That was not something Marissa had any desire to do right now. Or ever. But as she ran through all the excuses she could that wouldn't necessarily be considered rude, the blonde apparently saw her apprehension.

"I know this is probably a little weird and maybe even uncomfortable. But I kind of need advice, and I think you may be the best person to get it from."

Jesus, didn't this girl have friends? Wasn't she super close with Mel? That meant this was a relationship question regarding her ex-husband. Now she really wanted to say no. But as she opened her mouth to tell Kirstie just how inappropriate this was, she saw tears welling up in the young girl's big blue eyes. Instead, completely different words came out.

"I guess so."

"I'll buy lunch. My treat?"

Marissa's stomach churned at the suggestion of food. "Buy me a drink, and we'll call it even."

Kirstie nodded her head excitedly. "Thank you so much. There is a bar right around the corner," she rambled, motioning for Marissa to follow.

Marissa glanced off in the other direction, thinking about how much she hated herself already.

The bar was called The Hideout. All along the walls were paintings and artwork for sale. They grabbed a table, and Marissa got Ellie settled beneath it. Kirstie wiggled and looked over the menu, rambling about how this was one of her favorite places.

A waitress came over. Once Kirstie was done ordering enough appetizers for a small army, Marissa ordered a jack and coke. She figured she could keep it simple and, once the drink was done, be on her way. She had a ferry to catch, after all.

"So, you said you needed advice?" Marissa pushed, hoping to get this done sooner rather than later.

"I know it's a little weird because you and Jared ended on such bad terms and everything. And you don't know me from any other stranger in this bar."

Good God, this girl was long-winded. She bit her lip to keep from looking as bored and uninterested as she felt. Kirstie rattled on and on, Marissa only catching every few words, partially because of the noise in the bar but also because she was struggling to stay interested. The last thing she wanted was to be friends with Jared's new fucking live-in girlfriend.

"And I know it probably seems like we've moved really fast."

She was prattling on when Marissa's drink arrived. She thanked the waitress and took a sip, turning her attention back to Kirstie, who was still talking.

"And we haven't talked too much about the future. But what is his stance on kids?"

Marissa blinked, realizing she had missed the bulk of what she had said. "Kids?"

"Yeah." Kirstie rubbed her belly without taking her eyes off Marissa, as Marissa felt like the floor had given out under her feet. "Like I said, I had a blood test this morning to see and should know later today, but I don't know if it's something that he even wants."

Marissa's entire world was spinning, and her vision blurred as she processed the words again. "Oh." It was all she could manage as everything felt like it came crashing inward.

"I'm sorry. I know this is probably really inappropriate."

No, this girl had no idea just how inappropriate this was because she was basically a child. And now, she wasn't just playing house with her ex-husband, but they were going to add a baby to the mix. She blinked before removing the straw from her glass and shooting the rest of the drink down her throat.

"I just want to be prepared. Is this something he's going to want?"

Marissa had flashbacks to all those disappointing conversations that started with, "Nope. Still no baby," every month. They had tried so hard for a couple of years. They had been in the process of making appointments to see if a baby was even possible when everything happened.

Looking at the girl sitting across from her, she wanted to lie. She tried to tell her that it would be the last thing Jared would want. But again, different words fell out of her mouth. "He'll be thrilled." She managed. "Thank you so much for the drink, but I really have to get going."

"Wait!" She grabbed her purse and started digging around. A moment later, she pulled a silver band out and held it up to Marissa. "He was going to sell it. I thought maybe you would rather have it?"

Something about the expression on Kirstie's face made her wonder for a moment if she was trying to be hurtful. It was entirely possible. Cautiously, she took the ring, thanked Kirstie for the drink, and darted for the exit before the blonde could speak again.

Marissa didn't allow any of her new knowledge to sink in until she was back down by the docks. What the hell had just happened? She stared at the ferry they had only just missed and let out a yell of aggravation. People stared but just kept on with their business.

"Well, that's another two hours we need to kill." Marissa wished she had driven in, so she could have just gone home.

Instead, she found her way to one of her bars, The Owl N' Thistle. And while she only meant to pass the next two hours, she stopped drinking nearly four tall Guinness, a dozen shots, and six hours later. She drank a tourist under the table for the money, played some darts, and only almost got into one fight when someone got too handsy with her. By the end, the bartender was very kindly urging her to leave.

Sitting outside on the curb, she realized it had gotten dark when she wasn't looking. She tried twice to call Allison before she remembered why she wasn't answering.

"Fuck."

She fumbled with her phone, the sobering reminder killing the last of the fun buzz she had been riding for the past couple of hours. Ellie nudged her as she mumbled to herself, the shepherd whining through her nose impatiently. She flipped through her contacts before she landed on the only person in the Seattle area she could think would come to her rescue.

"Lydia. Hey." She sighed at the sound of her friend's voice on the other end. "I'm sorry to bother you. I'm downtown, at the pub. I... I was wondering if I could crash there tonight?"

After many reassurances that it would be okay, Marissa got to her feet and made the ten-block walk as it started to rain.

Lydia was waiting for her downstairs to let her in the building, giving Marissa a look of sympathy and understanding she didn't particularly feel like she deserved. Once they made it upstairs to the condo, Marissa gave the redhead a hug. "I'm so sorry for this."

"You don't ever need to be sorry. This is still technically your place. It's your name on the lease." Lydia smiled, disappearing momentarily before returning with a towel for Ellie.

Marissa glanced around, looking at the condo she had given up when she moved back into her mom's house. The condo she and Jared had shared for a time.

Once she had made her move final, she sublet it to Lydia Disher and her daughter. They needed somewhere they could stay, and as an ER nurse, Lydia wasn't exactly rolling in money. "How's Evelyn?" the daughter Tom hadn't gotten to witness growing up. He died before her first birthday.

"She's doing good. She's at Grandma Disher's for the weekend down in Burien." Lydia smiled, leading Marissa to a chair. "Sit. Do you want some water?"

"No, thank you," Marissa said, despite her dry mouth.

"So, what brings you up this way?" Lydia sat down on the other end of the couch.

She listened to Marissa as she talked about Allison, Natalie, and her run-in with Girlfriend Barbie. While she spoke, she hadn't even realized that Lydia set up the couch with sheets and brought Marissa a pillow, as well as a glass of water. Ellie curled up on Marissa's legs as she drifted off to sleep for the night.

Chapter 12

M arissa closed the door behind her, relieved to be home and overwhelmed by the past twenty-four hours. She took Ellie's leash and hung it up with her keys. She leaned against the wall for a minute, looking out as the giant shepherd jumped on the couch and rolled around, happy to be home. Marissa had slept on Lydia's couch until late in the afternoon. She woke up to an Evelyn greeting, which made the hangover worth it. She hadn't seen her in over a year and a half. The little girl was nearing three years old now.

On the ferry ride home, she got the call about a third body turning up behind the Palace Hotel. The body was found by a staff member at 12:30 a.m. Ironically, the Palace Hotel was normally part of the ghost tour. Jackson had left the file in her mailbox for her to go over when she got home so she would be caught up when she got back to the precinct.

She could feel Jackson's frustration. One murder was out of the ordinary, but three was too much to be a coincidence. She knew he had reached out to other agencies for assistance.

Brian was given the assignment to cover the story for Monday's paper, so she had texted him to let him know when she got off the ferry and was nearly home. They could look over the files together. Her understanding was that he had gotten interviews with witnesses and guests of the ghost tour.

She walked to the kitchen, dropped her phone on the counter, and continued to her back door; she slid it open to let Ellie sprint across the yard. She leaned against the door frame, breathing heavily. She folded her arms, closed her eyes, and took a moment to just let the last two days wash off her.

Brian arrived shortly, with shrimp-fried rice in hand. They exchanged information over their late lunch. Marissa shared with Brian all about Allison's secret affair, and Brian gave her the rundown on what it was like at the third crime scene. Crime scenes weren't something Brian had a lot of experience with. The way he described it was thrilling, exciting even, and with much more detail than she was sure she would have gotten from the officers on the scene.

The victim's name was Owen Rolley. He was a ferry worker who was visiting from Whidbey Island.

He was found by a hotel staff member along the route the ghost tour would've taken had they been operating. They hadn't seen his car, bags, or camera, as he was a hobby photographer—only his wallet and keys. There was not a whole lot to go on.

With their Chinese food, Marissa brought Brian upstairs to her office and showed him the whiteboard. Despite the hours she spent in the office, work always came home with her. She used to think it was dedication. If anyone saw what was on the other side of that board, they would call it an obsession. She added Owen Rolley to the board with his info. They ate and stared at the evidence, talking it through. Brian had the "Aha!" moment, realizing that Rolley was in town for a bachelor party the same night as Allison's going away party a few weeks earlier. Marissa was certain there was some kind of connection.

Owen Rolley's cause of death would come back as a self-inflicted gunshot wound to the side of the head. Yet another thing Marissa wasn't buying. It didn't feel right. They got so invested going over the details, she had almost forgotten to tell him about her run-in with Kirstie. So, she gave him a quick summary.

"Pregnant?" His face mirrored the feeling in her stomach when she said it out loud.

"We'll see." Marissa made a face, keeping her extreme opinions to herself. "It could still just be a scare. Obviously, don't say I said anything."

Chapter 12

"Speaking of secrets..." Brian sighed. "I don't want Mel to know I'm working this investigation."

That got Marissa's full attention. "Why not?

"She's already so worried and anxious. Three murders. And she's pregnant. You know what she's like." Brian shifted. "The last time I was on the crime beat, she was a wreck. And those were just some robberies."

Marissa did know what she was like. She gave Brian a sympathetic nod. "What are you going to tell her when your name is next to the story in the paper?"

"That someone else is following you around and taking notes. That I'm just putting it together."

Just what Marissa wanted. More secrets. At least they were mostly her own secrets. She was going to need a spreadsheet soon. "Okay. So, we don't tell her."

Over the next couple weeks, Brian and Marissa fell into a routine. Local cops were digging around and going from place to place, but Marissa was in the unique position to help the investigation while remaining on the outside. And truth be told, she couldn't have done it without Brian's help. He kept her focused and often had to remind her this was what she was good at. She must have been good to be promoted to detective in the first place. She had closed a lot of cases before her kidnapping. And yet, Marissa had no confidence in her ability anymore. She had missed far too much with Allie to be good. But whenever the local PD found something, it would find its way into Marissa's hands, and she would see where it would follow. Brian would come over, they dove over files together, and visit whatever new information would come in. Marissa had begun the difficult task of getting in touch with Allison's serious ex-relationships to start interviews after the upcoming holiday. She had gotten ahold of Matthew Carter, the boyfriend Allie almost married. She also scheduled an interview with Laura Seaver, one she was not excited about. To make that more awkward, she had to keep going to therapy to participate in the case, though she was bullshitting her way through her sessions.

By mid-November, Marissa had been looking over Owen Rolley's bank statements. She checked over all the activities of the bachelor party he had been involved in the weekend Allison had been murdered. She double-checked and triple-checked until her eyes were tired. His path had crossed several times with Allie, but nothing of real significance. The whole party had stayed at the Mansera, spending lots of money at the bar. They had hit all the hot spots over the weekend, taken a day trip out to the rainforest, and spent time at the beach.

It was a mixed bag, and only half of it involved the paper trail.

Marissa stared at the mess she had made at her dining room table; she paced around it, feeling like the answer was sitting right there. She had started in her study, but there just wasn't enough space in the room for more than one case. And even though it wasn't going anywhere, the Couple Killer's case owned that room. So, she took the pictures off the board and stuck them on her wall, surrounded by post-it notes. Chewing on her fingernail, she knew the three murders were connected, and the answer was somewhere in the details of Owen Rolley's life.

She recruited her brother-in-law for a trip to Whidbey Island. One that ultimately ended up being yet another dead end. There was nothing in Rolley's apartment, and his friend who let them in, Chris Erickson, had nothing of value to offer. His coworkers at the docks also didn't lead any-where. Rolley was a ladies' man, not the kind of guy who dated the same girl more than three times. His apartment was clean, organized, and bare. His camera was nowhere to be found. She had hoped to get in touch with the groom from the bachelor party, but he was out of town.

And it was during the ferry ride home that Marissa realized she might have been occupying a little bit too much of Brian's time. He looked exhausted, was trying to finish an article for work on his phone, and told her that he had come over to help fix a leaky toilet, if Mel asked. There was a tension that hadn't been present before, and she couldn't help but feel some guilt. Especially since working with someone else felt so natural. She hadn't worked a real case since coming to Port Townsend. She didn't have a partner anymore. She hadn't realized just how much she had truly missed this part of her life, even when the dead ends were stressful. She had even introduced Brian as her partner after identifying herself as a detective. It had just been force of habit. But now, Brian, who had always been one of her closer friends, even without the complications of whom they had married, was growing increasingly frustrated.

The gut feeling that she was stretching Brian thin proved to be true. A few days after the Whidbey Island trip, Marissa found herself glancing up from her table to see Melanie parking behind her car. Confused, she looked at her phone to see if she should have been expecting her before getting up and meeting her at the door.

"Hey, what's—"

"I need to talk to you." Melanie snapped, and Marissa suddenly wanted to go back inside.

"Is everything okay?"

"No. Everything is not okay," Melanie said as she reached the porch, standing in front of Marissa, her pregnant belly beginning to round a bit.

"I get you've been going through a thing, and everything has been crazy, but I feel like I got

Jared in the divorce. And you got my husband. And I don't know if you know this, but I'm pregnant, with four small children running around. I need my God damned husband at home. Instead, he's off galivanting with you, doing God knows what because he won't tell me anything anymore!" She paused, clearly retracing her words. "See, even when I say it out loud, it sounds absolutely ridiculous."

"He's just been helping me…" Marissa said with precise vagueness. Seeing the tears filling Melanie's eyes, she suddenly felt sick to her stomach. She hadn't given much thought to what Mel might have thought was going on. Marissa had gotten tunnel vision; it was what made her a great detective but also a terrible friend and sister.

"He's keeping secrets from me. He's never kept secrets from me. He's spending all of his time either here or at work." Her voice trembled, and Marissa's heart just continued to sink. "And like, I get that you are going through some shit. But you won't tell me anything either. And I never see you."

Marissa winced as Mel wiped her eyes free of tears.

"Mel…" Melanie threw her hand up and shook her head, not giving Marissa the chance to say anything at all.

"I mean, are you covering for him? Is he cheating on me?" Now tears were just flowing freely from her eyes, and Marissa felt utterly helpless. "Is he covering for you? Why are you both lying to me?"

159

Marissa went to give her answer, but nothing came out. Brain had asked her to keep it between them. And the longer that silence stretched out, the angrier Melanie grew.

"You can't even deny it! I came by when he was supposedly fixing a leaky toilet, and surprise, surprise. Neither of you was here."

"I—"

"Nope. Don't want to hear it. I just came over here to tell you to leave my husband alone. Get your shit together. And hire a fucking handyman!"

With that, her baby sister whirled around, stalked off the porch, and stormed back to her car.

Marissa was floored. She stood on the porch, processing. In the back of her mind, she heard a voice telling her to go after Mel, tell her everything. About Allie's case, about her own. All of it. But instead of going after her, she turned back inside, walked back over to her table, and stared at the mess stretching from her kitchen table to her kitchen island. She couldn't tell Melanie the truth. And maybe this was the push she needed to push her sister to a safe distance, just like she had done to Jared.

She had been trying to organize all the information she had, but the focus was gone. Mel had knocked her completely off balance. Now she was just overwhelmed with guilt. Thankfully, she had an appointment with Dr. Seaver today; otherwise, Marissa would have gone back to bed.

But an hour later, she and Ellie were back in that office. Too restless to stay still, Marissa stayed on her feet and took a good look around. It was a nice-sized office, with a desk she had never seen Laura Seaver sit at. The couch she usually sat on, the chair Dr. Seaver occupied, and bookshelves full of books: books, photographs, figurines, and a few bits and bobs. There was a beautiful, old type-writer, rock fountain, fancy camera, and an intricate wooden box. She glanced over the books, most of them psychology books. But there was a shelf dedicated to classics, such as *Of Mice and Men* and *Pride and Prejudice*.

"Are you going to sit down or just pace around my office?" Dr. Seaver broke the silence and Marissa's focus, or lack thereof.

"Sorry." Marissa sighed and sat down on the couch.

"So, what's on your mind? You seem distracted."

"I am. I feel … out of sorts," she said honestly. She noticed her mouth felt dry, and she felt almost restless.

"Out sorts how? Has something happened?"

Marissa was quiet for a moment, letting her mind catch up. "I got into a fight with my sister." She paused. "No, actually, she came over and yelled at me and then left."

Dr. Seaver waited, but Marissa didn't continue. It was like a fog had filled her mind.

"What did she yell about?" she asked impatiently.

161

Marissa blinked, having to figure out where to start. "Well. I've been investigating the murder of the ferry worker. I think that it's connected to the other murders from last month . . ."

"Allison," Dr. Seaver said quietly, a look of sadness washing over her face.

"Yes." She sighed before continuing. "Well, Brian was doing some of the reporting, so I sort of roped him into investigating with me. It's been helpful to have someone with me." She hesitated. "And I had told him the truth . . . about all the things. Because I just need someone to know." Someone who was on her side. Dr. Seaver did not count. "So, because of that, he's been keeping secrets from Mel. And I've never told anyone about—"

She dropped off. Two years later and she still couldn't get the words out. She could talk about what happened in factual terms, but she never spoke about what happened in those two days.

"I can't tell her about the investigation because it's ongoing. And Brian made me swear not to tell her about his involvement because she would be angry and worried." Didn't really seem to make a difference now, but she kept her word. "And I can't tell her about the pictures I keep getting because it would put her in danger. In more danger," she corrected, looking down at her hands in her lap.

"And what about talking to her about what you experienced?" Dr. Seaver gently nudged her.

"I can't tell her about the things that happened because she'll look at me differently. She won't mean to, but she will. Because if I say it out loud, it makes me a victim all over again." She wiped the tears from her eyes, taking a large breath. "And because I don't want her to hear those things that I had to experience. I can't—"

Dr. Seaver stared back at her, tapping her pen on her clipboard for a long moment before she spoke. "Are things going well with the investigation?"

"I can't really talk about it since it's still ongoing."

"You know whatever you say here stays in here," she said gently, giving Marissa a small smile.

Nodding her head, she finally continued. "It is progressing. I think they are all connected; I just can't prove it yet."

"That's good to hear," she said, looking past Marissa and sighing. After a long moment, she turned her attention back on her. "I miss Allison so much. I imagine you do, as well."

"I really do."

They sat in silence for a long moment before Dr. Seaver started again. "So, Melanie is angry that you and Brian are keeping secrets."

"Correct."

"What did she say to you?"

"She told me that she feels like she got Jared in the divorce, and I got Brian. She told me to leave him alone and to get my shit together."

Dr. Seaver adjusted her legs, making a face. "So, I guess my question is, what are you going to do?"

Marissa shrugged, feeling like crying all over again. "I don't know."

"Are you saying you can't solve these cases on your own?"

"Not at all," Marissa said almost defensively. "I just—"

"Let's look at this from Melanie's point of view for a moment. I mean, she knows you've been keeping secrets; now Brian is keeping secrets. She's completely in the dark from the two most important people in her life."

Marissa didn't say anything right away. She opened her mouth and closed it again several times before she attempted to say anything. "I—"

"You didn't think about how that would make her feel?" Dr. Seaver kept her face and tone neutral, but something felt like it had shifted in the room. "How often do you think about someone else before you take action?"

Marissa felt her jaw drop to the floor. "That's not fair."

"How is it not fair? What's the truth?"

Now she felt attacked. Standing back up, she shook her head. "No. I'm not doing this." She looked down at Ellie, who stared up at her before getting back onto her feet. "What gives you the right to attack me? Are you calling me a narcissist?"

she snapped, looking Laura Seaver in the eye. "Pot calling the kettle black?"

"Marissa, please sit down." She sounded exasperated.

With a heavy huff, she sat back down even though all she wanted to do was leave.

"Thank you." Dr. Seaver adjusted herself in her seat. "Now, let's approach from a different angle."

"Fucking angles," Marissa mumbled as she sat back, placing her hands in her lap, while Ellie curled back up at her feet, snorting her displeasure that she had been disturbed in the first place.

"I want to talk about your first marriage."

Marissa exhaled through her nose, keeping her body very still, but she could hear her heartbeat pounding in her eardrums.

"Now remind me, you graduated high school and got your acceptance into Seattle University. You majored in criminal justice, forensic psychology."

Marissa nodded.

"Jared was already in Seattle, at the University of Washington as a communications major."

Again, Marissa nodded but with a roll of her eyes. "Why is this important?"

Dr. Seaver simply gave her a look before continuing. "To celebrate, you two went to Vegas, got drunk, and got married on a whim?"

"Yep." She tried not to smile. Even though most of it was still pretty blurry, it had been one hell of a celebration.

"And from there, what was the thought?"

While everyone had been pretty upset with them, that time had been absolutely amazing. "We had always talked about it anyway. It wasn't how we planned on getting married, but there we were. We were doing it. We bought a house, we bought furniture. We went to school, worked. Mostly lived off our financial aid at the time. Ate a lot of ramen. For a while, it was actually pretty perfect."

Thinking back, it was possibly the happiest she had been. They didn't have a lot of money or a lot of free time. But the time they did spend together was more than perfect. They explored the city; they explored each other. They got to be together for the first time in a way they hadn't been able to before that point.

"So, what happened?" Her soft voice broke through Marissa's thoughts, bringing her back into the moment.

"It was too much too soon." A year or so in, she started to feel suffocated. It had been so hard to explain because, in one minute, she could be so happy, but the next, she felt like she had no room to breathe. Everything had just happened so fast. They hadn't experienced much of anything since leaving Port Townsend except each other. Now, she would have given anything to hold on to that. "Jared said he agreed with me, and we legally divorced. We agreed to see other people and to stay friends."

"Did you see other people?" Dr. Seaver had begun jotting down notes on that little pad of hers frantically, not bothering to look up at Marissa until there was a pause.

Blinking, Marissa shrugged. "I went on a few dates. I know he went out with a few girls from the university. Why does this even matter?"

"Did you ever have repeat dates?" Marissa just stared as Dr. Seaver ignored her question. "You know, like second and third dates?"

"Oh." Her mouth felt so dry again. Licking her lips, she again shrugged her shoulders, leaning further back into the couch. "I'm sure I did." She had to think about it, though. "There was this one guy, Troy; I think we went out three times?" Dr. Seaver raised an eyebrow. "Why does any of this matter?"

Putting her pen down, Laura Seaver straightened in her chair, giving her a very clear look of authority. "This matters because I want to get a clear picture of what you think a healthy relationship looks like. Because it is the very basis of how you view and treat other relationships. Such as your sister and brother-in-law."

Once Marissa was outside, she had no plans to go home. She couldn't. Looking at the time on her phone, she made the very conscious decision that now was the time to start drinking. She thought about going to the Mansera but couldn't bring herself to. The idea of being there without Allison was just wrong. So instead, she headed over to Sirens; she sat at the bar and ordered herself a rum and coke. She then silenced her phone as a call started to come through from her mom. Nope, she was going to put it on do not disturb. She had the evening off. It was fine.

"Do you want something to snack on? Maybe slow down on the drinks a little?" Tim, the bartender, asked, probably noticing how quickly she was making her drinks disappear. She barely paid him any mind. She had babysat Tim when he was still scribbling on walls; he certainly wasn't going to tell her how to drink.

"No, Tim. I just want another rum and coke."

"You know it's only like, five?" Before she could threaten him, he turned his attention to someone coming up to the bar.

"Her next drink is on me." She smiled at the sound of the familiar southern drawl as Jack sat down beside her. "Mind if I join you?"

"Please do." She smiled and resisted the urge to stick her tongue out at Tim.

Tim frowned at Jack but poured her drink anyway. "What can I get you?"

"I'll have the same." He gave Tim a polite smile before turning his attention to Marissa. "How have you been?"

Marissa shrugged her shoulders. "Okay, I guess."
"Well, that isn't very convincing." He rested his arm on the bar and met her eyes. Again, she shrugged. He was quiet for a moment before he glanced around. "Why don't we get a table?"
"Sure."
Marissa sucked down half of her glass. She got to her feet, drink in hand, and followed Jack to a table by a window. Sirens was an establishment upstairs to an art studio, so its view of the water was beautiful.
"So, do you want to talk about it?" His blue eyes searched hers with a small smile.
"It's just been a day." She hesitated. "My sister is mad at me. My therapist is awful. Things are just … stupid." She finished off her drink.
"Why is your sister mad at you?" He threw his hands up as her eyes snapped back to him. "Unless you don't want to get into it."
"I don't even know." No, she did know. Although putting it into words was not simple. "She feels I'm keeping secrets, accusing me of occupying her husband's time." She suddenly felt the need to quickly explain before he got the wrong idea. "He's a reporter for the local paper, and he's been following the murders around town. He was giving me a hand with the investigation."
"Ah." Jack nodded, finishing off his own drink. He motioned over to Tim for what she assumed would be more drinks. "How are the investigations going?"

Marissa huffed, dropping her shoulders forward. "Not as well or quick as I would like." She dropped her head onto the table between her arms. "I feel like I'm getting nowhere." Sitting back up, she sighed heavily. "Of course, I can't talk about it because it's an active, ongoing investigation." Marissa may have been saying it for her own benefit as a reminder.

"Of course." Tim came over with another drink, frowning deeply. She was pretty sure her glass was full of nothing but coke, but she didn't say anything.

"How have you been? Are you enjoying your time in our fun tourist town?"

Jack flashed her a charming smile. "I am. I really like it here. And I've done all the tourist things. Done the whale watching, checked out the rainforest, enjoyed museums, visited breweries and vineyards." He took a sip of his drink and seemed content enough with it. "I keep planning on heading out and visiting family around the states before I head back to Alaska but haven't brought myself to leave yet."

"Sounds like you've done literally all there is to do."

"Maybe. But it's nice and quiet. I like that."

Marissa shrugged. "I used to hate it," she admitted. "I counted down the days until I was able to get the hell out."

"You do seem like you've got more than this town can handle."

Marissa smiled and shifted slightly, not really into the flirting. "It's just too quiet here."

It didn't feel like they had been talking long when Tim made the last call.

"Jesus. Time flies." Marissa drank what was left of her sixth coke with maybe a teaspoon of rum and smiled. She wasn't nearly as drunk as she was hoping to be. Apparently, this was not the place to come for that when Tim was working.

Jack, on the other hand, was on his fourth drink, whatever it was. Marissa hadn't been paying much attention, but it looked like he was feeling a nice buzz.

"Especially when you're having fun." He grinned at her before finishing his own drink. "Why don't you let me take you home?"

Marissa thought about it for a long minute, weighing the pros and cons. She enjoyed his company, but there were expectations if she let him take her home. "No ... that's okay. I have to stop at my sister's place anyway." She hopped out of her chair and pulled her jacket closed. "Thank you so much for the offer, though." She noted his disappointed expression, but he gave her an understanding smile.

"Okay. But we should do this again sometime soon."

"Absolutely." He gave her an awkward sort-of hug, probably because of the yelping and screaming she had done in the past with physical contact. She still had a difficult time but kept her reactions inward.

She stiffened, and her blood ran cold. As he let go, she let out a breath, the urge to cry coming over her.

Once they were outside and said their final goodbyes, Marissa turned to look out to the empty street, turning to Ellie. "I hate this town," she muttered. Because the last call was at 11 p.m. Stupid tourist town. And this was a Friday night. During the week, everything would be closed by 9 p.m.

By the time they made it home, Marissa was exhausted and absolutely pouring sweat. As she reached the door, she stopped to look over at her swinging bench, a manila envelope propped up with her name written across it. She frowned, her head tilting to the side. It wasn't until she picked up the envelope that she realized what was different. They had never been addressed to her before. Taking the envelope inside, she made room on her counter and dropped the contents on the counter. There were four photos and a note. She blinked—a message. Putting on gloves, she carefully unfolded the piece of paper. It wasn't handwritten like her name but typed on a piece of paper.

I'm Still Here.

Cool. Not only did she have a murderous stalker, but he was talking to her now, too. Hissing between her teeth, she looked at the photos. There was one of her looking over all the papers spread across her table, probably taken from her porch. Another picture of her on the ferry to Whidbey Island, when she got out of the car and leaned over the side, looking at the water. There was a picture of her outside of Rolley's apartment, Brian, off to the side in the picture. There was also a picture of her sitting on her front porch. She wasn't sure when this one was taken, mainly because it became a real common sight—sitting on her porch, drink in hand, looking out as though she was searching for something. She resisted the urge to go straight for a drink and instead just left everything out on her counter, heading upstairs for a shower. She stood in there until the water grew cold, questioning why she wasn't more afraid of constantly being watched. It was enough to terrify anyone, but instead of terror, Marissa just felt numb.

Chapter 13

She spent most of the night tossing and turning, unable to sleep. Around 8 a.m. the next morning, she glanced at her phone, remembering she had put it on do not disturb. Taking that setting off, she watched as she got a couple of text messages and a voicemail. Scrolling through her texts first, she raised an eyebrow. The first one was from Madilyn, Marissa's other sister. She hadn't heard from Madi since she moved back to Port Townsend. The middle Ambrose sister lived abroad in London, where she had been for the past six or so years.

[Madi: *Rissa, I don't know what you did, but Mel is losing her fucking shit. I hope everything is okay, and if you need to talk, I'm here.*]

Marissa and Madi weren't necessarily close, but Melanie and Madilyn were *not* close. They hadn't been close since middle school. So, to get a message from Madi that she had heard from Mel meant Mel was really upset.

"Fuuuuuck," she said out loud. But rather than responding, she scrolled through the rest of her messages. Three from her mom, probably casually trying to pry rather than come right out and ask.

[Mom: *Hey honey, just wanted to see if you were doing okay. Call me soon.*]

The generic mom texts.

[Mom: *Hey Marissa. Melanie dropped the girls off this morning and was really upset. She wouldn't tell me why, just that you two got into a fight. Is everything okay?*]

She could hear this one in her mind in her mother's voice. Concerned but also very firm. No one was allowed to upset the golden child.

The newest text was from this morning.

[Mom: Hey baby, I was just wondering how you've been. Please give me a call.]

She also had a text from Jack.

[Jack: Hey beautiful, it was great spending time with you. Hope we can do it again soon.]

Closing her texts, she opened her voicemail and put the phone to her ear without bothering to sit up.

"Hey Marissa, it is Cooper from the SPD." He mumbled something that wasn't quite audible before continuing. "If you could call me back, I have some news that might interest you."

Marissa didn't bother listening to the rest before she hung up and dialed his number. Thankfully, he picked up, rather than making her go through Laura.

"This is Lieutenant Cooper. How can I help you?"

"Hi, Lieutenant. It's Marissa Ambrose—"

"Oh, Marissa. Thank you for calling me back," he said in a gruff tone. "How are you?"

"You said there was news?" She was not in the mood for small talk.

"Yes, yes. As you know, there had been an arrest made in Ohio. Well, he has been extradited back here, and the FBI would like you to come in as a formality and go over some things."

"The FBI?"

"Yes. I'm not permitted to say much more on the matter, but if you think you could plan to come down for a day—"

"Of course. I can be there in a couple of hours."

When Marissa hung up, she all but jumped out of bed, searching for clean clothes.

Within the hour, she and Ellie were on the ferry, on their way to her old precinct. Marissa could feel the fluttering of anxiety and excitement building in her stomach, giving her chills as she watched the Sound's choppy waters.

Upon arriving, she was escorted to the precinct's back office, just outside one of the interview rooms. Two very well-dressed men stood there, looking deep in conversation, until they noticed her presence. Marissa looked over at the taller of the two agents, recognizing him immediately. He had thick dark hair and soft brown eyes that made her smile without meaning to.

He caught her looking at him and smiled back. "Detective Ambrose."

"Agent Mackenzie." The world was very small indeed.

"'You two know each other?" the other agent raised an eyebrow.

"We worked together on the O'Rourke case. What was that? Four, almost five years ago?" He didn't take his eyes off her as he answered, and he hadn't stopped smiling either. "This is my partner, Clyde Bennet."

What he wasn't saying was that once they had closed the O'Rourke case, they had gone out for almost a year. After her second divorce. With many successful dates by Marissa's memory. But he was located in D.C., and Marissa still wanted to try to make things work with Jared.

"Something like that," she said before taking a deep breath through her nose. "So, what am I doing here?"

Agent Bennet nodded his head. "We've brought our suspect from Ohio to answer for the crimes here." He paused. "He has asked to speak to you." There was a long, weighty silence in the air. "You do not have to speak to him if you aren't comfortable. But he has offered to give us a list of his crimes to you."

"The suspect that you believe to be the Couple's Killer?" At least one of them. Even if no one believed her that there was a second unsub.

"That is correct."

She just stared at them in disbelief. "The man you think murdered my partner in front of me and held me captive for two days?"

"You are not under any obligation to talk to him," Mackenzie said gently, stepping forward, giving Agent Bennet something of a scolding look.

Lieutenant Cooper approached, frown on his face, looking exhausted. Knowing him, he was probably irritated with the FBI's presence.

Marissa looked from one man to the other. Agent Bennet looked annoyed, keeping his lips tight and his eyes focused on a spot on the floor. And desperate. James Mackenzie watched her with genuine concern. Looking past both of them, she looked through the one-way window at the man sitting in the interview room.

"That him?"

Agent Bennet nodded.

He didn't look like what she had pictured. She had only come face to face with one other serial killer, and he had more than fit the stereotype. He had been a grungy, hillbilly mess. This man, on the other hand, was well-groomed with a well-kept beard and clean clothes. He looked like someone she could have gone to school with. Not extraordinary but not bad looking. He seemed very casual sitting there, not like someone charged with not one but many murders.

"And he asked for me? By name?"

Agent Bennet nodded again. "He said he won't talk to anyone else."

"You really don't—"

"I'll do it," Marissa interrupted Mac and looked over at Agent Bennet.

"Does the dog need to go with you?" Agent Mackenzie asked, immediately nodding after seeing her expression. "Okay, but a few ground rules. You aren't allowed to discuss the crimes committed in Ohio that he was brought in for. If you feel too uncomfortable at any time, you can leave at any point. Anything you get can help us, names, dates, locations."

"Okay."

"I'll be in there with you, and Agent Bennet will be right here."

Marissa nodded and took a deep breath before following Mac into the room.

"There she is. My favorite detective." The man stood up slightly before the chains around his wrists and ankles forced him back down.

He looked so ordinary. Short, dirty blonde hair, gray eyes, broad shoulders. He looked like her high school quarterback. There was nothing out of the ordinary about him, but the way he watched her caused her body to stiffen.

"How have you been, detective? I'm glad to see you made a full recovery."

Marissa didn't want to be here. Mac pulled out a chair for her before sitting down in the other one. She stared at the top of the table while Mac spoke. "Daniel Fryer, you're here today because you have admitted to the murder of Detective Thomas Disher and the kidnapping and assault of Detective Marissa Ambrose. You were arrested in Ohio for the murder of Wendy Lupo, which we cannot discuss today."

"Yes, Agent Mackenzie. You already know this," he said with impatience, glaring at the recorder in the middle. He looked back at Marissa with a sly smile that drained all the blood from her face. "Do you think we could have space, Agent Mackenzie?"

Marissa went to speak up, but Mac shook his head. "That was not the agreement."

"Fine." He narrowed his gray eyes at Mac before turning his attention back to Marissa, causing her to flinch. "Tell me, how are you feeling these days?"

"I'm just fine." She made sure to keep her voice even. "They tell me you asked to speak with me. Why?"

"I was curious." He drummed his fingers.

"Curious?" Her head throbbed. She wanted to go home.

"I'd never left a victim alive before."

"Out of how many victims is that?" She needed to make the most of her time, but she felt like she was having an out-of-body experience. She didn't react to his words, keeping her face still.

"We'll get there." He was playing games. He had control of the room, and he knew it. They needed information, and there wasn't much they could leverage. "I'll give you a name at the end of each visit. All I have is time."

"I can't make those kinds of deals with you. But if you give me something worth giving them, I'm sure some kind of arrangement can be made." She swallowed, glancing over at Mac, who watched the convict closely.

"Okay," the man finally said after looking her over, leaning back in his chair. "Let me start with what I didn't do. I did not kill the Harrises, the Cochrens, or the Teens." He smiled at Marissa's evident confusion. "I admit to killing Detective Disher and being party to your subsequent kidnapping."

Glancing at Agent Mackenzie's raised eyebrow, Fryer looked very amused with himself.

"You didn't tell them there was more than one?"

The hair on the back of Marissa's neck raised, and her blood suddenly ran cold. She stiffened but kept her face as neutral as possible. It didn't seem like it was enough.

"Or they didn't believe you."

Despite her efforts, he was reading her like a book. Ellie sat up, resting her head in Marissa's lap and letting out a gentle whine of warning. Her anxiety was far too high.

"Is he sending you pictures?"

Marissa didn't say a word, but Fryer looked amused.

"What about that husband of yours?"

"Ex-husband." She hadn't meant to respond, but the words just fell out of her mouth.

"Interesting."

"Excuse me. I need to get some air. Can we get you anything?"

Marissa glanced at Mac before making eye contact with Fryer. He gave her a broad smile and shook his head, leaning forward, his chains shifting loudly with him.

"No, ma'am. Thank you for asking."

Marissa couldn't tell if he was taunting her or if he was trying to genuinely be polite. But she didn't care. Standing up very slowly, she nodded her head. "We'll be right back."

As the door closed behind her, Marissa sucked in a breath and immediately shot for the nearest garbage can. Foam and phlegm came up, her ribs aching from heaving. When she pulled her head out of the pail, she realized everyone was staring at her. Cold sweat covered her, and she shivered noticeably.

"Weak stomach?" someone muttered from their desk, though Marissa couldn't see who.

Mac stepped forward, placing a hand on her back, but before he said anything, Lieutenant Cooper slammed his hand down on the nearest desk.

"That's enough," he snapped before walking up to her, looking down at his feet. "Marissa, this department and I owe you an apology. For not taking your claims seriously."

She heard his words but didn't respond. There was nothing to say. Two years after the fact and all the shit they had given her, as crazy as they made her feel, finally, there was the truth. It didn't give her any relief whatsoever.

"We have to go back in," she mumbled and stood, taking a deep breath to collect herself.

"Is there anything you need before we go back in?" Mac's hand was still on her back supportively.

"A soda?" No faster than Marissa said it was there a coke in her hand. She took a few sips before nodding.

"Let's get back in there."

They talked in circles for another two hours, Marissa feeling like she wasn't accomplishing anything. Fryer knew he controlled the room. He took credit for over a dozen murders on his own. Murders that police would never tie him to or consider suspicious without his knowledge.

He had no demands in exchange for giving information, just visits with her. When she had asked him why, he gave her an unsettling smile that put her teeth on edge and repeated himself: "I've never left anyone alive before." He implied he hadn't planned on leaving her that way either but promised to discuss her stalker at their next meeting. He called him Ben. Having this name now felt like a thousand pounds being dropped on top of her. She couldn't begin to put into words how unsettled she felt.

"Let me give you a ride home." Agent Mackenzie stood beside her awkwardly, looking as though he didn't know what to do with his hands. She had brushed by everyone to hurry outside into the cold night air. She didn't want to talk to anyone at the precinct. None of these people had believed her—people who were supposed to be her friends and have her back. Now they were nothing but apologies. Two years of calling her crazy. She wasn't too fond of the FBI either, James Mackenzie aside.

"You don't want to give me a ride. I don't live in the city anymore."

"It's fine. You shouldn't have to be by yourself right now." He paused. "Is there someone I can call? Your husband?"

"Ex-husband. And definitely not." She straightened herself and swallowed, doing her best to look like she was okay. She was anything but fine. Ellie shoved her nose into her leg, urging her to relax. "Like I said, I don't live in the city anymore. It's a two-hour ferry ride."

"The last ferry to Bainbridge already went out. You take the ferry to Bainbridge, right? Then to Port Townsend?" Detective Sisto chimed in as he came outside, immediately looking as though he regretted opening his mouth and saying anything at all. "They are doing maintenance work," he added in a softer tone. "Have a goodnight." And he all but ran off.

Marissa rubbed her eyes in annoyance. Hell would freeze over before she called Jared. She could, in theory, call Lydia, but she was probably working. "I'll just grab a hotel."

"Nonsense. Let me drive you home." Mackenzie watched her with a raised eyebrow, waiting for her to agree. He looked like he had no intention of losing the argument.

Marissa narrowed her eyes slightly. On a different day, she probably would have continued to argue until she had gotten her way. Which was basically like cutting off her nose to spite her face. She didn't want to stay in a hotel. She would need to find one that would accept Ellie. And she also didn't have that kind of money at the moment. She had only planned for lunch, which she had now thrown up, and the ferry ride there and back.

"Okay. But it's a two-and-a-half-hour drive."

"That won't be a problem."

Marissa didn't bother looking up. "Great. I'll be back next week. Lead the way." And with that, she patted her leg and called Ellie to her side.

They walked without further comment to his car, a very predictable black SUV rental. Ellie stretched out on the back seat and immediately began snoring. Apparently, the day had been much too exciting for her.

Despite the brief excitement she had felt hours earlier when she saw him, they traveled in silence. Comfortable silence that Marissa was grateful for.

"The driveway there, you can pull up right next to the mini." She straightened in her seat, adjusting the seat belt, eager to get out of the car.

"Perfect," he said quietly, carefully pulling the car in and putting it in the park. "Do you know of any hotels open late?"

Marissa considered giving him a list of places to check but thought better of it. He had been kind enough to drive her all the way out here. "Nonsense. I have a perfectly good guest room you can use for tonight. It's the least I can do."

It may have been dark, but she was certain she saw relief wash over his face. Of course, whether it was because he didn't have to find a hotel or if it meant he could keep an eye on her, she wasn't sure. She didn't particularly care. She stepped out of the car and stretched while Ellie followed right behind her.

"Here you go." Marissa handed off the spare pillows and gave him a weak smile. "You are welcome to raid for the fridge or whatever you need."

He smiled back, taking the pillows. "Thank you again."

"Of course. Thanks for the ride."

His eyes lingered on her for a minute before he tossed the pillows on the bed. "Anytime."

"I'll see you in the morning." She sighed and turned to head into the hall.

"Marissa," he said softly, stopping her in the doorway. "Are you sure you're going to be alright?"

"Of course." She flashed him a smile, but he didn't look convinced. "I'm just going to shower and go to bed. I will see you in the morning." She didn't give him the chance to argue, hurrying out of the guest room and down the hall to her own. She looked over at her bed, contemplating skipping the shower, but she needed to wash the feel of the day off. She had to get it off of her.

How was she going to make this a regular thing? What the fuck had she been thinking?

Walking into her bathroom, she glanced back and saw Ellie jump up on the bed and curl up in the corner, exhausted from her long day. She didn't close the door entirely, leaving it cracked if one of the animals wanted to follow her in, and started stripping off her clothes. Marissa winced as she raised her arms to get her shirt off, and she didn't even bother unclasping her bra. She just pulled it off and tossed it into the corner.

After turning on the shower, she turned off the light, so the muted light from her bedroom seeped in. Stepping into the shower, she let the hot water run over her face, and she held herself close. The day had been like something out of a nightmare. Something she had watched but not experienced herself. She hadn't felt anything. She couldn't allow herself to, aside from vomiting once she left the interrogation room. She hadn't been able to stop herself from that.

Now that she was alone, she let all of it wash over her. The fear she felt when Daniel Fryer's cold eyes looked through her, his unfeeling tone as he casually spoke about torture and murder. His crooked, charismatic smile physically made her heave.

She couldn't even give herself a moment to feel relief that the truth was finally out there. That now everyone knew she hadn't been crazy. There was a second person there. The person stalking her now was one of the men who had held her for two days. It was not a comfort. But at least now they couldn't call her crazy.

Leaning against the wall, she slid down and allowed the water to run off her. Pulling her knees close to her chest, she struggled to breathe. It was ragged and strained, and before she knew it, she was sobbing, gripping her arms tightly. Trying to gain some control, she turned and bit into her arm, attempting to stop the panic that was spreading through her. She bit down for several beats, trying to use the shock of pain to ease the fear. When she finally let go, she could see the dark blood in the dim light running down the drain.

Marissa didn't know how much time had passed when the door was pushed further open, allowing more light through. The water that had been hot when she started was now cold, and she shook from the chill. She had assumed it had been Ellie but realized after a moment someone was speaking to her.

"Marissa?"

She saw his silhouette stand there for a moment before he turned the water off. He knelt down beside her, towel in hand. "Here," he said gently. "Let's get you warm."

Marissa accepted the towel and moved very slowly, trying to wrap herself up.

"Here," he said again, wrapping the towel behind her. He put his arm under her legs, lifting her up.

"No," she weakly protested, but he shook his head.

"You've been in here for over an hour and a half, Marissa. You're freezing." She hadn't even been aware. "And you're bleeding." He gently placed her down on the bed. She hesitated, feeling momentarily shy, until she remembered he had seen her naked before. "Do you have a first aid kit?"

Marissa had to think. "Downstairs bathroom, under the sink."

He disappeared, making his way down the stairs. Marissa took the opportunity to throw on underwear and a long tank top. Getting back into bed, she pulled the covers up to her chest. She hadn't even realized she had been in there so long. That the water had gone from scalding hot to ice cold. Ellie whined, standing and repositioning, so she rested her head on Marissa's legs, where she could easily receive pets. When Mac returned, he had gauze and a wrap in one hand, Neosporin in the other. "Here, let me get this bandaged."

She waited for him to ask what had happened or assume and lecture her, but neither came. He just quietly wrapped it up. Once he was content with his doctoring, he sighed and looked her in the eyes. "Now. How do you feel?"

"Warmer." She said with a sigh. "Thank you." She looked down at her hands, feeling over-whelming shame.

"Of course." He smiled at her and stood awk-wardly for a moment, seemingly unsure if he should leave her alone.

Marissa sighed and grabbed the remote off her nightstand. "Would it be too much to ask you to keep me company until I fell asleep?" The relief was immediate on his face. He walked around the bed and sat on the blankets on the other side of her. She thought she'd made the offer for his sake, but as they looked for something to watch, Marissa felt herself relaxing.

Chapter 14

She didn't realize she had fallen asleep until she felt James Mackenzie move. It was still dark, but she could hear the birds' morning conversations. He was trying to move carefully not to disturb her, pulling blankets back over her once he was on his feet and gently kissing her forehead, a habit that felt natural. Ellie raised her head and watched him leave, only lying back down once he had closed the door behind him. Marissa listened as he walked through the old house, the boards creaking under his feet. Once he was downstairs, she rolled over and looked at her phone. It was 5:50 a.m. Marissa had gotten a few hours of solid sleep, something she had not expected after yesterday. Adjusting, she hissed as she moved her arm, the ache radiating through her fingers. In fact, every part of her body ached; the tension from the stress of the day before was lingering.

Maybe she would just try to close her eyes and sleep a little longer. It was still early. Putting her phone back down, she rolled back over and closed her eyes. But sleep didn't return. It had obviously just been a fluke; pure exhaustion had taken over. But she laid there anyway, for no other reason than pure stubbornness.

Lying there, she thought back to the day she met James Mackenzie. She had been so pissed at the captain's insistence they bring the FBI on the case. But kids were going missing, so while she felt upset by the decision, she understood it. They were there only two weeks, and it hadn't been the FBI who brought the case to a close—she and her partner had found the kids. But in that time, she and Agent Mackenzie had built up a rapport full of fun flirtation and tension. And as soon as the case was closed, he asked her out to dinner. Marissa and Jared's divorce had been finalized for over a year, and he was out of rehab and doing well. He had already begun dating; Marissa had not. Though, she and Jared were back to being the best friends they had always been. For whatever reason, she had decided to say yes for the first time in a year of being single.

He had taken her to dinner, and then they went for a walk along the waterfront and spent some time at the Seattle arcade. It was all just so easy and natural with him; he made her feel relaxed. And they spent the next few weeks together, going out, spending time in, and exploring what a relationship looked like. He had to go back to D.C., but he continued to come out to visit her on the weekends and took days off here and there, and they talked on the phone nearly every day. They were exploring more and more what it was to be in a long-distance relationship.

And just like that, it was one of her niece's birthdays, Mac was out of town, and there was Jared. He told her he was sober, that he loved her. Jared wanted another chance. He needed another chance. And somehow, that was it. She said she needed to think about it, but from the moment he said he still loved her, that was it. Because somewhere in the back of her mind, they were always endgame. It would always be them.

She waited to tell Mac in person; she owed him that much. And he was amazingly understanding. Because he was all but perfect. Telling him goodbye was much harder than she expected it being. Still, they kept in touch as friends, talking every so often on the phone. But she had never realized that he hadn't necessarily moved on. Thinking back now, she could still see and feel that magic between them. That spark even existed. She had given up on them for something that hadn't worked out.

Not to say that it wouldn't have. Maybe she and Jared weren't the picture-perfect couple. They fought too much; they both felt passionate about almost everything, they were both insanely stubborn. But they loved each other fiercely. They could have really had a life together. Maybe not kids like they had wanted. Apparently, Marissa was the problem there. At least she knew now. But there was nothing like being married to your best friend. She loved him so much; she had let him go so that he had a fighting chance to have a whole life.

She had never considered anyone else other than Jared until Mac. That statement was still valid. Of course, none of this mattered one way or another anyway. She couldn't be with anyone as long as he was out there. Ben. She swallowed down the lump growing in her throat and forced herself to focus on her breathing. If she could just focus on that, think of nothing else, maybe she could just get some rest.

When she finally pulled herself out of bed three hours later, the sun was already up. She dug around her closet for sweatpants and eventually made her way to the stairs. She paused at the top and slowly descended down as her ankles locked up. Once she was downstairs, she let Ellie out and curiously looked around for any sign of Mac but didn't see him. What she saw was a cup of coffee on the kitchen island next to a post-it note.

I think I remember how you like your coffee.

Picking up her Ravenclaw mug, she sipped it and smiled. He did remember. Putting it in the microwave for a minute, she inspected the rest of her downstairs before seeing him through the front window. He sat on her front porch. Throwing on her hoodie and grabbing her now warm coffee, she stepped outside to join him.

"Good morning."

"Good morning." He smiled and stood as she came over, not sitting back down until she sat in the other chair. "Did you sleep okay? How are you feeling?"

"I actually slept," she honestly admitted. "Still a little drained but otherwise okay."

"Good." He took a sip of his drink. "How's the coffee?"

"Perfect. You remembered."

"Of course I did." He smiled at her in such a way that she had to look away from him, looking out on the empty street and hoping he didn't see the red in her cheeks. "I spoke to the director this morning as well as the SPD commissioner and Port Townsend's sheriff. Agent Bennet will be down later today, and we'll finish some details. Now that they are taking the threat on you seriously, we would rather have an agent across the street to keep an eye on you. You'll also always have an escort when you go into Seattle and ideally one around here."

Marissa just raised an eyebrow at him. "You know I've been managing on my own just fine. It's been two years."

"And you shouldn't have had to deal with any of this on your own."

She looked down at her coffee and sighed. "Maybe." Taking another sip, she shook her head. "It's been a hell of an experience," she muttered, unsure if he heard her.

There was a silence before Mac sighed. "You should have told me what was going on, Rissa."

"I'm fine, Mac," she said gently before taking a sip, but as she met his eyes, tears she didn't expect started pushing on her eyes.

He watched her for a long moment before he let it go. Though, she was sure it wouldn't be the last time they spoke about it. "How's your arm?"

Now she really worked to avoid his gaze. "It's okay. Good wrap job. Thank you." She blinked and looked every which way until she turned to look at him. His expression was unreadable, but she could see his mind was reeling with thoughts.

"Is there someone you should call? A friend, a relative? Maybe a therapist?" he said gently after a moment, free from any judgment in his tone. It annoyed her.

"No. I'm good. I was just ... having a bad moment." She took in a deep breath before sipping more of her coffee.

"You know, you really don't have to do this?"

When she raised an eyebrow at him, he sighed and continued. "I'm just saying, it might not be the healthiest thing—"

Raising her hand, she put her empty mug down. "I need to do this as much for myself as I do to help the investigation, especially if he can give me answers." She needed to change the subject. "So, you know most of everything that's been going on with me since I last saw you; what about you? What have you been up to?"

He looked her over for a long moment before smiling and leaning back in his chair. "Well, not much, really. Working, looking at a promotion. Thinking about buying a brownstone. Nothing to really write home about." He paused. "Just going to work and going home."

"How is Ethan?" Marissa loved watching his face light up when he spoke about his son. He and his ex-wife had been divorced for nearly a decade, but they were on good terms, and he had a close relationship with his son.

Now Mac grinned. "He's doing great. He just turned thirteen. And he's really embracing that whole 'teenage angst.'"

"You're not seeing anyone?" she asked casually. It had been a while since they had spoken. She hadn't realized just how much she missed his voice.

"Nope. Haven't found anyone worth my time." He grinned at her before also looking out into the empty street. "If you don't mind me asking, what happened with the ex-husband?"

Marissa said, looking down into her empty cup, "You know, we were making it work. And then everything happened, and I just couldn't deal. Especially when pictures started arriving on my doorstep. I couldn't bring myself to put him at risk."

"So, you told him the truth?"

"Oh god, no. I just broke it off. He actually still isn't talking to me." She leaned back in her chair and put the coffee mug down. "But it's for the better. He's got a girlfriend. A pregnant girlfriend that he lives with." She huffed. "It's fine. Can we talk about something else now?"

"Sure. What do you want to talk about?"

Marissa couldn't help but laugh. "I have no idea."

"Here, why don't we go and get some more coffee? I'm sure we'll come up with something to talk about."

"Sounds good."

She followed him inside, and as he went to pour them more coffee, she let Ellie back in. Sitting at the kitchen island, Marissa wrapped her hands around her mug, looking at the dark liquid. "I need to thank you."

"For what?" he asked gently, sitting beside her.

"For just being there last night." She looked up at him and met his gaze before dropping her eyes back to her coffee mug.

There was a pause as he seemed to carefully be picking his words. "You don't need to thank me, Marissa." He gave her a small smile. "I do think you might need to rethink this weekly visit plan with Daniel Fryer."

Marissa sighed before shaking her head at him, letting go of her cup, and rubbing her arms from an unseen chill. "You know I can't do that. For one, we don't even have a victim count for him yet, and I need to know more about what happened. Secondly, I need to know more about who he was working with."

Marissa's breathing had quickened without her taking much notice as she gripped the wound on her arm tighter. Mac placed his hand over hers and gave it a gentle squeeze, bringing her eyes back to his gaze.

"Hey..." His voice was gentle, and he waited until he was sure she was looking back at him. "You at least don't have to do it alone."

Studying his eyes, she knew he genuinely meant it. There was a slight, familiar flutter in the pit of her stomach, one she had felt when their case together had been closed and he had asked her out on a date.

Before she could respond to him, there was a knock at the door. Glancing down at the time on her phone, she frowned, not sure who the hell would be at her door this early. Getting up, she walked past Ellie, who barked twice and then excitedly whined at the door. Before she even opened the door, Marissa saw her sister through the glass window, standing there looking at the ground.

"Hey, what's up?" Marissa almost asked why the hell she was knocking, rather than just letting herself in, before she remembered Mel's last visit. Her sister had told her that she needed to leave Brian alone and get her shit together in no uncertain terms. Having been less than a week ago, she was surprised to see her back.

Melanie's jaw was tight, signaling that she was definitely still mad. "I just came by to make sure you're coming to Thanksgiving."

Marissa started at her blankly, trying to process. "Thanksgiving?"

"Yeah, you know, that holiday with all the food?" When Marissa just continued to stare, Mel rolled her eyes and huffed loudly. "Two days from now."

"Oh." With everything going on, she hadn't even realized the holiday was so close. "I mean. Do you want me there?" It was blunt, but she wasn't sure. And, of course, she immediately regretted asking. Melanie looked like she had been slapped in the face.

"Of course I do!" she snapped after a moment had passed. "I feel like we were closer when you lived in Seattle than we are now that you live two minutes away." She wiped her eyes. "I'm just tired of everyone lying to me! I'm not stupid. I know when I'm being lied to."

Marissa's heart broke as she watched her baby sister standing in front of her, falling apart. Mainly because of Marissa's actions. Mel shifted her weight from one foot to the other and sighed heavily.

"And I get ... that it's hard ... seeing Jared moving on so quickly. But you are both still my family, and we need to figure out how to make it work." Tears started falling from her eyes, despite her efforts to wipe them away. "I just need you there."

"Mel..." It was during that pause, while Marissa searched for something to say, that Mac came up behind her.

Melanie wiped the tears from her eyes again and smiled awkwardly. "I'm sorry. I didn't know you had company."

She saw the shift in her sister and sighed. "Melanie, this is James Mackenzie. Mac, this is my sister, Melanie."

Mac gave her a charming smile and extended his hand to shake hers. "It's so great to meet you. I've heard so much about you." Marissa had told him all about her family when they dated, but she doubted he remembered much in the way of details.

Melanie studied his face as though she were trying to remember if she had met him before. "It's so great to meet you. Are you staying in town for long?"

"As a matter of fact, I will be. I'll be renting the house across the street. I'll be finalizing the paperwork this afternoon. When I realized Marissa and I were going to be neighbors, I had to come by. It's been a few years since Marissa and I connected."

Marissa raised an eyebrow, giving him a curious look before giving Mel a smile, not that she was paying any attention to Marissa anymore.

"You should join us for Thanksgiving!"

Marissa was about to suggest that he had plans—
family holidays in general with a normal, functional
family were a lot, and this year was stacking up
to be a whole lot extra for her dysfunctional one.
But before she could speak up, he enthusiastically
responded, "That would be great! I don't really
know anyone else in the area."

Alarm bells were going off in her head, but there
was nothing she could do to stop this train now.

"Wonderful." Melanie's entire demeanor had
shifted, and Marissa could only imagine what was
running through her mind. Mel leaned forward to
pull Mac into a half hug before pulling Marissa
close into a hug. "I can't wait!" She started to head
off. "Dinner will be around four!"

Once Melanie was driving off out of sight,
Marissa turned to Mac. "You have no idea what you
just signed up for."

Shaking her head, she ran through the events of
their last conversation. She didn't understand how
quickly Melanie could turn it around. Maybe it was
the pregnancy hormones.

He gave her a half-cocked smile and shoved his
hands in his pockets. "You kind of seemed like you
needed a save there."

"You look like you're starting to make a habit
out of it."

He simply shrugged.

"Is that what Agent Bennet is coming down here
for? To finalize this rental arrangement?"

Mac nodded. "I told you, everyone agreed that you needed better surveillance, and if you insist on these weekly meetings, you should have someone with you. And while I'm sure Bennet can be good company, I insisted." He paused. "You know ... since we already know each other."

Marissa smiled. Something in the knowledge that he would be around was comforting. Not that she thought she needed anyone.

As though on cue, Agent Bennet, whose first name was apparently Clyde, arrived, and they sat around her living room discussing how things would go from here on out. Mac would move in across the street. It wasn't going to be regular surveillance because it was assumed that Ben, as they would now refer to him, already knew about the FBI's involvement. But the hope was that his presence would at least keep things from progressing any further than just pictures while they tried to learn his identity. Mac would also join her on her trips to Seattle whenever she met with Daniel Fryer. Next, they looked over all the photos she had received, the most recent envelope that she saved with her name, and the note that had come with it. Bennet took the envelope and the letter with him for analysis when he left. The pictures were useless.

Once it was just them again, Mac thumbed through the photos on her counter. Marissa glanced over before walking to the back door and letting Ellie out into the yard.

"I know that these photos are intrusive and taken by a stalker, serial killer, but some of these are pretty good."

Marissa raised an eyebrow and shook her head at him. "You're funny."

"This is the ex-husband, right?" She glanced over as he pointed out a few photos of her with Jared and the few of Jared alone.

"It is," she said flatly.

"You look really happy in some of these." She walked over, taking a better look at the photos he was pointing out. In one, they were sitting in her backyard laughing at something. In another, they were sitting on her kitchen floor eating ice cream.

"I have my moments," she mumbled. "It feels like that was taken a lifetime ago." She backed up and leaned against the counter behind him. "You know, hanging around here, you'll probably have your picture taken, too."

"Well, hopefully, he'll get my good side." He grinned at her, leaning his back against the kitchen island to face her, crossing his arms across his chest. When she made a face at him, he just laughed. "But seriously, I'm not too worried about it. I'm trained with a gun, so..."

She couldn't stop herself from smiling. "You're not nearly as charming as you think you are."

"You don't think so?"

"Nope." She grinned at him.

"Damn. I'm going to have to work on it."

"Stop it." She laughed.

He laughed with her, and she couldn't help but feel comfortable. He met her eyes and smiled.

"Okay, well, I've got to go get my things from the airport and get settled in." He gave her an odd look. "Are you going to be okay till I get back?"

"Yes, Mac." She rolled her eyes and gave him a shove. "I've been just fine all this time. I think I'll be fine till you make it back."

"Okay. But you have my number if you need anything?"

"Yes. Go. Get out of my house. I'll see you when you get back."

"Okay. I'm going."

She smiled and walked him to the door, where she watched him head to his car. She didn't go back inside until he had driven out of sight.

Chapter 15

Two days later, Marissa had already talked herself out of canceling at the last minute at least four times before she found herself on her sister's front porch. She turned around halfway to the house, but Mac hooked his arm into hers and fell in step with her until they reached the front door. Looking at him anxiously, she bounced on the balls of her feet.

"We could just go back, you know," she stated, only to be met with raised eyebrows.

"I'm sure it's not going to be as bad as you think," he said, his expression full of optimism that Marissa did not share.

First, there was the very one-sided argument with Melanie, where Mel had come and thrown hormonal rage at her and then left. She hadn't spoken to Brian since. She wasn't sure she should. Then there was Jared and his pregnant Barbie companion, who would undoubtedly be there. And potentially her ex-in-laws. And her own mother, whom Marissa had been casually dodging for a few weeks now. Then there was Mac, whom Marissa hadn't given any thought to explain. Thankfully, he was fully prepared with a story about who he was and why he was in town.

When she finally knocked on the door, she was greeted by her brother-in-law, who stared at Mac. Her former in-laws were already in the living room, listening to Blaire. Marissa's mom came out of the kitchen, trying to hush up her little dog, who was aggressively announcing their presence. Brian disappeared into the kitchen, where Marissa assumed Mel was cooking. The smells in the house were terrific, causing her mouth to water.

The four girls came running to see their aunt, whom they hadn't seen in far too long. Bethany jumped into Marissa's arms, while Blaire shyly smiled at Mac, referring to him as Prince Eric. She took a moment to introduce Mac to the family, who all watched him curiously. He was just an old friend, she insisted. It wasn't exactly a lie. And they simply ate him up, asking questions about his life and who he was. As far as they were concerned, he was a reporter for a travel magazine. Even Mel popped out of the kitchen to inspect him a little closer without paying Marissa any mind.

And then Jared arrived. She felt his presence before she saw him, the hairs on the back of her neck rising. Their eyes met for a moment before he turned to Mac, and Marissa saw his rage brewing. She realized what he must have thought. Because even though she had reassured Jared that she had never doubted her decision in choosing him over Mac, here they were ... together. It hadn't occurred to her what he would think when he saw Mac. Not only did he know Mac and Marissa's relation-ship history, but he also knew that Mac was FBI. Something they were making sure no one else knew. Her body tensed at the thought.

Kirstie was there on his arm, looking bouncy and perfect, although she narrowed her eyes at Marissa. Apparently, they were no longer playing nice.

Jared announced their presence, carrying pies and giving the girls big smiles as they all ran to him. Seeing him stand there made her heart drop. Mac must have had the same realization as Jared hur-ried past them because he turned to look at her. He didn't seem nearly as worried, stepping alongside her and placing his hand on the small of her back with a reassuring smile. Sighing heavily, Marissa didn't know what to do. She needed Jared to keep his mouth shut about Mac's actual profession, but she also didn't want to talk to her ex-husband alone.

Marilyn walked over to them before Marissa could decide, pulling her to her feet and into another hug. "Honey, you really are too thin."

"I'm fine, Mom." Mac nudged her gently, providing her with the out she needed. "Mac, this is my mom, Marilyn." She took a step back, letting them get appropriately introduced. "Mom, this is James Mackenzie."

"So, how do you know my daughter?" Marilyn seemed genuinely interested, and Mac was happy to once again provide false truths. Marissa hardly listened as he described a meeting a few years ago when he wrote a Pikes Place Market story. She was looking in the direction of the kitchen, still weighing her options. There were too many lies and half-truths involving her that were floating around this giant house, and it made the walls feel like they were closing in—and fast.

Marissa tugged at her hair anxiously, unable to hear anything going on around her. A ringing in her ears was growing louder and louder.

"Excuse me." Marissa gave her mom a smile and flashed Mac a look of reassurance before turning and heading to the bathroom.

Locking the door behind her, she leaned against the sink, closed her eyes, hung her head, and tried to breathe. Ellie whined and shoved her nose into her leg, concerned.

None of this should have been a thing. Marissa knew that there would be anger from Jared. She had made it easy for him to assume she didn't care anymore. She had done it on purpose because she knew anger would help keep the distance.

Opening her eyes, she looked at her reflection in the mirror before splashing some cold water on her face. Marissa didn't know how she would make it through this dinner. Every part of her felt tense and ached. Digging around in the tiny purse she'd been clutching since she hung her coat, she pulled out a pill bottle. Had she already taken a muscle relaxer? She couldn't remember; it was all a little foggy. It was always a little hazy. Considering everything still ached, if she had, it wasn't working. After popping the pill, she splashed more cold water on her face. She just needed to make it through dinner. Turning, she unlocked the door and started out of the bathroom.

Before she thought better of it, she found herself in the kitchen, where Brian was getting dinner ready to dish up and Jared was helping by carving the turkey. "Can I speak to you for a minute?" She didn't bother clarifying whom she meant to talk to but glanced up to meet his gaze and felt an ache as she rubbed the back of her neck. "It will just take a second."

She winced at the sound of a turkey leg he snapped and dropped on the cutting board. Definitely didn't need to guess if he was still angry. She glanced over at Brian, sighing. She hadn't spoken to him at all since Mel came over and told her off. Not that there was much to tell him; the case was growing cold, which left her feeling like a complete failure.

Chapter 15

Turning her attention back to Jared, she straightened herself up and swallowed. "I really need to talk to you. Alone." She couldn't leave the kitchen without doing so. She needed him to keep Mac's secret. Fuck, she was drowning in secrets.

Setting the leg down on the platter, Jared's attention was momentarily stolen by his brother, who'd pushed his way to the turkey to take over the carving without so much as a word.

"I'll pass." Keeping his words short with no room for interpretation, he went to the sink. He turned on the water, ensuring it was on at full blast to assist in partially drowning out any noises behind him while he washed the turkey off his hands.

Turning to Brian, Jared just continued to ignore her. "Looks like we're nearly ready. I'm going to go get the girls." And with that, he headed out of the kitchen past her.

Marissa took a step back when Jared pushed his way out of the kitchen and sighed heavily. She was about to turn when Brian spoke up.

"That went well," he said, working the knife and meat fork down the unfinished half of the turkey. "I don't know what kind of friends you and Mac are, but by bringing him here, you're probably lucky all you got was resistance. He's not happy. Mel's not going to be happy if you guys make a scene here."

She leaned against the wall and shook her head. "It is a really long story." She didn't want to give Brian any more secrets to hold, so she abruptly

211

stopped herself. "I wasn't planning on bringing him, but Mel insisted. She called me this morning to make sure he was coming." Shaking her head, she pushed the hair from her face. "I promise I won't make a scene. We'll eat, and we'll go."

As it was, Marissa didn't feel wanted there. Jared didn't want her there; Mel didn't want her there. She wasn't getting a great read on Kirstie, but she knew she didn't want to be around her.

But she could be an adult, at least. She wasn't planning on ruining Thanksgiving. So she could smile and stay quiet through dinner, spend some time with the kids, and leave. She probably should've followed her first instinct and called out of dinner sick. But it was too late for that. What she needed was a drink.

Back in the living room, she sat down next to Amanda, her ex-mother-in-law. Mac was still fully engaged in conversation with her mom and John, her ex-father-in-law. He glanced over to her and gave her that reassuring smile, noting the expression on her face. He was sweet like that. She sighed heavily as Amanda put a hand on her arm.

"Are you doing okay?"

"Yeah, I'm fine. I just have a headache." She gave Amanda a smile and grabbed her bag, considering taking something else for the headache.

Amanda had been the best mother-in-law a girl could have asked for. She had always been like a

second mom to Marissa, even through all the sep-
arations and divorces.

Everyone gathered at the table, the girls seated
at the kids' table right behind their parents. Marissa
stared at the food on her plate and tried to engage
in light conversation, but her heart was not in it.
She wasn't hungry; she didn't want to talk about
how things were going or what was new. She definitely didn't want to explain Mac. Or Allison's case,
or the others. She mostly wanted a drink.

Once everyone was seated, John stood up from
his place at the table, raising his glass of spar-
kling cider. "We've got a couple of newbies at the
table this year, so first, I'd like to welcome you to
the family."

He ignored the loud guffaw from his son and
continued on. "Brian, Mel." He gestured to the
house. "Looks beautiful, smells even better." He
beamed at his daughter-in-law, "Now. On to tradi-
tions!" There was some groaning, but he powered
through, "Grumble all you want, but we don't eat
until we share our thanks. I'll start."

He cleared his throat. "I am thankful for my
wife. For sixteen years of sobriety. And for getting
to be the Pop-Pop to the best granddaughters in the
world!" He glanced around the table with his ever-
charming smirk. "And I guess you kids aren't terrible." Sitting down, he leaned back and put his arm
around the back of his wife's chair. "Who's next?"

"Thank you, John. I'll go next." Marilyn looked around the table, full of pride. Marissa's mom always took a moment to beam with pride over everything she could. "I am thankful for this ever-growing family, my daughters, the sons I never had." She gestured to Brian and Jared, as she would always consider him family, even if he and Marissa weren't together. "I'm grateful for the most beautiful granddaughters in the world. And I'm so grateful we can all be together." Marissa could see her mom was beginning to get emotional and was thankful she sat down.

Marissa fought not to roll her eyes. She usually didn't care about this one way or another. Of course, Marissa saw the importance of showing what everyone was grateful for. Still, she was not feeling it this year, and it took every ounce of effort not to show that on her face. She felt exhausted. It seemed the muscle relaxers were finally starting to work. And she might have taken one too many. But it would be fine; they would eat and leave. Looking down the line, she watched her little sister stand up, beaming.

Melanie looked around the table, grinning at the compliments from her father-in-law. She had silently watched as just about everyone grumbled at the mention of going around the table, but Marissa knew her sister loved this tradition. Marissa smiled at her mom. Despite everything, she was grateful she had been able to be there. They had seen so much less of her since she gave Marissa the house and moved to Grays Harbor, and Mel missed her.

"I'm grateful for friends—true friends who really show up for you." She shot Kirstie a smile before continuing on. "And it may be redundant but needs to be said. I'm so thankful for this family—the best in-laws a girl could ask for and for my mom. For my beautiful girls, my amazing husband. For an honest family with no secrets between them," she said sweetly as she shot Marissa a look before sitting down.

She watched the color drain from Brian's face, going from a look of disapproval to surprise at the shots fired between the lines in his wife's words. Brian strained a smile when the family turned their faces to him next. He stood up and cleared his throat.

"Guess I'll go next," he said, chuckling nervously. "I'm thankful that we were all able to gather today. We're so lucky to be surrounded by family and to be able to get together. I'm thankful for good company, amazing food, my wife and her culinary wizardry, all of my girls, and all the great influences they have. My brother, my in-laws, and that all of us are safe and doing well. That's what I'm thankful for." He nodded once and sat down, looking thrilled to be done.

Jared was up next. "Alright. Well. I'm not gonna be cheesy and list off the family. That's obvious. But I do have someone I need to thank." His gaze turned toward Marissa and Mac. "Our law enforcement. Whom we would be lost without. Not only do they protect us from bad guys, but they're also the best people to call when you need help with your significant other. They just take them off your hands so you can relax."

Like Mel, shots had been fired between the lines, and then in bright neon lights that left most of the table confused.

Marissa shifted uncomfortably, shooting him a not-so-subtle glare.

Glaring at Jared, Kirstie stood and laughed. "He's hilarious." Her voice was strained. "I'm thankful for ginger ale, saltine crackers, and the Costco-sized bottle of tums." Her hand ran over her stomach in a circle. "And for Mel, for being such an amazing friend through this experience and helping my anxiety stay low." She reached out across the table for Mel's hand, giving it a squeeze when they came together. "You have truly become one of my best friends."

Before the next person around the table could speak, a smaller voice piped up loudly. "Is that because of the baby in your belly, Aunt Kirstie?"

Bridget, the second youngest of the girls, was looking at her from the small table behind them. The girls were seated back-to-back with Brian and Mel, but close enough to Jared and Kirstie that they'd heard everything quickly. Brian's eyebrows shot up, turning around to look at the girls and leaning over the back of his chair. His daughters burst into giggles as all the adults in the room looked in that direction. The parents all looked around at each other, jaws promptly hitting the floor with shock, despite the fairly obvious clues Kirstie dropped while she gave thanks.

Suddenly Marissa was grateful she'd had this information ahead of time. She didn't need to react in front of her family. Instead, she took a sip of her water, wishing it was something more potent. Anything stronger. She avoided her mother's eyes, which she knew were on her, and just stared at her plate, digging her nail deep into her cuticle until it started to bleed. There weren't enough painkillers in the world to make this tolerable.

"Congratulations! This is wonderful news!"

Marissa wasn't even paying attention to who was talking; she just kept staring at her plate. It felt like everyone was talking at once with surprise and excitement. After a moment, John quieted the table, reminding everyone they had three more people to go.

Mac got to his feet without hesitation, bringing Marissa back into the moment. "First, congratulations to the happy couple!" Then he turned toward John at the head of the table. "Next, I am thankful to be able to spend a holiday with a warm and wonderful family such as yours. You have such a beautiful family; it reminds me of my own back home on the East Coast." He paused and smiled at Marissa.

"Finally, I am very thankful for second chances. They so seldom come along, and I don't plan on messing it up this time."

Looking up at Mac as he spoke, her eyes grew wide before narrowing, and for a second, her mouth hung open. For fuck's sake. If it wasn't bad enough that Jared assumed Mac was the reason for their breakup, Mac was just fueling the fire. And he absolutely knew it. She shifted uncomfortably before getting to her feet, running her fingers over the palms of her hands, and clearing her throat. Her voice was hoarse, and her throat was dry. Whether it was because of the pills or from all the excitement at the table, she wasn't sure.

"I'm just grateful to be here." She didn't need to explain the statement further. Two years ago, she had died twice on a hospital table. Today, she was alive. And while this exact moment, she would have preferred to have been anywhere else, she was grateful to still be breathing. She went to say something else, but as she looked around the table, she instead forced a smile and sat back down, rubbing her face numbly.

Amanda got to her feet without hesitation, holding her own glass toward her husband and smiling at everyone at the table. "And I am grateful for this ever-growing family, whether it be by blood or not." She nodded toward Marissa before continuing on. "And for my husband, there is no one else I would want to spend my life with."

Dinner passed with lots of chatter, conversations across the table, and comments about most things. Mac held his own, answering questions and chatting mostly with Marilyn. Marissa stared at her plate, pushing the food around with her fork. She was pretty sure her heart was beating fast enough to break her ribcage despite the muscle relaxers that should have been coursing through her veins. She hoped the parents would take her silence and lack of appetite as nothing personal. Most of her food ended up under the table for Ellie. She just didn't have an appetite. No one was paying much mind, not that she really cared much at this point. Her mind was wandering. She couldn't help but feel a twinge of jealousy looking at Kirstie. It should have been her. With her plate mostly empty, she went to her bag and started to rummage through, searching for her pills, but she couldn't find them.

"You okay, honey?"

Her mom was staring at her.

"Oh. Yeah. I just have a headache. I was looking for my Tylenol."

Well, now she was lying to her mom. Cool. Looking up at Mac, he gave her a shrug but didn't deny taking them one way or another. She glared at him and huffed heavily.

Dinner shifted into cleaning mode, during which Brian stood and started gathering plates. Her former in-laws were chatting with Kirstie, and Mel had scooted herself closer to her new best friend, beaming with excitement. God, Marissa was going to have to figure out something else for Christmas time. She couldn't do this again.

Marissa had moved to the living room with everyone else and was sitting with her mom and Mac, half paying attention to her mom when her phone buzzed. Glancing down, she got back on her feet. "Excuse me for one moment."

She moved to the other end of the living room, closer to where Kirstie and Melanie sat side by side, chatting with her former in-laws excitedly. Marissa ignored them and answered Lydia's call.

"Hey Lydia, Happy Thanksgiving!" Despite the sadness she felt, the sound of her friend's voice made her smile. They chatted for a couple of minutes, and Marissa even got to wish Evelyn a happy holiday. Lydia explained that they were spending the holiday with Tom's family, and even though she felt supported and loved, it was a lot. She had called Marissa to take comfort in her voice. It left Marissa feeling conflicted; she was glad she could be there for Lydia but was also drowning in guilt that her partner couldn't be with his family during the holidays.

While putting the phone back in her pocket, she wasn't intentionally listening to the conversation beside her, but she heard Kirstie get really excited. "It's been just amazing. A real-life whirlwind romance. Everything has been happening so fast!"

"Getting knocked up must have been really convenient then."

Marissa hadn't meant to say it out loud; the words just stumbled out. And not even quietly. Mac and her mom didn't seem to hear her but noticed the now undeniable and uncomfortable silence in the room. Kirstie, Amanda, and John all wore expressions of surprise, but Mel looked furious. She got up from where she sat and stormed over to her.

"Kitchen. Now." There was no room for interpretation in her words, and if there had been, she grabbed Marissa by the wrist, just for good measure. Of course, Marissa was stronger than Mel, and maybe she was just trying to appease her to fix the situation, but she complied.

Once they were in the kitchen, Mel looked at Brian and Jared, who were cleaning, and pointed toward the living room. "OUT," she mustered forcefully, narrowing her eyes back on Marissa, waiting for them to leave before she ripped into her.

Marissa snatched her wrist free once they were in the kitchen. She positioned herself away from both Mel and her ex-husband, even though he was preparing to leave the kitchen. She folded her arms across her chest and leaned against the counter, feeling slightly off-balance. So much for not making a scene. Her eyes flashed apologetically to Brian. She hoped he understood. She hadn't meant for the words to come out of her mouth. Both men promptly darted out of the kitchen and into the living room.

Mel balled her hands into fists. "What the actual fuck is your problem?" She clenched her jaw, her face turning red.

"I don't have one. It just sort of ... slipped out. It wasn't meant to be malicious." She hadn't meant to say it out loud. Of course, it didn't make her wrong either, but that wasn't the point.

"You know you have no claim to him, right? No ownership? No say in who he dates or how he lives his life?" Melanie threw up her hands in frustration.

"I don't—" She didn't even know where this was coming from. It was only a few weeks ago that Melanie had been comforting her over their breakup.

"You broke up with him after two decades. And for what? That guy out there who none of us have ever met before?"

For fuck's sake, did everyone think so little of her?

"First of all, I'm not dating Mac. Didn't break up with Jared for anyone else." It was unbelievable. "You insisted I bring him."

"Then who is he to you?"

"I told you, he's an old friend."

"I don't buy it, Marissa. Try again."

"I can't tell you." It was closer to the truth.

"Okay. Then what did you break up with Jared for?"

"I can't tell you that either."

"Are these the secrets Brian is keeping from me?"

"I can't tell you that either."

"How dare you fucking make my husband keep secrets from me." She slapped Marissa right across the face.

Marissa's jaw dropped as her hand shot up to her stinging cheek.

"It wasn't bad enough you ruined your own marriage, not once but twice. Now you're fucking with mine."

"Not that it fucking matters, but Brian was my friend before he was your husband. And he was my brother-in-law before he was your boyfriend." Marissa all but spit at Mel, trying to keep her voice low. "Do not push your fucking insecurities on me, Mel. Your fucking husband adores you. He would never do anything to jeopardize that."

As she glared at her sister, she noticed the tears falling down her face. Despite the sting on her face, Marissa's heart briefly went out to Mel, the heartbreak, and worry that she knew Mel was carrying. "For what it's worth, Mel, it's my secret he's keeping. And I never meant to tell him. It was an accident. If I could take it back, I would."

"What about Allison?" Melanie said after a long moment of silence.

"What?"

"Did Allison know whatever this secret is?"

"Yes..." If Marissa had been on top of her game, she would have recognized this as a trap.

"Did you tell her by accident?"

"No."

"Exactly. That is my point exactly." Melanie hissed at her. "We aren't friends. You don't trust me with your secrets; you don't tell me about your life unless it's to complain." She turned away from Marissa, putting her hands on the counter. "You owe Kirstie a fucking apology. Just because you haven't dealt with your feelings doesn't mean you get to treat her like shit."

Melanie glared at Marissa, and when she said nothing, Mel gritted her teeth. "I want you out of my house. Say goodbye to the girls, goodbye to Mom, and get the fuck out of my house."

Marissa took a deep breath, trying to form words. But none came. So instead, she nodded her head and walked past her sister and out of the kitchen. She knew Melanie had been irritated with her, but she had no idea the level of anger her sister had been holding. She kept her head down, not making eye contact with anyone until she was all the way across the living room.

"So, I hate to do this, but I have to run." Everyone in the room literally knew that it was a lie, but she didn't care. She just wanted to get the fuck out of there.

The girls ran over. "But I don't want you to leave already," Bethany whimpered while grabbing onto her leg.

Marissa leaned down and picked up Bethany, giving her a tight hug. "I'll see you soon, little one."

Putting her back down, she made sure to provide all the girls hugs. Mac had also gotten to his feet and started saying his goodbyes. Amanda pulled her in for a tight hug, whispering in her ear and telling her to hang in there. When her own mother came over to give her a hug goodbye, she didn't bother to hide her concern. "Call me later," she said sternly. Marissa nodded, glancing past her mom at Jared, Kirstie, and Brian before nodding and heading out the door.

As they walked down the hill, Marissa folded her arms across her chest and sighed. Mac walked on one side of her, Ellie on the other, tongue hanging out of her mouth and tail happily wagging behind her as if absolutely nothing were wrong. At least she'd had a good time. They walked in silence for the most part, which Marissa was grateful for. There had been enough talking through the night, her brain was exhausted, and she didn't want to discuss what had just happened. But as they rounded the corner to her cul de sac, they both slowed their pace.

"So, thanks for letting me crash that fun dinner," he said in a light tone, laughing gently.

"I told you, you had no idea what you were walking into." Understatement. "To be fair, I wasn't prepared for what we were walking into."

"Are you okay?"

Marissa shrugged. "I guess." Sighing, she shook her head again. She paused. "Oh, and can I have my pills back?"

Mac made a face and shook his head. "I think I'll hold on to them till tomorrow; you can't take anymore till then anyway." He sighed, looking down at the ground for a moment. "You can't do things like that, Marissa. It can be so dangerous."

She met his gaze and challenged him momentarily before brushing the hair from her eyes. "I know. It was a mistake. I couldn't remember if I took one already."

He didn't look like he believed her, so Marissa narrowed her eyes at him. It had at least started that way. Then she had just wanted to make it numb.

"And what were you thinking?" She smacked him with a fist on his shoulder. "Fucking 'second chances.' Liar."

"I know," he said gently. "He had it coming, though. He was a dick to you."

Huffing heavily, she turned to face him as Ellie bounced up to their porch and waited patiently. "He thinks he's justified." Her voice was soft as she felt a twinge of sadness. "Besides, I doubt it affected him much at all."

"Well, he's not." Mac looked at her in all seriousness. "You didn't deserve any of that. You deserve so much better." He glanced over to Marissa's dark house, where Ellie waited. "Are you going to be okay?"

Marissa nodded her head, giving him a reassuring smile. "Of course. I'm just going to sleep this whole night off." He didn't look entirely convinced but nodded at her.

"You promise to call me if you need anything?" As she nodded, he gave her a small hug and left a quick kiss on her cheek. "I'll see you later."

"Have a goodnight, Mac."

She turned to head into the house, knowing he wouldn't go to his own door until he saw her go in. Once the door was closed behind her, she waited for a beat before heading into the kitchen to narrow down her drink of choice for the night. Because it was the only way she would get any sleep tonight.

Chapter 16

Marissa had stayed up way too late after Thanksgiving, drinking and watching the Lifetime Movie Network in bed. She could not get comfortable no matter what she did. She couldn't stop thinking about how Jared had looked at her that day with such disdain and resentment. Turning over, she grabbed her phone to look at the time. Only three minutes had gone by since the last time she looked. Even with the muscle relaxers she had taken over the course of the evening and the bottle of wine she had brought upstairs, sleep was still nowhere to be found.

With a groan she sat up, contemplating her options. Finally, she reached over to her nightstand and grabbed her laptop. She adjusted her pillows to sit up slightly and opened her email.

Jared,

I know I said—

Nope. Marissa held the backspace button down, deleting the words she had managed before trying again.

Jared,

I need you to understand, everything I said to you was a lie. It was meant to hurt you, because it was the only way I could think of to keep you safe.

She stared, rereading her words carefully a few times before she was satisfied enough to continue.

Upon leaving the physical therapy center, I started receiving photos. Just like the victims of my last case. So I came to Port Townsend. And they kept coming. The focus of the photos soon became you. The only thing I could think to do was cut you off and put distance between us. And it worked. I no longer receive pictures of you. Now they are only photographs of me. I'm working on putting distance between myself and everyone but

Marissa paused.

the truth is I'm not ready to be alone.

And while some of her family had made appearances in the background of some of these photos, they were never the focus, which was something she could cling to.

"What the fuck am I doing," Marissa growled softly to herself.

With a sigh, she held the delete button down and watched the email disappear. No good would come from it. He had moved on. He was happy with medical assistant Barbie. They were living together and starting a family. What good would the truth do now? Their friendship may never recover, but he could live a full life. Telling him the truth would only serve to place him back in danger.

She slammed her laptop closed and wiped the wetness from her eyes. Running both her hands through her hair to wrap around her temples, Marissa shook her head. This was pointless. She rolled onto her back while different thoughts floated across her mind.

Second chances. The universe certainly had a sense of humor.

As morning arrived, she decided that no, she was just going to stay in bed. Ellie and Wicket didn't seem to mind spending the day snuggled up with her. She kept all the curtains closed and lights off,

Chapter 16

the only light coming from the TV. It wasn't until nearly midnight that Marissa her way downstairs to really scrounge around for food, finally feeling some pangs of hunger. She hadn't been wandering around her kitchen for more than ten minutes when a knock at her door made her jump. It was late; who the hell would be knocking at her door? Grabbing her phone to investigate her Ring app, she couldn't help but smile to see who was standing there.

"Hey, what's up?" She opened the door to see Mac standing there with his hands in his pockets. He was much more casual than she was used to seeing him, in sweatpants and a black hoodie, his hair messy enough to make it look like he'd just rolled out of bed.

"I saw your light on. Wanted to make sure you were okay since I didn't see you all day."

Marissa huffed. "Yeah, I just couldn't sleep." She scratched the back of her head, loosening the previously tightly pulled hair. "What are you doing up?" She raised an eyebrow at him.

"I spent most of the day sleeping. Recovering from that food coma your sister put me in." He paused. "Plus, it's my job to keep an eye on you."

"Right," she said, shifting her weight from one foot to the other.

"Okay, well, if you're okay, I will just head home." His eyes lingered on hers before he started to turn around. As he did, she hesitated.

"Wait," she said, bouncing onto her toes. "Do you like old movies?"

He turned and smiled at her, looking interested. "What?"

"Do you like old movies?" she repeated, potentially looking impatient until she gave him a small smile. "When I can't sleep, I run through TMC streaming and watch old movies. I was debating between *McLintock!* and *El Dorado*. Feels like a western kind of night."

His smile brightened. "Love John Wayne films."

"Why don't you join me?" She opened the door a little wider and moved out of the way, allowing him to enter the house. As soon as he closed the door behind him, Ellie was in the hallway, whining in excitement.

She watched them for a moment and felt herself relax a little. Having someone else in the house calmed her nerves a lot more than she expected. "I'm going to make some popcorn and get a drink. You want anything? I have..." She looked into her kitchen. "I have wine. Lots of wine."

"Wine is good then."

"Good. Have a seat, and I'll be right there."

A few minutes later, Marissa joined him on the couch, sitting on the middle cushion. "This way, we can share," she explained, as though she needed to, handing him the popcorn. He smiled at her. "Do you have a preference?"

"Let's start with *McLintock*."

Chapter 16

"Start with, huh?" She laughed as she passed him his glass of wine.

He shrugged, taking the wine carefully. Marissa took a large sip of her wine before putting it on the coffee table and shifted as Ellie jumped up on her other side. The shepherd put her head in Marissa's lap and huffed in contentment as the movie started.

She didn't feel drained anymore. They watched the movie quietly, laughing together. At some point, Ellie stretched out, pushing Marissa closer to him. She waited for him to protest or tell her to move over, but he did neither. The two hours had flown by before she was even aware.

"One more?" She glanced at her phone to look at the time. It was just after 3 a.m. She should have sent him home and gone to bed.

"Yeah, why not?" He smiled at her and stretched out, leaving his arm around the back of the couch as she leaned forward to put on *El Dorado*. She finished her wine and sat back on the couch, pulling a blanket over her legs, and throwing them up on the sofa under Ellie, who huffed in annoyance. "Are you cold?" She held up her blanket, offering to share.

"I'm good." He nodded and smiled at her before looking back at the TV.

She stared at him for a moment longer, briefly wondering what her life would have been if she had made different choices. Second chances, indeed.

It wasn't as though she didn't enjoy *El Dorado*, but somewhere in the middle of the movie, Marissa started to drift off. Sleep that so often eluded her finally came. It was a restful sleep. It wasn't until the sunlight from the front window shone on her face that she opened her eyes again. She wasn't sure where she was at first. Ellie was sleeping curled up in the chair, and Marissa had, at some point, stretched out her legs. She had also curled into Mac's chest, his arm around her. Sitting up, Marissa wiped the drool from her mouth and sleep from her eyes, surprised. As she shifted slightly, she felt him move beneath her.

"Good morning." He stretched out his arms and yawned before he looked down at her and paused as though waiting to see how she reacted.

"Morning," she said slowly. "Sorry."

"For what?"

"I think I might have drooled on you a little," she said sheepishly.

"I think it's okay." He gave her a confident smile, his arm still around her. "How did you sleep?"

"I actually slept," she admitted, a little surprised.

"Good. I'm going to take a little credit for that."

"You should." She nodded, allowing herself to relax a little, leaning into him.

Chapter 16

He was about to say something else when Marissa felt her phone vibrate before she heard it. She grabbed it quickly. It was a text from Veronica.

[Veronica: *There is a report of an abandoned car in Upper Big Quilcene Trail #833. Matches the description of your victim Rolley's car. You wanna check it out?*]

"They found my murder victim's car." She stared at her phone for a long moment. She wanted to call Brian but didn't feel comfortable after Mel's bitch-fest at Thanksgiving. Maybe if they actually found something in the car she would. She looked up at Mac, bouncing where she sat. "You want to go with me? It's about an hour and a half drive."

Mac nodded. "Sure. Let me just run home, change, and freshen up?"

"Sounds good." She smiled at him. She was grateful for the interruption, too, not yet ready for this conversation. She wasn't prepared to give it any kind of thought, give it labels, or any finality. Instead, she'd just ignore it. She would continue to pretend there was nothing but professionalism between her and Mac.

Once he was out her door, she ambled up the stairs, her legs feeling stiffer than ever. She washed her face, threw her hair up without bothering to brush it, and found some clothes that wouldn't be too tight on her skin. She could already feel a flare-up coming on, probably from the Thanksgiving stress settling in. Heading back down the stairs, she stepped into the bathroom to grab her daily meds, grabbed Ellie's vest, and walked out the door, locking it behind her. Mac came out of his front door moments later and met her by her car. "I figure I'll drive since I know where we're headed." She paused, looking around the interior. "Sorry, the car is an absolute mess."

"Sounds good to me," he said, flashing her that charming smile of his, which she turned her head to ignore as she sat down in the car.

Marissa settled into her mini, turned the radio on, and smiled as she started the car. She loved her little, fast car. While the hour-and-a-half-long ride wouldn't have been long to begin with, Marissa made it in forty-five minutes. As she started to slow down along the service road, Mac let out a small laugh.

"You've got a serious lead foot."

Marissa just shrugged and gave him a smile. "She likes to go fast." She grinned before turning back to the road. They didn't have to go too far off the road before they saw it. Pulling over, she knew right away that it was the car they'd been searching for.

The little silver Honda was pulled off the side of what would be considered a service road, the front wheel in a ditch. Veronica was standing behind the car, looking down the hill. She walked over as they got out of the car, shaking her head. "I don't know how this ended up here, and his body ended up behind the Palace Hotel. It makes literally no sense."

"Have you looked inside yet?" Marissa felt a slight flutter of excitement, pulling her jacket closer as the cold coast breeze blew through.

"No, I figured I'd wait for you." Veronica nodded her head at Mac, acknowledging that he was there. "Hey." She stood to the side, giving Marissa space. "Oh!" she said after a moment, digging in her pocket and pulling out a pair of keys. "You'll need these."

"Yes." She took the keys and looked at the car. Taking a deep breath, she unlocked the car door and began the initial search. The forensic team would tear the vehicle apart later. Still, Marissa, Ronnie, and Mac searched under the seats, in the glove box, and in the trunk for anything left behind. She hoped they would find something that would lead to answers.

"I got something," Mac said, awkwardly straightening his long body after leaning down to look under the front passenger seat. He held up a bracelet very carefully.

Marissa stopped her search of the driver's seat and stared. The silver chain dangled and glistened, the familiar A charm twirling as he held it up.

"That's Allison's bracelet," Marissa said quietly, without taking her eyes off the band.

"Allison Drake?" Mac asked, obviously trying to keep up on a case that wasn't his.

"Yeah." Marissa pulled herself out of the car and met Mac around the vehicle's front, taking the bracelet in her gloved hand. She examined it closer, but she had no doubts. This was Allison's bracelet. She never took it off. It was a gift from her dad on her sixteenth birthday.

Veronica came over, looking uncomfortable as she eyed the bracelet. "The tow is coming for the car, so we can have our forensic team look through it."

Marissa nodded, dropping the bracelet into an evidence bag that Ronnie held open. Marissa then took the bag and stuffed it in her pocket.

"I'm gonna take a look around the area," Marissa announced, following the direction the Honda's wheel was facing, hoping there was some sense to the madness. There wasn't much to see, just more forest: tall trees, dried-up leaves of all colors scattered on the forest floor. There was no path here, only dense woods.

Marissa walked just far enough that she could still see the car, Mac, and Veronica in the distance when she turned back, but they seemed small. Ellie's nose was high in the air as Marissa shoved her hands in her pockets, the sinking feeling of disappointment washing over her. The scene around her was beautiful; the quiet forest should have calmed her, and the fresh air hitting her lungs should have felt refreshing. Instead, as the air filled her lungs, her breathing grew frantic and shallow. She could feel her heart pulse against her breast, hard enough that she thought it might burst right out. Pain exploded through her, shattering through her body. She felt it in her legs, her back, in her throat, in her head. She was frozen in place where she stood.

Ellie immediately started nudging her, urging her to get on the ground, and whining loudly. Despite the pain that she logically knew was from panic, she sat on the floor, laying out her legs so Ellie could lay across them and lick her face while she tried to reassure her. As Marissa breathed in through her nose—inhale calm—she tried to isolate the feeling or thought that had put her on the ground. Letting out a heavy breath—exhale worry—she shuddered, closing her eyes. Inhale calm. It was quiet. It was the calmness that surrounded her. Exhale worry. Marissa opened her eyes to see Mac kneeling beside her.

"You okay?" He didn't reach out to touch her, though he looked like he wanted to.

Marissa swallowed, feeling her heartbeat. It was nearly back to normal. Still quick, but typical for her, at least. "Yeah."

"You want to talk about it?" he asked, uncertain if he should.

Marissa let out another slow breath before she answered, her voice low. "It's too quiet."

Mac looked understandably confused.

"I don't know how to do calm and quiet anymore. Everything about my life is chaotic and loud and in constant motion." At some point, tears had begun falling down her cheeks. "I have no idea how to do quiet anymore. It makes me panic. Fight or flight mode."

Mac looked at her for a long moment, his face still before he held out a hand to help her up. Ellie jumped off her lap as she stood and brushed her pants off. Marissa looked up at him to see he was watching her, and he gently brushed the tears from her eyes. Mac looked like he wanted to say something, but he sighed and took a look around the forest, keeping his thoughts to himself. Instead, he held out his hand to her.

She hesitated before slipping her hand into his, and they made their way back to the car. Veronica was busy talking to George, who had arrived with the tow truck, and giving him instructions.

By this time, Marissa had snapped herself out of it. She handed Veronica the evidence bag with the bracelet. "Here. You take this down to the station. Let Jackson know I'll be in first thing in the morning. I think I just need the afternoon. I'm not feeling great."

"No problem. Go home and feel better." Veronica obviously tried not to look concerned, but she gave Mac a look that said it all.

"So you're gonna let me drive, right?" Mac flashed her a charming smile that melted any resistance she had planned on putting up. Though it wasn't much, she felt weighed down and exhausted now.

"Sure." She gave him a half-hearted smile as she handed over the keys. "But she is my baby, so you better treat her right."

"Yes, ma'am." He grinned.

Chapter 17

"You're sure you're feeling better?" Mac stared at her, leaning against her bedroom doorway, looking unconvinced as she did her best not to wince while she put on her shirt. It took more effort than she was willing to admit, and just lifting her arms felt like someone was twisting a knife in her back. But she forced a smile for him anyway.

"I'm great." She got to her feet, grateful for Ellie sitting beside her, keeping her steady. "We've got to get down to the station. There is way too much to do, and I can't do it from here." She walked over to him and stared up at him, hoping even if he didn't buy what she was saying, that he would at least understand.

He stared down at her, arms folded in front of him, a skeptical expression for a long moment before he sighed and pushed off the doorway. "You know I'm just worried about you, right?"

Marissa gave him her best smile, leaning up to give him a quick kiss on the cheek. "I'm fine."

He groaned but followed her down the stairs.

It had taken her more than a day to recover, but thankfully she was feeling better, just in time for the rest of the interviews.

Once they arrived at the station, there was plenty to do. Jackson had assigned Stalinski and Donaldson to dig deeper into a connection between Allison and Rolley although Jackson openly admitted he was pretty sure the bracelet was planted there. Marissa and Veronica were tasked with interviewing Allison's serious ex-relationships for a second time just in case anything had been missed: Laura Seaver, Natalie Beckett, Ryan Cooper, and Troy Stone. Even though Mac had wanted to stay, he had been summoned to Seattle with Bennet to check in on the surveillance status. Marissa was disappointed to see him go, even if it was just for the day.

Around the time she was entering the day's first interview, Marissa realized she had never really been a fan of any of Allie's exes. If she had to choose one she liked best, it would have been Natalie, and she barely tolerated her. Ryan Cooper was their first interview. He was also their shortest. He had been Allie's first high school boyfriend, with whom she had shared many of her firsts. But Ryan was happily married with their second baby on the way. He had married the girl he had begun dating right after Allie, and they had been together for over a decade. When Marissa asked, Ryan said he didn't remember Allie ever seeming distant or feeling like she was with anyone else when she was with him. It was so early in her dating career that Marissa doubted that the manipulative relationship they were looking for had begun yet. Marissa's impression was that he felt a genuine loss when they spoke of Allie and that he didn't have anything to hide. But Marissa was also second-guessing herself. Thankfully, Ryan also had a solid alibi of being in California visiting his sister-in-law on the night of the murder.

The second interview was with Laura Seaver. Marissa let Veronica lead this one, feeling uncomfortable with the idea of interviewing her own therapist. However, she did interject more than she had planned. Dr. Seaver was collected and relaxed and spoke of Allie with great admiration and sadness. She said that when she thought Allie was distant, she felt maybe Allie had been seeing someone else, but she always denied it. Laura Seaver was currently in a relationship with a woman who lived in Tacoma, only a couple hours away. Marissa couldn't get a read on her one way or another, but she said she was in Tacoma the night Allie had died.

Chapter 17

Before Marissa could go through another interview, she decided to call Brian. It had been long enough. She had kept the radio silent since Thanksgiving and obviously still wasn't talking to Melanie. Heading out of the station, she texted her brother-in-law with the idea of lunch, although the thought of food made her feel nauseous. He responded quickly, and they planned to meet at the sandwich shop in his building.

Marissa got there a little early and popped into the bathroom to adjust herself. The interviews left her looking as drained as she felt. Marissa hadn't bothered with anything more than some concealer to try and hide the bags under her eyes and some eyeliner. She also hadn't bothered to brush her hair, just threw it up into a bun. Marissa let it down and frowned at the mirror. She didn't know who the hell was staring back at her; she barely recognized herself. She fixed her hair, threw it back up into a messy bun, then splashed some water on her face.

Exiting the bathroom, she looked presentable, maybe just a little tired. She decided to wait toward the sandwich shop's front, anxiously picking at her fingernails. Thankfully, she didn't have to hang around long.

Brian gave her a smile she could see was forced and tried to hide his concern as they got in line for sandwiches. She didn't even know what she ordered, but she did get a Sprite to sip on.

"I've got some small updates for you," she said as she grabbed a table and sat down. Ellie curled beneath the table comfortably without cue as Marissa sat down and stared at her wrapped-up sandwich.

"Before we get into that, though." She sighed. "I'm really sorry about Thanksgiving," she admitted. It was hard for her to get the words out. She wasn't necessarily sorry about her behavior or anything she had said but more for the fallout she imagined Brian probably had endured after. She could only imagine what the house must've been like if Mel was still in a rage, which she figured she probably was. "I didn't mean to cause such a commotion."

He seemed both grateful and relieved for the apology. Then came the question Marissa knew would be next. "Are you going to tell me the truth about that 'old friend' you brought with you?"

She stared at Brian for a long moment, folding her arms in front of her and frowning back at him. She hadn't wanted to overload him with any more secrets, but if he was going to ask for them, she might as well be honest with someone.

"We are old friends," she started as he rolled his eyes at her. "We met on a case about five years ago. He works for the FBI. He's here for work. They are finally taking the stalking photos seriously, and he's here on surveillance." She paused with a heavy sigh. "We also dated after that case for several months, after Jared got out of rehab. He was the guy I was seeing when Jared wanted to give us a try again."

She came to a stop, picturing that moment in her head. It felt like a lifetime ago.

"But he and the FBI are now camped out at the house across the street from me. And even though our infamous photographer knows he's FBI, it would be best to keep it quiet."

She watched her brother-in-law's jaw drop. "You dated a guy for months, and none of us knew? How did we all miss that?" He blinked. "Although I guess Jared knew."

Marissa sipped the Sprite she ordered, leaving the sandwich wrapped and untouched. Adding a slight shrug, she shook her head. "You didn't miss anything. I didn't tell anyone."

At the time, she told herself it was because of his job. The truth was she wanted something that was just hers.

"Jared did know. It had actually gotten pretty serious." She paused. It had been the only reason she had introduced Mac and Jared in the first place. "It's not really a big deal. It's been, like, five years. He's moved on; I've moved on. He's just here for a job. Mel just happened to invite me when he was checking in. She saw him, got excited, and invited him." She sighed. "My guess is Jared probably thinks I broke it off to go back to Mac. Because he apparently thinks that little of me."

She couldn't help it. She hadn't been able to let that train of thought go. Everyone had apparently thought very little of her in that sense. At least here, she could be honest, or so she hoped.

Instead, Brian scolded her. "No, look, don't go there. You know he doesn't think little of you. Marissa, you broke his damned heart, and you knew you did it. Whether you have good reasons to do it or not, it's not fair of you to put any of this on him. You know it's not about that."

Marissa shifted, trying not to noticeably sink in her seat. She knew he wasn't wrong, but on some level, it just didn't seem fair. Fuck. She was just so tired. For half a second, she thought about coming to her own defense, but she let the thought pass. There wasn't anything she could say that made a difference.

She let a moment pass, taking a deep breath and still shifting uncomfortably in her seat. Ellie sat up under the table and rested her head on Marissa's lap. With one hand, she pet the shepherd, feeling her heartbeat speed up and return to normal.

"We found Rolley's car about an hour away. No camera, no evidence in there." She let out a grumble. "We did, however, find Allison's bracelet in there. It was more than likely planted." Marissa cracked her neck, feeling the stress rising back up. "I've also started interviewing all of Allison's serious ex-relationships."

Honestly, she wasn't sure which was more frustrating—planted evidence or interviewing her best friend's past partners.

They spent the rest of the time discussing Owen Rolley's suspected suicide and how neither bought into it. It was all speculation, but everything pointed to murder.

Glancing at her phone, Marissa sighed. "I should probably head back."

She got to her feet slowly, Ellie instantly on her feet and at her side to steady her. Marissa grabbed her soda and gave Brian a melancholy smile. "Again, I'm really sorry about the whole Thanksgiving fiasco. I will find a way to make it up to you, I promise. And..." She paused. She had almost asked him to give Mel a hug for her, but right now, that was not something Mel would be receptive to. "Take care of that beautiful family of yours."

She hurried through the goodbye and disappeared out of the building before giving Brian the chance to do much, leaving her sandwich sitting on the table.

Once outside the building, Marissa walked along the main street and past the precinct. Needing a minute, she turned down one of the boardwalks. Marissa faced the sea, watching the ferry heading out and boats off in the distance, taking advantage of the beautiful day at the end of November. Looking down at the water, she watched it splash against the pier and wondered just how cold it must be. Marissa should have felt cold now, the wind was blowing off the water, and she knew what November breezes felt like along the coast. Still, it wasn't touching her for whatever reason. In fact, her cheeks were growing hot as she stood there, leaning against the railing, watching the water quietly.

The next thing she knew, she was sitting on her front porch, holding a bag of ice on her wrist with Ellie sitting beside her. Mac was pulling into the driveway across the street. He closed the door and ran his hand through his hair. He made his way over, smiling until he saw the ice pack.

"What did you do?" He sat down next to her on the step, petting Ellie as she shoved her head into his hands.

"I..." Marissa pulled the ice pack off to reveal a dark black bruise that wrapped its way around her wrist. She had absolutely no memory of how she got it. She had no memory of how she made it home. "I don't know," she answered honestly, choosing not to go into detail.

"Jesus," Mac muttered, running his finger gently on it. He looked up at her but must have seen something in her face that kept him from prying further.

"Come on, why don't we get inside?" He helped her up and led her into the house. "Are you hungry?"

He didn't wait for an answer, heading straight for the kitchen. He had stocked her fridge at some point. "How did the interviews go?" he asked as he dug through the fridge, picking out ingredients.

"Um..." Marissa paused, scraping the corners of her memory to find an answer.

Grabbing her phone, she opened her texts, seeing the last conversation with Veronica.

[Veronica: *Hey Ronnie, I'm going to head home. I really don't feel good. Can you handle the last few on your own?*]

Marissa had no memory of sending the text, but based on the time, it was shortly after she had left Brian. The clock on her stove told her it had been over four hours ago.

"I did the first two," she finally said, answering Mac as he stood in front of her. "I wasn't feeling too great, so Ronnie finished."

"How about your hand?" He raised an eyebrow, gesturing to her swollen wrist.

Looking down at the bruise, she again frowned. "It's fine," she said quietly, offering no explanation of what happened.

"Let me look at it," he said. She could tell he was trying to keep his frustration to a minimum. If Marissa hadn't been feeling that same frustration, she would have thought it was cute. Mac took her hand in his gently and ran his fingers over the swelling and bruising. He eyed her for a long moment, the uncertainty clear on his face.

"Keep the ice on it." He frowned, clearly not pleased. "Are you feeling okay?"

The question felt out of left field. "Yeah, I'm fine. Why?"

He watched her closely before shaking his head. "So they need us both in Seattle tomorrow. Are you up for interviewing Daniel Fryer?" he said finally, letting out a breath and turning back to the stove, preheating the oven.

Marissa nodded, sitting herself down on a stool and leaning her elbows on the kitchen island. "Of course."

"Are you sure? Because I can always insist we put it off a week..."

"It's fine, Mac," Marissa insisted, giving him a small smile. "Now, what are you making for dinner?"

Chapter 18

Marissa took a deep breath and walked into the interview room, followed closely behind by Mac. Daniel Fryer was seated there, looking a little amused, his cuffed hands in his lap as he sat back in his chair.

"You look nice, detective. Rested."

"Thanks," Marissa answered curtly, sitting down in the chair that Mac had pulled out for her. Once she was seated, he sat in the chair beside her. "Shall we get started?"

Marissa didn't want to bother with small talk today. She had also been ordered to get straight to the point. She was supposed to steer the conversation toward victims rather than get the answers she wanted. She and Mac had spent the last hour on the phone with ADA's and the FBI's offices about how things should be handled.

"Lets. But I think today we should do things a little differently."

"Oh?" Marissa raised an eyebrow. "What did you have in mind?"

"I'm thinking of a question for a question." He leaned forward with a crooked smile that made her shift uncomfortably.

"I'm not sure that's a good idea." Mac leaned forward, shaking his head.

Fryer raised an eyebrow at him. "I mean, we don't have to do this today if you don't feel like it..."

"What kind of questions?" Marissa interjected, giving Mac a look. The last thing they needed was a wasted trip. What they needed was to start getting information out of him. And soon.

"I just want to know a little bit about you."

"We can try. But a question for a question, an answer for an answer."

"Deal. You can even go first."

"Who was your first victim?" She all but sputtered out the question, feeling suddenly cold and uncomfortable.

Fryer seemed surprised. "This isn't the question you want to ask."

He wasn't wrong. But if she wanted to remain part of the process, it was clear she had no choice but to ask the approved questions.

"Her name was Jenna Spheres. I saw her hitch-hiking off a beach road in Oregon, took her, and buried her in Washington State, 1996. Her remains can be found in the Olympic National Forest. She is still listed as a missing person."

As he spoke, Mac took notes without looking up.

His willingness to talk caught her off guard. It also made her sick to her stomach.

"My turn."

Marissa nodded.

"Ben has been sending you pictures, making a real hobby out of his voyeurism habits. What did you do when he started leaving you pictures of your ex-husband?"

She stiffened. "I broke it off."

This was apparently not the answer Daniel Fryer was expecting; the surprise was written on his face. "You broke it off with him because you were receiving pictures?"

"Yes. My turn." Marissa was not enjoying this game. "Why Jenna Spheres?"

"She was alone. She told me she was setting out on her own, running away from home. No one was expecting her. It gave me time." He smiled as though reliving a pleasant memory. "She was a sweet girl." He leaned forward, cocking his head to the side. His beard had grown since they had last been there. "So, are you seeing anyone else?"

"No, I don't see how any of this is relevant." Her irritation was beginning to bubble, but this entire arrangement was already uncomfortable. It was personal.

"Let me explain, detective. You see, Ben has a type. Each woman he set his sights on — all brilliant, strong, independent women, right? Miranda Harris was a lawyer. Pretty brunette, loud screamer. When Ben started sending her pictures, she ignored them. And when pictures of her boyfriend started to arrive, she continued to ignore them. And then she found him dead. And she was killed shortly after. You already know all that. Christine Cochren, the journalist. Another brunette. She got the police involved right away. Her husband was murdered much faster. Amy Teagan, the cardiac nurse, got the police involved right away. Always with the brunettes. I prefer redheads." He paused to shrug. "You, the police, suggested a safe house or protection. Boyfriend said no, dead less than a day later. Amy Teagan was supposed to be the one lured to that warehouse and, instead, it was you. Now, as you know, she died shortly after you were found. It took a while to find all of her. She was a fighter."

Marissa was going to vomit. She could feel it rising in her throat, and it felt like the walls were closing in around her. She kept her eyes on Fryer, but she knew they were glazed over. "Is there a point to all of this?"

"There is." He smiled, drawing the tension out just a little longer. He was getting a sick kick out of this, watching her squirm. "Every one of those women fought it. Your ex-husband becomes a target, and you kick him to the curb. You're playing his game. You're complying with him."

Marissa just stared. She felt every inch of her body tighten up, and that lump threatened to rise further in her throat.

"If I had to venture a guess, I'd say he probably thinks he has a real relationship with you."

"Enough," she said, shaking her head. Mac looked at her full of concern, and Daniel Fryer kept grinning with amusement. "Jenna Spheres. You said 1996. How many victims do you have?" That was a vast timeline. Twenty-four years.

He just shook his head. "I honestly lost track at some point. Hopefully, these little visits will refresh my memory."

"How many did you kill by yourself?"

"Most of them."

"Why?"

"Why not?"

Marissa backed into the precinct wall, holding herself, still trembling. Ellie sat right beside her feet, looking up at her and nudging her with her nose, gently whining. Marissa had forced herself to make it through but only lasted an hour before the interview ended. They had gotten the details of Jenna Spheres's kidnapping and death, as well as details on where to find her remains. It was all Marissa could take. She had answered his questions, too. Questions about the photos she had received and more information than she wanted to give about her relationship with Jared.

Mac came through the doors, looking around for her. He barely had his arms open for a hug before she rushed to him. The second she felt him against her, the wall she had built over the hour came crashing down, and she sobbed into his chest. He wrapped his arms around her, holding her close and stroking her hair, occasionally telling her it would be alright.

"Hey." He spoke gently, still holding her close. "Why don't we go for a walk? The waterfront isn't far from here, right?"

Marissa pulled her face from his chest and looked out, needing to remember where she was. Wiping her eyes, and probably some snot from her face, she nodded, trying to bring the tears to a stop.

"Come on." He hugged her before letting her go but took her hand as they walked. They walked in silence, Mac on one side and Ellie on the other. Her phone buzzed in her pocket. It was her mom. Declining the call, she shoved it down into her pocket.

Chapter 18

Marissa closed her eyes after a long afternoon on the waterfront. First, they walked through the Ye Olde Curiosity Shop, stared at the Seattle Great Wheel, and discussed their mutual hatred of heights. They had an early dinner at the Crab Pot where Marissa only sipped on a single glass of wine. They ended the evening with a walk through the Aquarium. There was something amazingly calming about watching sea creatures in the water. If it hadn't followed a horrible, skin-crawling interview with a serial killer, Marissa would have considered it one of her most successful dates. Not that dating was an option for them now. They were working on a case together. They made their way back to the car and drove back to Port Townsend.

He pulled into the driveway and put the car in park, turning to her. "You're home."

Marissa pulled herself up, breathing deeply, and nodded. She looked at her dark house for a long moment before turning to him. "Will you stay with me tonight?"

A look of relief flashed across his face before he nodded. "Of course."

Inside, Marissa fed Ellie before letting the shepherd out. She headed to the bathroom to grab her meds, popping a muscle relaxer into the mix. Her entire body felt tense, and the dull ache that followed was getting stronger and stronger.

Once everything was shut down, she headed up the stairs, Mac following behind. He stopped outside her guest bedroom, but she picked up his hand, leading him into her room. She pulled her hoodie off and disappeared into the bathroom to change into her tank and shorts for bed. Mac was still standing in the doorway awkwardly, unsure what to do.

She crawled onto her bed, pushed the covers down, and waited quietly. After a moment, Mac came over, pulled his shirt off, and lay down next to her. She hesitated but then lay her head on his chest, listening to his heartbeat. He pulled the blankets over them as Ellie jumped on the bed. She seemed confused by the extra body but circled until she found a comfortable spot. As he wrapped his arms around her, she started to cry again, unable to stop herself.

"You know, that's not usually the response I'm looking for when I get in bed with a beautiful woman," he said after a long moment of just letting her cry in his arms.

"Shut up." Marissa let out a soft laugh and wiped the tears from her eyes, unable to hold back the smile. "This is strictly a sleeping situation."

"Of course. Anything more would be breaking protocol." She felt him sink down and adjust, getting comfortable.

Marissa sighed, closing her eyes. "Exactly." She took one heavy breath, followed by another. She was exhausted.

"I'm sorry you've had to go through this," he said in almost a whisper. "But you're not alone anymore."

It was the last thing she heard before she drifted off to sleep.

She wasn't sure how long she had been asleep, but she shot up abruptly, screaming. Marissa grabbed her side and let out another yell, clawing at her own skin. She felt resistance and realized that there were arms around her, holding her hands from clawing at herself. Opening her eyes, she couldn't catch her breath, feeling like the air was being pulled from her lungs. It took another moment for her to realize that Mac was holding her arms and talking to her. As the realization washed over her, she struggled to slow down, pushing breaths out, trying to bring air in. Her heart was pounding hard against her chest, everything feeling like it was on pins and needles, and her mouth was dry as she let out another wail.

She hadn't noticed until that moment that Ellie was whining and was shoving herself in front of Marissa, licking her face with fierceness.

"Marissa."

She heard his voice through the piercing ringing that was screaming at her eardrums.

"Marissa. You're safe. I'm right here. You're safe."

As she listened, she felt herself relax although her body was still cramped from being tense.

"Easy. I've got you."

Marissa felt finally able to get air with slow, long breaths even though everything in her body remained tense. She could feel herself closing more and more into herself, every part of her frozen in place. Her hands balled into tight fists, and she had begun to double over, although Mac was doing his best to hold her. Her knees came up to her chest, and she froze into a ball. Ellie shoved her nose below her chin, trying to push her way between her legs as her body continued to tighten.

"Hey," he continued, rubbing her arms as though trying to help her regain warmth.

Ellie nudged Marissa, still whining and giving her cheek kisses.

"There you go." Mac didn't bother to cover up the relief in his voice as Marissa felt her shoulders drop. Once that happened, whatever tightness she felt that forced her into a ball seemed to release, and she melted into him. She was still breathing heavily, pins and needles racing over her body.

Once he was satisfied that she had calmed down enough, Mac leaned back onto the headboard, rubbing her arms as he held her close. Ellie crawled into Marissa's lap, but being a massive shepherd, half of her was on top of Mac.

"Okay," he said after many silent moments of nothing but the sound of their breathing. Pushing himself up a little, he looked down at Marissa. "Are you okay?"

Marissa nodded, still breathless. What she was, was exhausted. She closed her eyes and took several heavy breaths before meeting his gaze again.

"Downstairs bathroom. I have Clonazepam for emergency anxiety. Top shelf."

He nodded, very carefully moving her to the bed before jumping up and running out of the room. Ellie took the opportunity to lay on top of her, nudging Marissa's face with her cold nose.

It wasn't the first time it had happened, probably wouldn't be the last. But it was the first time Marissa wasn't alone for it. Hurrying back up, he had a pill in one hand and a glass of water in the other. Reluctantly, Ellie moved to Marissa's legs as she very slowly pushed herself up, wincing a little as she did so. She popped the pill and sucked down half of the glass of water.

"Thank you," she said, carefully putting the glass down on the nightstand as Mac climbed back into bed beside her.

"Are you okay? Really?" He was no longer bothering to mask his concern.

Swallowing, the back of her throat still felt dry as she nodded. "I am." It was a reactive response, and he knew it based on the look he was giving her. "I will be," she eventually said with a sigh.

He seemed more receptive to that answer as he nodded and settled back in. "Do you want to talk about it?" he said a little more gently.

Marissa shook her head. Even though she couldn't remember the exact details of whatever nightmare she had had, she knew. Marissa knew the details of what had actually happened. And she refused to voice them out loud. She would not put it into words.

"No," she said softly.

That was enough for Mac, who wrapped his arm back around her, pulling her into him. "You know you're safe, right?"

She nodded her head against his chest. And she honestly felt it, at least for that moment. There was a long silence as they shifted back to being comfortable, and she felt him lean down and give her a slow, gentle kiss on the top of her head.

When Marissa opened her eyes again, the sun shone brightly through her bedroom window. She felt groggy, as she often did after taking Clonazepam. It took her a minute to remember the absolute panic attack she had experienced in the middle of the night. And to realize she was in bed alone. But before she could worry that she had chased Mac off, he came into the room, still shirtless, coffee in hand.

Chapter 18

"Hey," he said gently, offering her the coffee cup as she pushed herself into a sitting position. "Are you feeling any better?" He sat himself down next to her, eyes full of worry.

"A little. I've got a headache. Still a little tired."

"Did you want to sleep more?"

"No." She smiled, shaking her head. "I shouldn't really sleep anymore. What time is it?"

"It's 9:30ish?" He shrugged, grabbing his phone and taking a look. "Yeah, it's 9:37 exactly."

"You been up long?" She raised an eyebrow as she sipped her coffee, which he had made ideally once again.

"Not too long. Just long enough to make a few phone calls. Made coffee. I also fed Ellie."

"Jesus. You're some kind of awful morning person, aren't you?" She smiled before taking another sip.

"You could say that." He smiled at her before he let out a sigh. "I do have some news, though."

"Oh?"

"I have to fly out to DC this afternoon to check in with my bosses. Two days, three tops."

"Oh." Marissa didn't mean to sound as disappointed as she felt and turned away from him as he turned to look at her.

"But I was thinking." He waited until she met his gaze before continuing, making sure she was looking into his dark brown eyes. "What if you came with me?"

265

Marissa blinked. She, almost without a thought, said yes, but instead bit her lip.

He gave her a smile, noting her hesitation. "Hey. You don't have to. I'll be back before you know it."

"Yeah," She nodded her head. "I have an appointment with Dr. Seaver later today, and I should keep working on Allison's case..."

"Okay. Then we have a couple of hours until I need to head to the airport." Standing up, he grinned at her. "Come on downstairs. I'll make you breakfast."

He turned and left her bedroom, leaving her sitting on her bed staring after him. Allison would tell her he was too good to be true, and she was inclined to believe that. Fuck, she missed Allie. She missed having someone to talk to.

She changed from her shorts to sweatpants and considered changing out of the tank top. She didn't usually wear anything that left her shoulder and chest visible anymore. The scar that ran from the left side of her collarbone across her chest made her extra insecure. She worked hard to make sure she kept it covered. But since Mac had slept in the same bed with her, it didn't matter anymore.

She made her way downstairs, stopping in the bathroom to grab the necessary morning pills, and headed into the kitchen. Mac had made himself at home in her kitchen, cooking food that she didn't usually have in the house after having restocked the fridge. She sat down on one of the stools in the kitchen and watched him for a long moment as Ellie padded her way into the kitchen to join them.

"Is there anything you can't do?"

"I can't draw or do crossword puzzles. And I don't get Sudoku." He grinned at her, leaving Marissa to shake her head and turn her face so he couldn't see her cheeks flush.

They spent the next hour talking about nothing in particular as he made a spectacular breakfast, complete with bacon, eggs, and pancakes. When it was time for him to leave, he lingered in her doorway.

"So I'll see you on Sunday."

"Yes. Sunday." It wouldn't be that long, but she wished she had agreed to go with him. She hesitated but leaned forward to pull him into a hug. Physical contact was something that Marissa didn't find herself craving much of these days, but something about him made her feel safe.

As he pulled away slowly, he lingered for a moment and left a slow kiss on her cheek. By the time Marissa opened her eyes again, he was already walking out the door.

Sunday wasn't that far away, and she was excited to get through the weekend.

Chapter 19

Marissa headed into Dr. Seaver's office feeling like she finally had something to share, something positive, after all the bullshit and that shitshow of a holiday. But when she entered the room, Laura Seaver was sitting at her desk. Marissa was reasonably sure in all the time she had been coming into this office that she had never actually seen her sitting at her desk.

"Good afternoon, Marissa." She looked up from her computer with a weak smile.

"Hi," Marissa said, sitting down on the couch. "I'm sorry about our last session." Even though she hadn't stormed out, she hadn't been pleasant either.

"Water under the bridge," she said passively. "But I do need to talk to you."

"Okay." Ellie settled down at Marissa's feet while Dr. Seaver shifted awkwardly behind her desk, observing Marissa.

"There is no easy way to say this. But after our interview last week, I realized I'm not taking Allison's death as well as I thought." She sighed heavily, looking down at her hands folded in front of her. "I need to take a step back from the practice, meaning I can't treat you anymore."

Marissa stared at her, mouth hanging open.

"I'm sorry, I know this isn't convenient, but I will give you a list of qualified names in the surrounding areas."

Marissa closed her mouth and sighed. "What are you going to do now?" She wanted to ask why now. It had been months.

"I don't know. Travel maybe? Go visit places on the bucket list? I haven't really decided yet."

Marissa didn't even bother taking advantage of the final session. She had been too stunned by the announcement. Instead, she made small talk and looked one last time at all the things Laura had collected and displayed around the room. Books, figurines, a really nice camera with a Space Needle sticker, that old typewriter. So now she was without a therapist. She needed one to remain on the force, though she was sure she would be allowed the appropriate time to find a new one before it caused her any problems.

Once she was back home, she didn't waste any time looking at her alcohol shelf. One rum and coke wouldn't be the worst thing in the world. She flipped through her phone. She couldn't call Mac; he would be in meetings most of the day. She couldn't call Mel. It was probably better if she didn't call Brian. She couldn't call Jared. Instead, she made herself another drink and got comfy on the couch.

The next thing she knew, her phone was screaming at her. Jumping up, startled, Marissa flailed around, trying to grab her phone on the night-stand, nearly falling off the bed. Her head was throbbing as she stumbled over the buttons on her phone.

"Hello?" Oh, her head was pounding.

"Marissa. It's Sheriff Jackson. I need you to come in." Marissa noted the stern tone as he spoke. It definitely didn't sound good.

"Right now?" She tried to remember how much she had had to drink the night before, but it wasn't coming to her. Had she even slept? When did she come to bed?

"Right now," he added with extra urgency.

"Okay. Give me fifteen minutes, and I'll be on my way." She hung up the phone and stumbled out of bed. For a minute, she wasn't sure if she was hungover or if she was possibly still drunk. But she managed to get herself dressed and stumbled through her house, trying to hurry downtown.

"Marissa, please have a seat."

Marissa sat down quietly, leaning back in the chair with her hands in her lap, sunglasses over her bloodshot eyes. Sheriff Jackson sighed heavily and stared at his desk.

"We received a package from Christopher Erickson in regard to Owen Rolley, addressed to you and 'Detective Brian Shaw.'"

Oh, fuck. But Marissa kept her expression neutral, swallowing.

"Now, correct me if I'm wrong, but we don't have a detective here by that name, do we?"

"No, sir. But—"

"Did you introduce a reporter as a detective? In an ongoing investigation?"

Marissa thought about her words very carefully. "I did not introduce him as a detective." Not a lie— she never said the words *Detective Shaw*, but she knew this was a fine line. "It may have been implied that he was accompanying me on semi-official basis. But I did not say he was an officer, and he definitely did not impersonate one."

Herbert Jackson looked angry. This was not a good sign. "In what capacity was he there? Was he there as a reporter, or was he there as your brother-in-law?"

When Marissa didn't answer, he rubbed the bridge of his nose, closing his eyes and letting out a hefty sigh.

"Marissa, I know you know the rules. Civilians are not welcome on ongoing investigations. Reporters are not allowed to participate in active cases. You know this."

"I—"

"It's also come to my attention that you are no longer in active counseling. This was the condition for you to remain on the force."

"But—"

"No. I understand that Dr. Seaver is stepping back from her practice and that you need time to find a new doctor. However, I've spoken with Dr. Seaver at length about your progress, and I'm not confident that it is in your best interest to be on the force right now."

"Please don't do this."

"Therefore, I am suspending you, with pay, until you have at least six weeks of regular counseling. And I forbid you from working on Allison Drake's case. I take full responsibility for my poor judgment in letting you be on a case you are too close to." He briefly made eye contact before looking at the top of his desk. "I need you to turn in your badge and gun."

Marissa sat there, staring at the top of the desk and blinking. "I understand," she finally said, getting back to her feet as she grabbed her gun from her holster and pulled her badge out of her wallet.

"You need to take it easy. Take a break. Maybe go on a vacation." He leaned back in his chair, resting his arm on his desk. "Why don't you go visit Madilyn? With the holiday right around the corner, it's a great time to spend with family."

"Sure," Marissa responded without any interest in doing any of those things. Although she loved her sister, she wasn't leaving town any time soon. "Is that all?" she asked, wanting very much to get out of there.

Jackson watched her for a long moment before finally sighing. "Yeah, that's it. Please take it easy, Marissa. We'll update you when there is something to update with."

"Of course. Thanks." She didn't wait for anything else, heading out of his office, closing the door behind her.

Sighing heavily, she was about to head to the exit when Ronnie called her over quietly. "Marissa." She was almost whispering and avoiding looking up.

When Marissa walked over to her desk, Ronnie stood. "I know why you were in there," she said quietly. "I just wanted to give you a hug."

Marissa stared at her suspiciously but nodded slowly. "Okay..."

Veronica came around her desk to give Marissa a hug; she felt something drop in her jacket pocket. As Ronnie leaned into the hug, she whispered in Marissa's ear. "I'll say it got misplaced when being thrown into evidence. Go."

Marissa nodded, and once Ronnie pulled back, she turned and headed out of the precinct.

Fucking suspended. She felt the frustration and anger building as she walked home, Ellie keeping pace with her, her long legs making it effortless. She had known that if Brian's involvement had gotten back to the sheriff, it was possible trouble would follow. At least she hadn't gotten fired.

But fucking Laura God-Damned Seaver. As though quitting on her wasn't enough, telling her boss she wasn't fit to be on the job?

"Fuck her," Marissa mumbled under her breath, pulling her jacket tighter against her. She didn't dare pull the package out of her pocket until she was behind closed doors. She always knew Ronnie was her favorite.

She hurried back into the house, locking the door behind her. She let Ellie into the backyard and didn't bother pulling the envelope out of her pocket until she was at the kitchen island. Grumbling, she unsealed the envelope and dropped the contents onto the counter. There was a key taped to a piece of paper that read:

Chris,

This is the other key to the lockbox at Puget Sound West Bank if anything happens to me. In it, you will find everything you need to know about what happened. Thanks for every-thing, man.

Owen

And on that note was a sticky note addressed to her.

Hope this helps.

Marissa stared at the letter, reading it over and over again. Grabbing her phone, she did a quick Internet search for the bank's phone number and dialed.

"Puget Sound West Bank. Ericka speaking, how may I help you?"

"Yes, I'm calling on behalf of the Port Townsend Police Department. I am Detective Marissa Ambrose. I was wondering if I could ask you a couple of questions?"

"Of course, detective! What can I do for you?"

"I have a key to a lockbox here under the name of Owen Rolley. He is the victim in a homicide we are currently investigating, and I was hoping you could help me out with the contents of that box."

"Well, ma'am. I can confirm we had a box under Mr. Rolley's name and that the contents were removed by his fiancée this morning."

"His fiancée?" Marissa blinked.

"Yes, ma'am."

"Can you give me her name? Or tell me what was in there?"

"I would love to, ma'am; however, we are going to need a warrant before we can divulge any of that information. I'd be happy to give you all the information once we have one in hand."

"Of course. We will get right on that; thank you so much." Marissa hung up with a huff.

What felt like a significant lead had landed her nowhere. Jackson wasn't going to take anything she had to say with any seriousness, so even if Ronnie tried to get a warrant, it was going to take forever. She knew the contents of that box could have only been a handful of things. And Marissa was willing to bet her life on it that the missing computer, cash, and maybe photos were among them. She shot Ronnie a quick text, letting her know to start the process of getting a warrant for the bank. But seeing as it was already Saturday afternoon, the soonest anything would happen would be Monday.

Marissa let Ellie inside and plopped onto the couch, flipping through channels. She felt defeated and heavy. Ellie jumped onto the couch and lay down on her feet. She should probably eat something. Frowning, she tried to remember the last time she had eaten but couldn't remember. The night before was still fuzzy. But she didn't feel hungry. She stopped flipping through channels, landing on *Ocean's Twelve*, and tossed the remote to the coffee table. She adjusted, getting herself as comfortable as she could manage. Marissa picked at her cuticles, not realizing that she had picked them enough to make them bleed.

Three movies later, her phone started to buzz. She hoped it would be Mac, but it was Jack.

"Hey, beautiful. I just wanted to check-in. Make sure you're doing okay. Last time I saw you, you were having a hard time."

Smiling slightly, she shrugged to no one. His honesty was refreshing. "I'm alright, I guess. Tired but nothing too interesting to report. Are you still in town?"

"For the moment. I'll be heading out in a week or two. That was actually the other reason I was calling," There was silence on the other end of the

277

line for a moment. "I was wondering if maybe I could take you out for a proper date before I go?"

He sounded so hopeful.

"I'm sorry, Jack," she said slowly. She almost said she was seeing someone else. But that wasn't true. "I just don't think I'm in the right place at this point. Life has been a lot lately."

She heard him sigh on the other line. "I understand, but I had to try." He chuckled, laughing it off. "Maybe when I return, you'll let me try again?"

"Sure. No promises, but you're welcome to try."

Why was she giving him hope? He was nice enough, and his southern accent was charming as hell, but no. Even if he had been her type, there was still that whole "serial killer stalker" thing to contend with. And then there was Mac.

"You've been a good friend Jack. Thank you for checking in." She meant that. It was nice to have people on her side.

They chatted for a little bit longer about nothing of any importance. It was just mindless gossip, and Marissa found it made her feel just a little lighter. By the time she hung up the phone, she felt almost relaxed.

She pushed the call button on Mac's name, but it went directly to voicemail. That wasn't surprising. Chances were he was in a meeting or something to that effect. She began scrolling again, stopping at Jared's name. She stared at it and shook her head, thumbing through the rest. Jared wouldn't answer

Chapter 19

her call, and even if he did, what the hell would she say? She stopped at Brian's name and hit the call button. At the very least, she could give him an update.

The phone rang three times before someone picked up the other line. But instead of Brian, it was Mel. And she sounded annoyed. "What?"

Marissa hesitated, surprised, but gathered her composure momentarily. "Is Brian there?"

"He's putting the girls to bed. You know it's late, right?"

Marissa pulled the phone from her ear and looked at the time. It was 8 p.m. Not that late, but it was the younger kids' bedtime. "Sorry, I just needed to talk to him real—"

"No," Mel said flatly.

"No?"

"No," she repeated. "Listen to me very carefully. I love you, Marissa, but I need you to just stop."

Something about the direction of this sounded familiar. Marissa's heart sank. She considered just hanging up but allowed Melanie to continue.

"I need to remove the toxic people from my life. And you are my sister, and I love you, but we need space. I'm not going to tell you that you can't see the girls because they absolutely need you in their lives. And I'm not going to tell you that you can't speak to or see Brian. We're all adults here. But I hope you can respect what I am saying to you and just leave my husband and me the fuck alone."

She was speechless. She had known Mel was pissed at her, especially after the Thanksgiving debacle, but to call her toxic. She was cutting her off. "Mel..."

"No," Mel said with force. "I know you've gone through some shit, and I know you're having a hard time. And I have done my best to be here for you as much as I can, but I can't do it anymore, Marissa. I can't. I would appreciate it if you would respect what I'm saying to you."

She blinked. It was surreal. Nodding her head to no one, her grip tightened on the cell phone. "I don't understand. How the hell did we get here?"

"Honestly, Riss? I don't know. But I just can't do this with you."

"Yeah. Okay," she managed.

"Thank you." And with that, Mel hung up on her.

She pulled the phone from her ear and tossed it across the room without giving it much of a second thought. She watched as the phone crashed and broke open.

"Of course," she muttered under her breath as she stood from the couch. Ellie snorted at her but got up and followed her into the kitchen, where Marissa started taking a mental note of how much alcohol she no longer had. Apparently, she had had more to drink the night before than she thought. At least she had a couple of bottles of wine left.

Chapter 19

Marissa looked around the empty house and shook her head, bottle of wine in hand. There was an answer, right on the tip of her tongue. Somewhere. Bottle in hand, she wandered upstairs to her office and stared at the whiteboard. She stared at the individual pictures, focusing on Allie's. She was shooting back a mouthful of wine directly from the bottle when something struck her.

Pictures.

She hurried back down the stairs and ran to the lockbox full of photographs taken of her. Every single image over the past two years. She finished off the bottle and grabbed another before she started spreading them out. There were far too many for her kitchen table. So instead, she shoved them back in the box and moved to the living room. After moving all of her furniture to the edges of the room, she started spreading them out. She needed to put them in order—two years of her life in photographs, taken from afar.

It took her much longer than she had anticipated. She had finished the bottle of wine before she was even halfway through organizing them. By the time she had them all laid out in her living room and most of her dining room, Marissa couldn't remember why she had done it. Standing on her stairs and looking down, she stared at the images that stared back. She couldn't stop the ringing in her ears, and what had started out as a dull ache now felt like something was stabbing at her.

Rubbing her face, she turned and walked the rest of the way up the stairs. She glared at her office, and she walked by before heading into her room. She looked at the bed, where Ellie had curled up and fallen asleep hours ago, and just shook her head. She wasn't tired. Instead, Marissa made her way to her bathroom and stared at the reflection that stared back.

Interestingly enough, in the images covering her downstairs, she looked like she was okay. The reflection in the mirror, on the other hand, looked like a ghost of her former self. She was pale, with dark circles under her eyes and scars all over her body. Scars that were nearly impossible to hide. Scars that made it hard to pretend nothing had happened. The longer she stared, the less she started to see. Until everything went black.

Chapter 20

She had no idea how much time had passed. Marissa was utterly disoriented, curled up in an empty bathtub with her knees pulled close to her chest and a cat lying at her feet in the dark. She blinked, the ringing in her ears finally seeming to quiet. She had heard nothing else for hours. Maybe it was days. She hadn't been able to sleep or focus, for God only knew how long. She was taking rapid, short breaths, rocking herself slightly back and forth.

Outside of her bathroom, she heard a loud crash and Ellie barking. She jumped, but the sounds seemingly stopped. She felt her heart leap into her throat, but when Ellie began whining again, she felt herself settle down. But then the whining came closer, and she stiffened again. Ellie pushed the door open with her nose, letting in the dim light from her room, whining loudly as she turned in circles, yipping a little as she did.

A moment later, Mac emerged through the door, his eyes wide and worried.

"Marissa," he said gently, kneeling next to the tub without turning on the bathroom light. "Are you okay?"

She didn't move, holding her knees tight to her chest, unsure if he was actually there or if she was just imagining him being there. But he reached out a hand and touched her shoulder gently. "Hey."

She felt herself twitch and met his eyes.

"Mac?"

As he nodded his head, Marissa slowly moved forward before jumping into his arms, startling Wicket, who bolted out of the bathroom. Mac caught her and held her close, letting out a heavy sigh of relief.

"Are you hurt?" he asked without letting go at first. She shook her head against his chest, but he pulled back, unconvinced. After a moment, he seemed to realize it was too dark to see anything, and he carried her out to the bedroom, setting her down on the bed. Taking a step back, he let out a gasp as he looked her over. "Marissa, what did you do?"

She pulled her knees back up to her chest, not answering him.

"Okay. The pictures downstairs. Did you do that?"

Marissa nodded vigorously, mumbling in response. "I figured it out. I figured it out."

Chapter 20

She repeated herself a few times, speaking much faster than she realized before Mac nodded his head. "Okay. Just come with me. We're going to take a ride."

Everything started to move very fast. Marissa felt like she was sitting in a bubble where nothing was moving, but someone had pressed the fast-forward button outside that bubble. He got her sweatpants and hoodie, and it was the first time she realized she was wearing nothing but a tank top and underwear. Mac helped her get dressed slowly and helped her put shoes on before carrying her downstairs.

As they came downstairs, she saw he had already gotten Ellie into her service dog vest and had left all the photographs spread throughout her first floor. He took her to the car, her heart leaping back into her throat, panic beginning all over again. She begged him not to take her to the car and began to cry once he got her in there.

Marissa was lying on her back, dim lights filling her vision. She tried to pull herself up but couldn't move her arms, and Ellie shifted as she tried to move her legs. Letting her eyes adjust, she realized she was in a hospital bed, and her arms were restrained.

"Easy honey," she heard a woman's voice before seeing the nurse. A kindly, older woman, she almost

285

reminded her of her mom and made Marissa wish she was home. "Take it easy."

"Where am I?" she asked, her throat hoarse and her voice sounding foreign to her ears.

"You're at the medical center in Port Angeles," she answered as she ran a thermometer over her forehead and started the blood pressure cuff.

"What happened?"

"You were experiencing what we call a manic episode. The doctor will be in tomorrow morning to talk to you about it more, but you had gone nights without sleep and were putting yourself in harm's way. Thankfully for you, this knight in shining armor over here brought you right in."

She nodded, smiling over to Mac, who was smiling back with sleep in his eyes as he stretched in his chair.

"It's nothing to be ashamed of, dear," she said reassuringly as she moved the blood pressure cuff. "Now, can I trust you and take these restraints off, or do you think you need to keep them on?"

Marissa glanced at the restraints that held her wrists before looking back at the nurse. "You can take them off."

"Don't make me regret it now, you hear?"

Marissa nodded, and once the nurse was satisfied, she removed them from her wrists.

"The doctor will be in to talk to you in about four hours. Try and get some more rest. Can I get you anything, honey?"

She turned to Mac, who just shook his head and smiled. "No, thank you, Dolores."

Once the nurse was content and checked everything that needed checking, she lowered the light even further and closed the door behind her.

When she was gone, Mac moved his chair closer to Marissa's bed. The confusion must have been plain on her face because he gave her hand a reassuring squeeze before he explained. "My little sister is bipolar, so I've experienced a few manic episodes in my day." He brushed the hair from her eyes. "Have you ever experienced that before?"

Marissa just shook her head. "How long have we been here?"

"It's been two days. They had a difficult time sedating you at first, but once it finally kicked in, you've been sleeping soundly since. What do you remember?"

Marissa tried to recall when he had found her, but it was all blurry. "I—I don't." She huffed in frustration.

"Hey. Don't push. You were in pretty bad shape when I found you."

"Bad shape?" She realized no one had explained to her why her hands had been restrained, and she tried to sit up but winced as a sharp pain shot through her chest.

"Easy, Marissa," he said gently, stroking her hair. He paused, assumedly weighing what he wanted to say next. "It looks like you were trying to tear through the scar across your chest. You did enough damage that you required some stitches. You also had some smaller gashes. It looked like you had just been scratching at them for hours."

She didn't know what to say. She didn't remember any of that. And while she would willingly admit she hadn't taken great care of herself lately, she had never been the kind of person who would do something that drastic before.

As though he could read her expression, he gave her hand another squeeze. "You're going to be fine. You're meeting with the doctor in the morning, and they'll get you on some more effective meds, and then we'll get you home, okay?"

Marissa nodded, but she wasn't feeling reassured.

"Do you know where your phone is?"

She blinked and stared at him, processing the question. Her brain felt lost in a fog, and it was a little hard to keep hold of her thoughts.

"My phone..."

"I got a text from your phone on Saturday night at 11:36 saying, 'She needs you.' Obviously, you didn't send it. But when I found you, I couldn't find the phone," Mac explained.

Marissa scrunched her face, frowning, trying to remember. "I threw it." She swallowed. Her throat felt dry. "It broke. In the living room?"

Mac shook his head, looking concerned. "It wasn't there. I did look. And I sent Clyde in once I got you here." He sighed heavily, concern still all over his face. But when he saw her worry mirroring his, he forced a smile for her. "Everything is going to be fine, Rissa."

He watched her for a moment before leaning forward and giving her a kiss on the forehead. "You're going to be okay."

The next morning, the doctor checked out Marissa, who gave her physical the all-clear after looking over her vitals and stitches. She was then taken to visit the on-call psychiatrist. She was a kind-faced, older black woman with thin, black-rimmed glasses.

"My name is Dr. Gardner. I understand you experienced your first manic episode."

"I guess." She shrugged. "I don't remember a whole lot of it."

"That's not really surprising. It's actually quite normal." Nothing about this whole situation felt normal. She nodded wordlessly. "And I understand you're also coming off a lot of traumas, am I right?" Again, Marissa nodded. "There is nothing to be ashamed of."

Marissa heard her words but felt tears beginning to form in her eyes.

"The meds you've been on, your doctor didn't talk to you about the possible side effects or warning signs to watch out for?"

Marissa shook her head.

"Irresponsible," Dr. Gardner muttered angrily, flipping through her paperwork and shaking her head with a heavy sigh. "This could have all been so much worse," she said, mostly to herself, before looking back at Marissa. "That must hurt," she noted gently.

Marissa looked down at her chest, where fresh stitches sat. She was largely grateful that she couldn't remember the incident. She couldn't imagine doing something like that to herself, but here they were, her chest heavy and stitches unbearably itchy. There was a small part of her that wanted her memory back, wanting to know what had to go through her mind to try to literally tear the scar off her body.

"It hurts, and it itches."

Dr. Gardner was quiet for a long moment. Marissa assumed the next question would be how she got the scar. To her surprise, the doctor took a different route. "Tell me, what do you think about when you look at that scar? What do you feel?"

Pausing, Marissa blinked. She hadn't given it much thought before. "It makes me feel like a victim all over again," she finally admitted, tears running freely down her cheeks. "It's a reminder that I failed. I failed to save those people, my partner. That I failed to save myself. I allowed this horrible thing to happen to me and that I had no control."

"You aren't a victim. You're a survivor. You survived a horrible trauma," she said gently. "It may not feel like it, but you need to know it is an amazing accomplishment."

When Marissa didn't say anything, she continued. "You need to know that first and foremost." She cocked her head to the side, looking at her. "When you look at that scar, what else do you feel?"

Shifting uncomfortably, she looked to the side to avoid the doctor's eyes and scratched Ellie's ears.

"Like it's a lie. Like I never made it out of that warehouse. Like I still have no control." She swallowed, pausing. "We use words like *violated. Molested. Assaulted. Raped.* You hear them all the time, on the news, on TV shows. For this job, we have to label people with them. But even after years on this job, seeing what one human can do to another ... I guess I thought maybe the badge kept them from touching me. Or just arrogance that made me think it could never reach me." Marissa shook her head. "Now I feel like it defines me. Because I didn't fight hard enough. I couldn't save myself from that situation. So what does that say about me?"

Dr. Gardner simply listened, letting Marissa get out things she wasn't aware she had been holding in.

Chapter 21

Once she had her session with Dr. Gardner, she agreed to a seventy-two-hour hold for evaluation, otherwise known as the ITA, Involuntary Treatment Act. They didn't need her to approve, but she did, nonetheless. Convinced she was no longer a danger to herself, they discharged her. Newly diagnosed, she was allowed to go home. Mac had stayed with her the whole time and tried to make light conversation on the drive back to Port Townsend. She didn't know what she was feeling. The entire ordeal had taken two weeks, from the morning Mac got her into the medical center to the ride home.

As he pulled the car up to her driveway, she experienced the same feeling when she had first come home after the experience from the warehouse wash over her. It wasn't a great one. She opened the back door of the car for Ellie, who bounded happily to the front door. Mac unlocked the door but paused before opening it.

"I made sure that nothing was touched. So it looks like it did that night." He was warning her. And it was a good thing he did so. When he swung the door open, she was greeted by the sight of photographs strewn all over the floor. They were in some kind of order, starting from the living room to her dining room and finally, into her kitchen. There were even photos on the stairs. Surprisingly, Ellie walked very carefully through the minefield of pictures and waited at the backdoor, in desperate need of running out some energy. Mac followed her while Marissa stood in her front hall, her eyes scanning over the photographs.

She vaguely remembered spreading them out. They were in a timeline order. From the first photograph to the most recent. If only she could remember why.

"Do you remember where you threw your phone?" Mac's voice broke through her thoughts.

"Over here." The conversation with Mel drifted across her thoughts, the hurt she had felt, and the sudden reaction of throwing the phone. "I just left it here." She pointed to the floor, where no phone could be seen.

"Okay." Mac hesitated, looking out toward the backyard. He was avoiding her eyes.

"What is it?" Marissa asked as he turned to look at her, and she could see it all over his face. He had something he didn't want to tell her. "Tell me."

Walking over to the counter by the back door, he picked up an envelope and handed it to her. "This was in the mailbox this morning, according to Clyde."

She took the manilla envelope, still studying his face before turning her attention to the package in her hands. It was the same as all the others, her name written across the front, but immediately, she realized it felt heavier than they usually did.

Opening it very carefully, she pulled the photographs out, letting out a gasp and nearly letting them slip through her fingers.

The top image was of her looking at her reflection in her bathroom mirror. Taken from directly behind her. The image was dark, taken from the shadows. He had been standing right behind her that night. Flipping to the following picture, she shuddered violently. It was a photograph of her face, looking directly at the camera as she cried. The camera couldn't have been more than six inches away from her face. She flipped through several more of just her face, one where she was clearly trying to push the camera away from her and one of her sitting in the bathtub, rocking herself.

"He was here," she said quietly, her voice shaking more than she anticipated. Flipping to the next, she found a picture of Mac helping her out of the tub.

The photo had been shot from the ground. Maybe under her bed? The final image was of her and Mac outside the SPD from weeks earlier when Mac had just arrived. Scribbled in the corner were the words *I'll be seeing you.*

She handed the photos to Mac, whose horrified expression matched her own. "He was here," she repeated, looking to the back door where she could see Ellie running laps in the yard, her toy in her mouth.

"She knew him." The realization washed over her, looking over at Mac. "He couldn't have gotten in without Ellie realizing. He's someone she knows."

Marissa felt all the breath get sucked out of her lungs. Her knees wobbled beneath her where she stood, and Mac took her arm gently, making sure she didn't lose her footing.

"You should sit down," he said finally, putting the photos on the counter, but Marissa shook her head.

"No. I need to remember what the hell I was doing with these photographs. We'll address those," she gestured to the pictures on the counter, "later."

She walked back into the front hall and looked at the photographs spread throughout, unable to remember what it was she felt had been so important.

She walked along with the photographs, eyeing each carefully. Seeing her life over the past two years summed up on the floor was surreal. She stopped to stare at the photo of her and Allison at the Mansera, the night of Bree's birthday party. That was when it hit her, like a shockwave through her body.

She made her way to the pictures from the night of Allison's going away party, closer to the dining room. Sure enough, in the first picture she saw, Owen Rolley and the bachelor party were in the background.

"There!" She snatched up a picture. She was the focus of the image, laughing as Allison whispered something in her ear on a night that felt like it had been decades ago. But in the background of the picture, there was Owen and his camera. And she had seen that camera before. It had a cheesy Space Needle sticker on the side of it.

Marissa's mouth all but fell open. "I've seen that camera!"

Mac stood next to her, looking at the photograph with her. She looked up at him with big eyes, her hand shook.

"It's in Dr. Seaver's office." She pointed directly to the Space Needle sticker. "The camera we never found."

Mac took the photo from her hands to take a closer look while Marissa breathed very carefully through her nose, struggling to process. She walked over to the table and sat down. It didn't make any sense, thinking back to the interview at the police station. Laura Seaver had been calm, collected, and appeared to be nothing but helpful. Her breathing had been controlled; she didn't do anything to raise alarms with her body language or words.

"Okay." Mac sat beside her, placing the picture between them on the table. "What do you want to do now?"

She wanted to approach Laura Seaver by herself and potentially strangle her with her bare hands. Instead, she shook her head. "I don't know. I don't..."

Her eyes wandered back to her kitchen, to the photos sitting on the counter. She couldn't stop thinking about how he had been in her house. He had been right in front of her.

Forcing herself to focus, she looked at Mac, shaking her head. "I don't know."

Mac knelt down to be eye level with her, directly meeting her gaze and taking her hands in his. "Hey. One step at a time, okay?" He watched her, waiting for her to respond.

Marissa took a deep breath, finding herself momentarily lost in his dark brown eyes. She had to focus, grounding herself before she nodded her head. Inhale, calm. Exhale, worry. Inhale, calm. Exhale, worry. The stupid mantra she was supposed to recite every time she felt that panic in the pit of her stomach.

"I'll call Ronnie and give her everything I have. We'll wait for them to pick her up and hope they let me in an interview room with her."

She let out a breath, catching a quick flash of relief on his expression.

"Here. You can use my phone." He handed it to her and stood up. "I'm going to get all of that picked up." Before he walked off toward the dining room, he leaned down and kissed her forehead. "You've got this." He gave her a reassuring smile and squeezed her hand before he started picking up the photos scattered all over the first floor.

Marissa reluctantly dialed Ronnie's direct number, which she had thankfully memorized. It rang enough times that she was afraid it would go to voicemail, but finally, she answered.

"Ronnie!" She didn't even give her enough time to finish saying hello. "It's Marissa."

"Oh, hi, Marissa. How are you feeling?" Cool, she was up to date on how things were going.

"Never mind that now. I know who killed Allison, Cindy, and Owen Rolley."

She told her about the photograph, along with the potential motive. Ronnie promptly put her on hold while she went to talk to Jackson. Marissa counted beats while she waited, watching Mac anxiously, bouncing on her toes while sitting in her chair. Inhale calm. Exhale worry. Inhale calm. Exhale worry. She felt slightly irritated that it seemed to be working. Mac was picking up the last photos when Ronnie came back to the phone.

"Okay. I'm going to come by and pick up the photo. Dylan and Dale are heading to her office, and Jackson is trying to call her in now. I'm pretty sure she left town last week, but she won't have gotten far. We'll bring her back, Marissa. I promise."

Marissa let out a breath of relief. She hadn't been sure she would be taken seriously.

By the time she had hung up the phone, Mac had all the photos back in the box, except for the newest ones. "I think we need to get these to my supervisor. I'm going to make some calls and see what they want me to do." He paused and looked at her. "What do you need?"

She looked up at her and sighed. She didn't even know. Suddenly, her mouth was unreasonably dry.

"Ronnie is coming by to grab the photo of Rolley. But I think after that I need to take a shower. I need to get the hospital feel off of me." She involuntarily shook as Mac nodded, watching her.

"We'll have to get you a new phone..." He glanced at the clock. "But it's Sunday. What are the chances that there is somewhere open?"

"None," Marissa said flatly. "Stupid tourist town."

"Okay, we'll get it tomorrow then." The concern on his face hadn't lessened. "Are you hungry? Do you need something to eat?"

Marissa smiled. "I'm okay. You can sit down, you know." He didn't look convinced. "Or even go home and rest."

"Now you're talking nonsense." He grinned at her.

They stayed in the kitchen and talked quietly, passing the time until Ronnie arrived. Marissa had hoped Ronnie would just come, take the picture, and go, but she noticed Marissa's appearance. After two weeks in the hospital, her hair was ratty and dry, she was pale, her lips were chapped, and the circles under her eyes made her look like she hadn't slept in weeks.

"Are you doing okay now? Is there anything I can do?" She was trying to be helpful, but Marissa felt herself tensing up again.

"Just tired mostly." It was honest. She felt exhausted. But thankfully, Ronnie took the hint.

"Okay, well, I will let you go. Let me know when you have a phone again, and until then, I'll call Mac. But I will keep you updated when there is anything to update."

"Sounds good. Thank you for everything, Ronnie."

"Of course." She gave Marissa a hug and headed back out the door.

Marissa had hoped she would feel some kind of relief when Ronnie took the photograph, a sense that it was close to being over. They knew who it did, but Marissa didn't feel any better. There was no relief. In fact, if anything, she was feeling restless.

"I need to take a shower."

Mac nodded but hesitated. "Let me just ... check things out upstairs first. We've walked through several times since the other night, but I just want to triple-check." He wanted to make sure her crazy stalker wasn't still in the house.

She nodded with a sigh and allowed him to head upstairs first. Ellie followed behind him before

Marissa could make her way up the stairs. She stopped on the bottom step and turned, deciding to lock the front door's deadbolt.

By the time she made it to her room, Mac seemed content that everything was okay, but still, he hesitated. "How about I stay and make my phone calls out here?"

Marissa wondered for a moment what he would say if she had said no. But she smiled and just nodded. "Of course." His presence always made her feel better anyway.

She walked into the bathroom, letting Ellie follow her in before she closed the door behind her. Ellie curled up on the mat and watched her as she stared at her. Marissa had been at the hospital long enough that the stitches they had to put over the scar had already been taken out, but it still looked red and irritated. She was pale and thin, and she was looking more and more like a ghost of her former self. Marissa started the hot water and disrobed slowly, the fabric irritating her. Stepping into the walk-in shower, she let the hot water run down her body, leaned her hands against the wall, and closed her eyes.

Allison's killer had been identified. Not only was it someone Allie had trusted, but it was also someone who had all of Marissa's secrets. Someone who had been in control of her medication, who had kept her from getting better. Someone who had allowed her to get worse and nearly lose the remainder of the life she still had. She had violated her trust. She had violated Allison's trust. For years. She had made Allison feel as though she had no other way, that there was no out in that relationship. And when she finally made it out, she fucking killed her in a rage. Clenching her fist, she hit the stone tile.

It had been just over two years ago that Tom Disher lost his life in that warehouse, and her life had been spared. But again, she had been violated. Repeatedly. She had experienced things she would never put to words. Someone just as vile had sat across from her in an interview room to confess to her, and only her, all the horrible things he had actually done. And the one who had actually done those things to her had been here, in her home, less than a few feet away.

He had taken pictures of her at her most vulnerable, as she was literally trying to tear herself apart.

He had been right there. He had touched her.

He had stopped her. Chances are he had texted Mac and taken her phone.

But he had been right there.

And Ellie knew who he was.

She hadn't acted upon a stranger entering the house. Ellie hadn't warned Marissa of anyone's presence. She knew who he was.

Again, her fist met the stone wall. Again and again and again, unaware that she was letting out a feral scream as she did until she felt her legs give way beneath her. But instead of dropping to the ground, she felt arms catch her. Looking up through the water that was still running down her face, Marissa saw Mac standing there, holding her up. He helped lift her back up, and while her ears were ringing, she could feel he was telling her to just let it out. So she screamed again and again. She cried out until she had no voice left, and all that remained were tears. And Mac just held on to her.

He helped her out of the shower, and once he got a towel wrapped around her, he took his own soaked shirt off and dropped it to the floor.

"I'll be right back," he said to her gently. "Get comfortable." He was speaking so softly to her. The ringing in her ears had stopped.

She nodded, holding her towel in place as he left her room. She felt weak. And embarrassed. She had never allowed herself to appear so vulnerable in front of someone else. Now her head was beginning to throb. She waited a long moment before grabbing a pair of underwear and a loose tank that she could manage. Ellie rubbed up against her legs and whined, probably less than pleased with her screaming.

By the time she sat back down on the bed with her back against the headboard, Mac had come back in, now wearing dry sweatpants and a shirt. It took Marissa a minute to realize he'd had a bag with him from staying with her at the hospital. Wordlessly, he sat down on the bed next to her. Ellie was more than happy to jump up and curl up on the edge.

A moment passed before Marissa broke the silence. "I'm sorry," she said in a whisper.

"Why are you sorry?" Mac seemed shocked by the admission.

"I'm just so afraid..." She choked the words out.

"Hey..." Mac turned his body slightly to face her and took her hands in his. "You remember when we worked the O'Rourke case?" Marissa nodded. "Melissa Jensen. We needed her to ID him in a line-up, and she was terrified. Do you remember what you told her?"

Marissa blinked. Honestly, she would've needed to give it thought to remember what she said, but apparently, James Mackenzie did not.

"You told her that being scared didn't make her any less of a badass. That being a badass, even though he scared her, was something he wasn't going to ever be able to take away from her. That she had all the power." He gave her hand a squeeze. "I'd been working for the FBI for nearly a decade and never had met anyone with so much compassion for people. You never treated them as victims. You treated them like survivors. And that's exactly what you are. It was the first thing I admired about you. You never have to apologize. Not to me. Not for anything."

Before Marissa could remember how to form words, his phone rang. Pulling his cell off her nightstand, he sighed. "It's my boss. I have to take this. I'll just be in the guest room. Why don't you try to sleep?" He leaned down and kissed her forehead, his lips lingering there for an extra beat before he headed out the door, answering the phone. She listened to the sound of his voice as he walked down the hallway to the guest bedroom, processing.

It had been about five years since the O'Rourke case. And he still remembered.

She grabbed the pillow beside her and held on, feeling the need to hold on to something. The adrenaline from the shower was fading, and exhaustion was quickly taking over. One day she was going to stop having meltdowns in front of him, particularly ones in her bathroom. Flexing her fist, she realized she'd probably bruised the knuckles on her hand. She'd have to take a look when she woke up.

Breathing deeply, she forced herself not to think about the photographs, Daniel Fryer, Allison, or Laura Seaver. She couldn't, or she would never sleep. Instead, she let herself think about that extra beat when his lips touched her. The way he was there to catch her. The way he looked at her. The way he took care of her while always following her lead. Wicket mewed as she jumped up on the bed, happy her new human was home, and curled up by her pillow.

Chapter 22

Marissa spent most of the night tossing and turning; after spending nearly a week stuck on a tiny hospital bed, it was nice to be able to do so. On the other side of the pillow, she had fallen asleep holding on to Mac, shirtless and sound asleep on top of the covers. She peeked over the pillows, watching and listening to him breathe. Ellie was stretched out on top of her legs, probably trying to keep her restless moving in check as much as possible. It must have been early; the sun was just coming up. Biting her lip, she rested Ellie on the pillow and just watched him.

There was a part of her that kept expecting him to leave. Eventually, it would be one meltdown too many, too much drama. Marissa knew she was a lot. And it's not like he was getting anything out of this. It wasn't a relationship. He was doing a job. And yet...

His phone went off on the nightstand beside him, causing her to jump and hide her face in the pillow. He sat up with a start and grabbed his phone, instantly alert. "Agent Mackenzie."

She couldn't hear the other side of the conversation but slowly pulled her face from the pillow as she watched him. He was frowning.

"Okay. Right now?" He glanced over at her without changing his expression. "Yes, sir. I understand." He nodded to no one in particular. "We will be there." He glanced at his watch. "Sounds good, sir. You, too."

He hung the phone up and sighed before turning to her. "We have to go see Fryer."

"Now?"

"Now." He nodded. "We have to take the pictures with the writing on them. And Agent Bennet."

"Okay." Marissa sighed. She didn't want to see Daniel Fryer. She wasn't sure she was ready to face him again after the last breakdown she had.

As though Mac could read her mind, he reached over and squeezed her hand. "You're going to be fine. Get ready and meet me at the SUV."

Marissa nodded her head, looking down at his hand. "I'll see you in a few minutes," she finally said. That seemed enough for him to release her hand although his gaze lingered a second longer before he left her room. Once he was gone, she grabbed her pillow and squeezed it.

Inhale calm, exhale worry. Inhale calm, exhale worry.

Marissa was feeling a flood of emotions at that moment. Most of them were full of negativity, anxiety, and fear. But there was a slight flutter that Marissa was very much ignoring. Throwing her legs over the bed, she groaned as Ellie jumped off. Her body still felt stiff. She had been told to expect some flaring side effects from the medication changes and adjustments. Flexing her hands, she winced. She had almost forgotten about the breakdown in the shower. Her knuckles were bruised, and she had a pretty deep cut over her index finger. Once on her feet, she made her way into her bathroom.

It took her twenty minutes to throw her hair up, throw clothes on, wrap up her hand, and make sure she took all the correct meds she was supposed to before she and Ellie made it to the car. Clyde and Mac were already outside, standing by the car talking. Clyde looked less than pleased as he got in the back passenger seat. Marissa let Ellie, who loved all the space the SUV provided, in before hopping in herself.

The ride felt like an eternity. Both men were completely in FBI mode, so they insisted on remaining inside the vehicle during the ferry ride. Neither seemed to be in the mood for talking. It felt like the longest ride ever, and the air was heavy.

It seemed like the two men might have had some kind of disagreement before she had come out, but neither was speaking. She tried to turn the radio on once, but Agent Bennet just complained about a headache. Even Ellie shifted and whined uncomfortably. It did nothing for Marissa's nerves.

When they finally arrived at the precinct, Marissa jumped out of the car, thrilled for some fresh air. Clyde went straight inside, but Mac approached her, running his fingers through his hair with one hand, the other in his pocket.

"There is something you should know." There it was. Whatever the heavy mood was about, this was it. "There's a new ADA involved. He's rescinded FBI presence, and since they haven't been able to prove Fryer's story about Jenna Spheres, it's not technically our jurisdiction."

"What does that mean?"

"It means I won't be able to go into that interview with you. It also means that we are here to gather our stuff, close out our files, and go back to D.C."

Marissa's heart dropped. She went to say something, but words just didn't come out.

"Hey ... it's not over yet. We'll figure it out." He gave her his best reassuring smile.

Marissa just nodded and followed him into the building, Ellie nosing her the whole way, feeling her tension.

Marissa stared at her feet while they waited, picking at the beds of her nails nervously. They were approached by a tall man in a dark suit with brown hair and small eyes. This had to be the ADA. He gave them a thin smile with his thin lips and quick, uninterested handshakes. "Hi. I'm Assistant District Attorney Gorden. You must be ... Agent Mackenzie?"

"Yes, sir." God, he was so polite. Marissa huffed.

"And you must be Detective Ambrose."

"I am." She gave him a half-hearted smile.

"So, as I'm sure you know, the FBI is no longer needed for this investigation. I've asked for Ms. Ambrose—"

"Detective." Marissa had no issue correcting him. Mac looked like he was holding back a smile.

"Forgive me. I've asked Detective Ambrose here as a courtesy to see if our suspect is willing to give up any relevant information. Particularly about the Couple's Killer case or to the supposed stalker photo you brought with you."

Marissa went to say something, but Mac half shook his head at her, and she stopped herself. Who the fuck did this guy think he was? Supposed stalker?

"So shall we get this over with?" He stared at her impatiently.

She glanced up at Mac before nodding her head slowly. She didn't like the idea of going into that room without him. She liked the idea of going in with this man even less. Shaking her shoulders, she took the envelope from Mac containing the picture and followed the attorney into the interview room.

Daniel Fryer was sitting back in his chair, knees spread apart, looking bored and unimpressed, staring at the table. But he snapped to attention as she entered the room.

"Detective! It's so good to see your bright face compared to this one."

ADA Gorden looked apathetic at best, leaning back in his chair as he drummed his fingers along the table. "Let's move this along already?" He looked at Marissa expectantly.

Reluctantly, she put the envelope on the table. "This was left at my house since the last time I was here." She opened it and held it up, so the photograph fell out on the table. She had no desire to touch it.

Fryer leaned forward, bringing his cuffed hands to the table, looking closely at the photograph. Of course, there wasn't much to the picture itself. It was taken at night when Mac offered that first ride home after their first interview. It was the writing over the image. *I'll be seeing you.*

"Interesting..." Fryer said after what felt like several minutes of uncomfortable silence, rubbing the beard that had begun to grow in.

"Interesting?" Marissa raised an eyebrow. She needed a hell of a lot more than *interesting*.

"Very." He stared at the photograph for a moment longer before smiling at her. "He thinks I'm going to give him up. Something about the FBI's presence made him nervous."

If Marissa didn't know any better, she'd think he were amused by this revelation.

"So, is it over?" Marissa didn't mean to sound as hopeful as she did, and she felt it even less.

"Not even close." Daniel Fryer met her eyes. "In fact, this says the exact opposite. The FBI presence makes him nervous, but he is far from being done with you. He'll be back for you."

"Why?" she asked quietly. She already knew the answer but hearing him say so made her feel sick.

"I could tell you if you really want to know." Fryer gave her a toothy smile that made the pit in her stomach drop even further and made her blood run cold. But she needed answers.

"Tell me."

"That is not what we're here to discuss." Marissa stared at the ADA in disbelief, but he just stared back at Fryer. "Can you give us a name? Or tell us where he is?"

Daniel Fryer raised an eyebrow before shaking his head and leaning back in his chair. Marissa recognized the change in his body language. This interview was over.

"Then let's get back to what we came here to discuss."

Marissa stood, nearly knocking the chair over, grabbed the photograph from the table, and left the interview room with Ellie on her heels. Once the door was closed behind her, she could feel herself beginning to panic. Mac was standing right there, but Marissa couldn't hear his words. She shoved the picture into his hands and hurried into the bathroom.

Once Ellie was in behind her, she locked the door. She threw up everything she had until the aching that had already been there in her ribs became unbearable. Marissa sat on the floor, letting Ellie curl up in her lap and try to soothe her. She wasn't sure if panic or anger was charging her emotions right now, but she felt so overwhelmed, and every part of her body could feel it. A few minutes passed before she got to her feet and managed to splash her face with cold water and take a few deep breaths, shaking it off before she walked back out of the bathroom, collected and composed.

Mac, Clyde, and ADA Gorden were all standing in the hallway, along with Captain Cooper. It was not a reassuring sight. Despite the extreme urge to just head for the exit, she joined them as though nothing out of the ordinary had happened.

"So nice of you to join us, detective." There was a bite to the attorney's words, but Marissa smiled.

"What did I miss?"

"Well, we were just discussing the fact that since your stalker has, in fact, left the area, there really is no need for the FBI presence at all," Gorden remarked.

"And I was reminding him that the only reason he's supposedly gone is because of our presence in the first place," Mac replied.

"If you really feel threatened, you could always ask for an agent to stay with you. But I am sure agents as decorated as Agent Mackenzie and Agent Bennet here have more pressing matters to spend their time on." He eyed both agents, who didn't offer anything of the contrary. "And since Daniel Fryer refuses to talk about any of our current cases, you will no longer be needed for these interviews. If we need anything from you, we will call. But we will handle this case from here."

Marissa had to fight to hold her jaw in place. She looked from Gorden, who wore a smug smile, to Captain Cooper, who looked exhausted, to Agent Bennet, who really looked bored, to Mac. Mac avoided her eyes altogether, but he bounced on the heels of his feet, his hands behind his back, and his jaw was clenched.

With a heavy sigh, Marissa nodded slowly. "Sounds like you have it all under control." She glanced at Captain Cooper, who seemed no more pleased than they were. "I will be on my way then." And with that, Marissa walked out of the precinct and resisted the urge to just scream. She stormed over to the SUV, got into the passenger side, let Ellie in with her, and slammed the door behind her.

Only moments later, Mac came in behind her, getting into the driver's side. "Hey, are you okay?"

"I'm great." She was not great. She was fucking angry. As she met his worried gaze, leaning on the armrest of her seat, she let out a breath and felt a little bit of that anger start to melt away.

"Listen, this isn't completely over. I'm not leaving, even if I use my vacation time."

"You don't need to waste your vacation. And I mean, you probably do have better things to do than babysit, waiting to see if he comes back." She hated saying it, but it was true.

"First of all." He leaned on his armrest, only a few inches away from her. "I can't think of a better way to spend my vacation time. I never use it anyway." He smiled at her. "And second, with you no longer working with the FBI and the FBI is no longer on the case, if I were to stay for say, just surveillance, the protocols are different."

She stared at him for a long moment, confused, but the longer she looked into his eyes, it became clear. When they were working on cases together, protocols were very strict and precise. There was no room for romantic entanglement.

"If you were interested, at least." There was a flash of self-doubt over his expression.

Before Marissa could respond, his phone went off, and they both jumped.

Mac fumbled around to grab the phone and answered, while Marissa took a minute to look out the window. She was not in a place to be with anyone. She was such a fucking trainwreck; it should have been the furthest thing from her mind. And instead, she was now thinking about his lips.

"Fuck," she mumbled to herself.

"Here, it's Ronnie." Mac passed her the phone, looking as flustered as she felt.

She took the phone and took a deep breath. "Hey, Ronnie, what's up?"

"We've got her, Marissa. She made it to Victoria. Border Patrol is escorting her back on the ferry now, and Jackson and Dylan are picking her up. She'll be here in a few hours."

"Damn. That's great!" That was faster than Marissa had even thought possible.

"So we'll see you down at the station, right?"

"Damn straight, you will. I'll be there soon. We're leaving Seattle now."

"Sounds good. I'll see you then!"

She hung the phone up and turned to Mac, full of excitement. "Laura Seaver is being brought back in from Victoria. She'll be in Port Townsend in a couple of hours!"

Mac went to say something, but as he opened his mouth, Clyde Bennet plopped into the back passenger seat and shut the door behind him. "Shall we go?"

Looking forward again, Marissa sighed. Whatever moment they had nearly had was behind them now. She put the phone down and adjusted her seat to lean back slightly, closing her eyes. She wouldn't be able to sleep, but she could at least rest. The rest of the day was shaping up to be just as eventful as the morning.

They had been sitting in the ferry line for what felt like an eternity before she heard Clyde from the back. "Hey," he whispered. "Is she sleeping?"

There was a silence in which Marissa assumed Mac was examining her to see if she were awake. She closed her eyes and focused on her breathing, making sure it was even. After a moment, Mac seemed confident enough that she was, in fact, asleep. "I'm pretty sure."

"This all feels sort of ... off, right?" She heard Bennet murmuring from the backseat.

"Oh, you mean how they're sending us packing and leaving her vulnerable? Absolutely." Mac grumbled. "Gorden is making a power play. Suppose he can prosecute a case before they find something tying him to any other cause outside the jurisdiction. In that case, he'll be a shoo-in for district attorney come election time." She heard him huff. "It isn't right."

"I agree, man, but there isn't really much to be done, is there?"

"I'm not leaving, Clyde." She felt the shift in Mac's tone and held her breath.

"James, she'll be fine. She can hold her own. She'll have backup. She'll happily tell you she's done fine for the past two years without us."

"I'm not leaving."

"This is more than just a stalker. This is about her." There was a long silence, and Marissa could feel the tension building in the car. "Dude. Don't go there."

"It's really none of your business. But nothing is going on there."

"There better not be. That girl fucked you up so hard the last time, or have you forgotten? And now she's got even more fucking baggage."

"Again, it's none of your business," Mac said softly. Marissa could feel his eyes on her, and she let out the breath she had been holding, making sure to keep it even and continue to appear sleeping. "I can't explain, man."

"Okay, yeah, but again. Do you remember the last time? You didn't have another date for like ... two years. And it happens once in a blue moon now. And what happens when she doesn't need you anymore and runs back to that ex of hers?"

"I'm telling you, it's not like that. I couldn't live with myself if something happened to her. Especially if it was because I just walked away. She's had enough of that already."

Again, there was silence. Marissa wished she could see what was going on during these long, quiet stretches; it didn't even sound like they were breathing.

"What's so special about *her*?" She could imagine the face Clyde was making with his emphasis on the word *her*.

Chapter 22

"I wish I could explain to you. But I just can't." Something in his tone had shifted. "I'm not sure I know the words to describe it... I just..." He let his words drop off.

"You're fucked, dude." She could picture him shaking his head. "This is why I don't ever invest in anything serious."

"No, you just string married women around until you get bored."

"Well, that felt judgey."

"This whole conversation feels judgey."

"Look, man, I just want to make sure you don't make a rash decision based on your feelings. That you're making smart decisions and not putting your career or life in jeopardy for no reason. Or me. That you aren't making a mistake with her for a second time."

"And I appreciate that. But I can assure you, I don't do anything without thinking it through."

Marissa couldn't listen to this anymore. She sighed heavily and shifted, trying to hint that she was waking up. Thankfully, they took the hint and were quiet.

Chapter 23

Marissa rubbed her eyes and lifted the seat as they pulled up to the station. She had managed to get some restless sleep: restless due to both the uncomfortable passenger seat and the conversation still playing through her mind.

"Hey, you ready for this?" Mac took her hand in his and gave it a slight squeeze. She heard Bennet grumble from behind them before he exited the car. "Ignore him." Mac gave her a reassuring smile.

"Yeah." She nodded, biting her lip before turning, pulling her hand from his. "Let's do this." She took a deep breath and opened the door. She stepped out, letting Ellie jump out beside her, and waited for Mac to come around the car; she bounced anxiously on the balls of her toes.

"Let's go." He gave another reassuring smile and shoved his hands into his jacket pockets.

She pulled the doors open to the small station to see everyone was moving around all at once. There weren't more than two or three officers in sight on a typical day, and everyone was usually stagnant. Today, everyone was on the move. She saw Jackson on the phone in his office; Ronnie and Dylan were gathering papers. Other officers talked to what Marissa assumed must have been Border Control. Agent Bennet had made his way straight for Ronnie, who, upon noticing his arrival, jumped up and ran to Marissa.

"She's in the interview room! We got her!" It was hard not to smile. For what had felt helpless only a night before, Laura Seaver was now just one room away in handcuffs. "There was an anonymous tip called in regarding a homicide suspect, and sure enough, they found her at a bed and breakfast under a different name."

"They don't know who called it in?"

"Nope. Whoever he was called from her room at the bed and breakfast. But she hadn't checked in with anyone or met with anyone that the staff knew about."

Before Marissa could respond, Sheriff Jackson walked over, trying hard not to look at his feet as he approached.

"Marissa. I'm glad you're here," he started uncomfortably. "It seems I owe you an apology."

She simply raised an eyebrow and resisted the urge to cross her arms. "Considering Dr. Seaver was the one in charge of your medications and the one whose recommendations I was taking, I am lifting your suspension and reinstating you." He handed over her badge and gun.

He held on to the handgun for a moment longer. "But this doesn't go into that interview with you."

"Yes, sir." Marissa smiled, letting out a breath of relief. It felt good to have her belongings back in her hands. She grinned at Mac and Ronnie and gave Ellie a good pet behind the ear before turning back to business. "Has anyone talked to her yet?"

"Nope, waited for you. Figured you earned that right." Sheriff Jackson almost seemed to be avoiding her eyes while looking directly at her. The excitement she felt was already wearing off as she thought about the interview she was about to have.

"Let's go then." She handed her gun to Mac. "Keep this for me?"

He nodded, giving her a smile.

Ronnie handed her the file, and Marissa headed into the station's only interview room, Ellie at her side.

Laura Seaver looked tired but in control as always. She had dyed her hair red but still wore it back in that tight ponytail, pulling her face back. Her hands, while handcuffed, were calmly folded in front of her, and she stared at the table, barely paying Marissa any mind when she came in. Marissa sat in the chair in front of Laura and leaned against the table, clasping her hands together wordlessly on top of the closed file in the middle of the table where she had placed the file folder.

"Marissa," Laura said casually, a small smirk on her face.

"Laura." She put on her best smile. "I hope you haven't been waiting long."

The corner of Laura Seaver's mouth twitched, but she gave Marissa a forced, small smile. "Not too long, although I would love to know what I'm doing here. I was on my way—"

"Right, I'm so sorry about that." She didn't bother to let her finish and leaned back into her chair. "There are just some questions we would like to clear up."

"Of course. Anything you need," she said politely with her perfect smile. "But are the cuffs necessary?"

"It's protocol," she offered with a small shrug, running her fingers over the manila folder. "I wanted to ask you about your camera."

"I'm sorry, a camera?"

"There was a camera in your office. A Nikon D7500. A few years old, a sticker of the Space Needle on the left side."

Dr. Laura Seaver's lips tightened, and the color had begun draining from her face.

"When and where did you get it?"

"I um..." Laura paused and swallowed. "I've had it for a while. Picked it up somewhere."

Marissa had to bite back her urge to smile. "What would you say is a while?"

"I'm sorry?" The smile turned to a deep frown.

"A few weeks? Months? Years? What is a while?"

Laura Seaver let out a heavy sigh as she shifted in her seat, but she said nothing. The chances that the woman across from her would lawyer up were pretty high.

"Okay, let's talk about something else then." Marissa paused. "Let's talk about Allison."

This time, Laura looked like she was going to say something, her eyes dropping down to the table. But her mouth closed.

"Nothing?" Marissa straightened back up in her chair, making sure to catch the other woman's eyes with her own. "You have nothing to say?"

"I'm pretty sure we already covered everything there was to cover."

"I want to focus more on your breakup." Marissa drummed her fingers on the table, raising an eyebrow. "And I don't mean the first one."

Laura Seaver's mouth twitched slightly, but Marissa could see the crack starting to form in the woman's walls.

"You never really let her go." Marissa let her voice drop and soften a little, forcing herself to relax her body language. "And I understand. Allison was the most amazing person I've ever known. She had the most infectious smile. And the best laugh."

Chapter 23

The woman across from her shifted, and the hint of a sad smile formed on her lips.

"She did have the best laugh." Her eyes dropped down to the table, and her shoulders slumped forward slightly, her perfect posture gone.

"So I can't imagine how much it hurt to see her move on with someone else. Like really move on." She let her words hang in the air for a moment before continuing. "That was the real breakup. When she told you it was over and she was going to Seattle, right?" She waited, but Laura Seaver didn't move. "Why don't you tell me what happened?"

Dr. Seaver sighed heavily, blinking a few times while staring at the table before meeting Marissa's eyes. They were wet and full of tears. She looked like she was ready to say something, but she clamped her mouth shut once more.

"Did she give you a reason, or did she just say it was over?"

But again, the woman said nothing.

Marissa glanced down at Ellie, who had relaxed at her feet, before opening the manila folder she had placed on the desk. She pulled out the pictures one by one: first Owen Rolley's scene, then Old Lady Cindy's scene, and finally, Allison's scene down in the Shanghai tunnels.

"I want to know how you can do this to someone you claim to love." She pointed at the photos of Allie's crime scene. "I want to know how someone whose entire profession is to make people better,

with the promise to do no harm, can do this to innocent bystanders?"

Laura Seaver's eyes fell on the photos, looking
at them one by one before she landed on Allison's
crime scene.

"How do you *do this* to someone you love?"

"Stop." The woman snapped, keeping her body
still. "Just stop."

"I just want to know why," Marissa simply said.
"We have everything we need, Laura. If you talk now,
we avoid a trial. Who knows what kind of leniency
you could see?"

They both knew she would never see the light
of day again. She was just lucky the death penalty
was no longer an option in the state.

She lifted her once-again-cold-eyes to look
at Marissa and stared through her for a moment
before cocking her head to the side.

"It was an accident," she finally said. "She wanted
out of the relationship; she was leaving me. I told
her it was never an option, but she kept trying to
prove her point. Packing her things, signing a lease."
She looked at Marissa. "I loved her deeply. And she
loved me. I never meant to hurt her."

"So what happened?" Marissa managed softly,
trying to keep herself as removed as possible, but it
felt like a hundred-pound weight had been dropped
in her stomach.

"I waited until her party was over, and she was
headed home. We started arguing, and she started

hitting me, and I just saw red. I shoved her against the brick wall and grabbed her by the neck until she stopped breathing."

"And Cindy?"

"She saw the whole thing." That was what they had figured from the beginning—just an unfortunate effect of being in the wrong place at the wrong time.

"And Rolley?"

"He got the whole thing on camera. Had pictures, proof. He was extorting me. I paid him off once, but he came back for more. And when you told me that it might have been one of her exes, I thought maybe I could set him up to look like that guy. Two birds, one stone."

Laura wiped her wet eyes as her expression went cold again.

It was nauseating, but it was over. It was fucking over.

Passing over the paper and pen, Marissa sighed. "Are you willing to write all this out and sign your name, admitting that this is the whole truth that you have willingly given?"

"Yes, ma'am."

"I will leave you to it then." She grabbed the pictures, shoving them back in the file. Marissa sighed softly but got to her feet. Ellie, without hesitation, got to her feet, as well. "I'll send someone in to finish processing you."

"Before you go." Laura Seaver straightened up once more, looking Marissa over slowly before she shook her head. "I don't get it."

"Get what?" she said with honest confusion.

"What it is about you. You should be locked up in a padded room, and instead, you're here. Because of him. I don't get it."

Marissa blinked, confusion washing over her face. "What? What are you talking about?"

Laura Seaver shook her head, the smallest hint of a smile on the corner of her lips. "Nothing, Detective Ambrose. Nothing."

Once the door closed behind her, Marissa let out a heavy, shaky sigh. Ronnie took the files from her and gave her a sympathetic look. "I'll take it from here."

Mac pulled her into a hug as Jackson came up alongside them.

He sighed heavily. "I won't lie. I wouldn't have considered Laura Seaver a murderer in a million years. But then, I guess you don't ever really know people." He shook his head. "It should be smooth sailing from here on. Sentencing should be quick. I'd be surprised if she doesn't get three consecutive life sentences. This Saturday, we'll have a press conference and should be able to give out all that information. I want to credit you with the arrest."

He looked at Marissa, but she shook her head.

"I'm just glad it's over. I don't want any more attention on me. I'll be there, but you don't need to single me out."

Jackson nodded. "If you're sure."

Marissa smiled and nodded.

"Alright. Why don't you get out of here? There's nothing else going on right now; take advantage."

Marissa nodded and didn't need to be told twice.

Mac turned to Clyde, "You want a ride home?"

But Clyde glanced at Veronica, who shook her head.

"Nah, I think we're gonna go get drinks. You two wanna join?"

Mac glanced at Marissa before turning back and shaking his head. "Not today."

Marissa smiled. The man could read her mind.

They drove back to her house in silence. It was a silence Marissa felt strange about. She couldn't help but wonder if maybe Clyde's words were sinking in for him.

As she got out of the SUV and let Ellie out, Mac hesitated. "I've got a couple of errands I need to run, but I will be back shortly, okay?"

Marissa tried not to frown and nodded her head. "Oh, sure. I'll see you in a bit."

She felt strange as she watched him drive off but, with a sigh, turned and headed into her house. She went to text Brian to tell him the good news and then remembered she had no phone.

So instead, she pulled out her laptop, got herself comfortable on the couch, and sent him a quick email. They hadn't spoken since that time after Thanksgiving, right after Rolley's car was found. He had no idea about her little breakdown, time in the hospital, a stalker in her home, or today's news—the arrest. She stared at her computer screen, wondering how much was appropriate for a quick email. It wasn't like she could just go to his house anymore. Mel had all but banished her.

Hey Bri,

Sorry for being MIA lately. If you've tried to call or text me in the last couple of weeks, my phone was stolen.

She deleted that.

My phone has been missing.

She deleted that, too.

It's a long story. But more importantly, I wanted to let you know that Laura Seaver was arrested and confessed today to the murders of Allison, Cindy, and Owen Rolley. There will be a press conference Saturday, so you can't run with this info yet, but I wanted to let

*you know. It's over. I'll have to fill you
in on the whole story sometime.*

*I have decided to stay home for
Christmas this year, just spend my
birthday at home. Don't take it personally; it's been a year. I'll make sure
to deal with my mom before Christmas
Eve, so you don't have to deal with any
of that fallout. I do have presents for all
of you. If you want to come to get them
at some point, let me know. I don't
want to upset Mel by bringing them by.*

I hope you guys are doing well.

Rissa

It was ridiculous that she had to keep their conversations on the down-low to avoid upsetting her
stupid pregnant sister. But here they were. Thank
God this stupid year was nearly over. It wasn't the
worst she had experienced, but it certainly wasn't
doing her any favors. She refused to even list it off
in her head.

Staying home for Christmas was definitely
the right choice, though. She couldn't do another
family gathering. She was still adjusting to the
new meds, and while she felt fine right then, Mel's
hormonal rage and the sight of Kirstie with Jared

were just too much. It was too much to think about. Thankfully, she could get away with it. But only because it was her birthday. Had it been any other holiday, her mother would never have allowed her to just not show up.

She wasted time scrolling through her socials for a good half hour before she found herself restless. Ellie nudged her and whined, but Marissa just scratched her ear. "I'm alright, sweetheart." She knew the dog was reading her anxiety. It was still much higher than it should have been.

"Let's clean up upstairs." She gave the dog a small smile and made her way up the stairs, though stiffly. The med changes she was undergoing seemed to be finally kicking. Her underlying fibromyalgia meant the next few weeks were going to be really uncomfortable, though.

At the top of the stairs, she made the right into her office and, with a heavy sigh, took a look around. The entire room was cluttered with the mess that was the Allison Drake case. She started grabbing all the post-it notes she had stuck up across the room. She also took down the pictures she had hanging on her whiteboard, and the police files literally strewed about the room.

It took her over an hour before it felt like she could breathe in the room again. She put everything into files, carefully organized and labeled. She took great care with everything, finally allowing herself to feel that last stage of grief. Acceptance.

Chapter 23

She would never be okay with how it happened or that she had missed all the signs. Looking back, she could see them clear as day because hindsight was everything. But at least there was closure. And not just for Allison, but for Cindy Jenkins and Owen Rolley, too. The last thing she put inside the box was the quote she had planned to say during Allie's funeral but couldn't bring herself to. Taking the piece of paper, she quietly read the words.

"No one ever told me that grief felt so much like fear. I am not afraid, but the sensation is like being scared—the same fluttering in the stomach, the same restlessness, the yawning. I keep on swallowing.

"At other times, it feels like being mildly drunk or concussed. There is a sort of invisible blanket between the world and me. I find it hard to take in what anyone says. Or perhaps, hard to want to take it in. It is so uninteresting. Yet I want the others to be about me. I dread the moments when the house is empty. If only they would talk to one another and not to me.

"—C.S. Lewis."

It was what Allison had read at her parents' funerals only a few years earlier. Later that night, she declared her expectations that it also be read at hers. Marissa hadn't been able to make the words come out on the day, but the intention was there. The words were there in print. And the meaning was still just as deep and meaningful now as it was then. Gently, she placed the paper on top of the contents in the box and closed it. Labeling it, she put it on top of the other boxes of her solved crimes.

Plopping down in her office chair, which was finally free for the first time in months rather than covered with files and trash, she stared at the clean whiteboard before flipping it over and revealing her notes on Seattle's Couple's Killer, a.k.a. her personal stalker. There wasn't much there; she had pretty much left it alone since Allison's death. And she had no desire to start digging back into that. Wicket stopped at the door and mewed at her before jumping up in her lap and letting her know she was deeply in need of attention.

But then she heard Ellie whining from downstairs. She had to push Wicket off her lap, the cat making her loud protests known as she did. Before she could think to panic, she heard Mac's voice from her back door. "Hey, Riss. It's just me."

She exhaled. She had forgotten she had told him where she had the spare key. Making her way down the stairs, she smiled at the sight of him standing there in her kitchen, Ellie yipping at him like a puppy for attention.

"So I got you a new phone; the guy at the store said you just have to put in your password, and you should be able to get all your stuff back up. He did lock down the old phone, so whoever had it won't be able to do much." He offered her a box with a new phone.

"Thank you!" She let out a sigh of relief. She hadn't wanted to go out into public to get one herself.

"How are you feeling?" he asked, doing his best to look unconcerned. It brought a smile to Marissa's face.

"A little tired but fine." The expression on his face didn't change.

"Maybe you should lie down?"

Marissa shook her head. "No, it's okay." She let out a slow sigh, sitting down on the stool. "I closed up the case files and cleared the board upstairs." If anyone was going to understand the ritual that was the end of a case, it would be Mac. He smiled at her and nodded.

"What do you want for dinner? My treat?"

"I don't know," she said lightly, smiling back at him.

"Alright, I'll make you a deal. Why don't you go lie down and get some rest because we both know you're exhausted, and I'll surprise you."

Marissa thought about arguing, but the truth was, she was tired. Nodding, she let her shoulders slump back and got to her feet. "Okay. But only because I want to and not because you're telling me to."

Mac threw his hands up and laughed softly. "Of course."

"Alright. Don't let me sleep too long. Please." Mac just nodded, but she touched his shoulder, and he put his hand over hers and gave it a shake.

"I promise."

Marissa curled up into bed, Ellie snuggling in alongside her, resting her chin on her stomach. She felt like all she had done the last few weeks was sleep. She didn't really want to waste any more time lying around in bed, but her aching body had other plans. Grabbing her new phone, she turned it on and signed back into her accounts, effectively restoring everything she'd had on her old phone. Once she confirmed the phone number, text messages came rushing through. She had several from her mother, a couple from Madilyn, from her dad, a few from Ronnie, from Brian, and even a message from Jack.

[Jack: *Hey, Beautiful. I wanted to check-in. I came by, but you weren't home. I had to head out of town before heading back up to Alaska, but I plan on coming back through town in April. Hopefully, I'll see you then, but I'm sure I'll talk to you before then! Take care, lovely girl.*]

Lydia had also checked in.

[Lydia: *Hey, Rissa. I just wanted to check-in and make sure everything was good. Give me a call when you can, I was thinking maybe we could hang out soon.*]

The sound of her voice in her head left her with an ache, that tiny voice insisting that it was her fault Lydia didn't have her husband.

Marissa sighed and kept scrolling through, glad to see at least one message from Mel.

[Mel: *I don't know what's going on, Riss but give Mom some kind of sign of life. She's freaking the fuck out. I'm sure you're fine. Just let her know.*]

Most of the messages were the same. With a heavy sigh, she put the phone on the nightstand and grumbled as Wicket made her way over. The cat mewed and circled on the pillow until she found just the right spot and curled up beside Marissa's head. She rubbed the cat's face, closing her eyes and falling asleep to the sound of her purring.

Chapter 24

The next day and a half went by quickly. Mac ended up spending the night with her on the couch once again, watching old movies on TCM. It was the most relaxed she had felt in months. He even got up early in the morning, went shopping, restocked her fridge with food, and cooked her food. He may have done it because if he hadn't, she would have passed on eating altogether, but it was still sweet.

And then his phone rang. Something about the way he was nodding and frowning told her it was work-related. He got off the couch, headed off into the kitchen, talked low, and left Marissa on the sofa with Ellie cuddling alongside her. Glancing down at her phone, she looked at the time. It was still considered early in the day.

Chapter 24

When Mac returned to the living room, he shoved his hands into his sweatpants' pockets. Before he could say anything, Marissa sighed. "Work?"

"Work." He nodded, running his hand through his hair. "I have to fly out later today and meet with my boss. Bennet and I need to make our case on why leaving would be a mistake."

Marissa got to her feet reluctantly. "If you can't stay..."

"No. We aren't going over this again." He shook his head. "You are still in danger, so I will be back."

Marissa studied his stubborn face and stared into his eyes before nodding. "When do you have to leave?"

"I need to get everything together now and head to the airport." Marissa must have looked disappointed because he took a step toward her. "But I promise, I will be back before your birthday," he said gently.

"You remember my birthday?" She hadn't meant to sound so surprised, but she had barely remembered it was coming up except to tell Brian she would be spending it alone.

"Of course." He almost seemed offended by the question, but she just blinked at him. He remembered the way she liked her coffee. He remembered all her favorite things. Of course, he had remembered her birthday.

Marissa looked down at her feet for a moment before glancing back up at him, taking another step toward him so she was standing directly in front of him, forcing him to look down at her. She bit her lower lip before pushing up on her tiptoes and pressing her lips to his. At first, she was hesitant, but as he wrapped his arms around her waist and pulled her closer, she welcomed the fierceness with which he kissed her back.

She had no idea how much time had passed when she felt him reluctantly pull away from her, looking as breathless as she felt. He gaped at her, wide-eyed, and she could see the confusion written all over his face.

His mouth opened and closed several times before Marissa finally took a deep breath, resting her hands on her chest. "You have to go. Just ... hurry back. And we'll figure things out then."

Blinking at her, he processed her words and slowly nodded his head. Marissa couldn't help but smile at his confusion, gave him another quick kiss, and laughed lightly as she pulled back.

"Now get out of here and call me when you land. Go."

She had to urge him out the door and watch him walk across the street. Once he reached his door, he stopped and turned to her, giving her a grin, before disappearing on the other side. Touching her lips with her fingers, she smiled and closed her door behind her, Ellie staring at her expectantly.

Sighing heavily, she leaned against the door and closed her eyes. Her heart was beating rapidly against her chest, but for the first time in months it wasn't in panic. It was like their lips had been magnetic; it had been the most natural thing in the world. She was so overcome with surprise and emotion; tears had begun falling down her cheeks without her noticing.

As promised, Mac called when he landed in D.C. It seemed he'd thought as much about that kiss as she had during his flight. "Everything is okay, right? That wasn't like, goodbye or anything?"

"No." Maybe she should have considered that he might think that, but it hadn't even crossed her mind.

"You promise? You're okay."

"I promise. I'm okay."

She could hear the uncertainty in his voice. "And you're going to be there when I come back."

"I will be here when you get back."

"And we're going to talk?"

"Yes, we will talk. We'll figure it out." Marissa couldn't help but laugh. "It wasn't my intention to make you more anxious about leaving."

"I know, I just…" There was a long silence. "I can't tell you how long I've been thinking about doing that."

He couldn't see it, but she smiled, curling further into the corner of the couch. She needed to change the conversation, or they would sit in silence. "Are you going to see your son while you're there?"

"Yeah. Kim is going to meet me tomorrow afternoon after the meeting."

"Good." She smiled, knowing how much that meant to him. They talked for over an hour, a lot like they used to when he had to fly back for work. Eventually, she heard him try to hide his yawn and glanced at the time. "I should let you go. It's so late over there. Plus, you're jet-lagged."

"You don't have to," he said, yawning again. "Oh. Before I forget, Veronica is coming over when she gets off work."

"Oh?" Marissa was confused.

"Yeah, I didn't want you to be alone while I'm out of town."

"Okay." She wasn't going to argue. "How long do you think you'll have to stay?"

"Meeting with the boss tomorrow, then the director in the next day or two after. So not too long."

Good. It wouldn't be too long. "Okay. Get some sleep. Give me a call if you get a chance tomorrow. And have a good time with your son."

"I will." She could hear him smile. "Hey, Marissa?"

"Yeah?"

There was a pause on the other end of the line. "Have a goodnight."

Chapter 24

She could feel the familiarity of this conversation, but they had said things differently then. "You, too," she said softly.

Hanging up the phone, she put it down on the end table and pulled the nearest pillow close to her, finding herself needing to hold something. Ellie was already sound asleep at the other end of the couch, and Wicket was sleeping on the back of the sofa behind her. She looked toward her stairs and considered walking upstairs to bed. Still, as though her body felt her considerations, every inch of her ached at that moment, and she decided to remain on the couch for the night. It was comfortable enough. She could also see the doors from there, and it gave her a sense of calm. It wasn't real, just an illusion of safety, but it was enough to help her rest.

Chapter 25

Her thirty-seventh birthday felt like it had snuck up on her out of nowhere. It might have had something to do with the last six months being utter hell, but she wasn't much in the mood for celebrating. She had hoped that Mac could make it back in time, but it looked less likely with his ex inviting him to spend Christmas Eve with his son. She wasn't going to ask him to miss that for her. She knew how much that time meant to him.

Typically, she would have spent the day with her family, being treated like the birthday princess because the Ambrose women took their birthdays seriously. At least they all had until this year.

Once her feet hit the floor, she was grateful to be spending the day alone, as every inch of her heavily ached. The physical toll that med changes took was a lot and something many people didn't discuss, but the struggle was real today. Birthday or not.

Making her way downstairs, she was about to let Ellie out when her Ring alarm went off. Glancing at her phone, she saw it was some kind of delivery person. Opening the door, Marissa was surprised to find a young delivery man on the other end, holding a long flower box in one hand and his pad in the other. "Marissa Ambrose?"

"That's me," she said, glancing at the box. It was from some sort of floral shop she didn't recognize.

"If you could just sign here." He extended out the pad for her to sign before handing the sleek, long box over to her. "You have a great day, ma'am."

"You, too." She shut the door, fighting the urge to shudder at the label of ma'am. Sometimes it made her feel so old.

Making her way over to the kitchen island, Ellie sniffed the box as Marissa carefully opened it. Inside were long-stemmed red flowers that bloomed from the tip of the stem halfway down. She didn't recognize them as flowers she had seen before. They were paired with beautiful violet Forget-me-nots. Wrapped in the middle of the bouquet were the flowers' names and explanations.

Forget-me-nots represent true love, and giving someone this flower means you genuinely love and respect this person. It is a testament to your relationships and promises the other person that you will never forget them in your thoughts. They are a symbol of fidelity and being truthful to someone you love. This connection can't be broken or shaken by anything or anyone.

Red Salvia or Scarlet Sage is a rare find, much like the one you give this to. The meaning behind this dark beauty is very simple: forever mine.

Something in the way it read, or maybe it was the way the bouquet was arranged, made Marissa suddenly very uncomfortable. At the bottom of the box was an envelope. She took it carefully and unfolded the typed letter from inside.

Marissa.

Merry Christmas, My Love. I knew you could do it, though you couldn't have done it without me. I'm so glad you finally took a closer look at our pictures. I was happy to detain the good doctor while border patrol caught up. This is my Christmas present to you. I hope this closure can bring you just a little bit of peace.

For your birthday, I have something I think you'll like even better. For your birthday, I give you time. I give you space. I have big plans for you, my love. But I give you time to live your life as you see fit, for some happiness before I come back for you.

Enjoy it. I'm still here. I'm always watching.

In the meantime, I'll have to find ways to keep myself busy.

Marissa took a deep breath and looked around, feeling uneasy, as though there were eyes on her. Going around the house, she made sure all the windows and doors were locked and made sure all the curtains were closed. Dropping the flowers into the garbage can, she left the note on the counter. She would need to figure out what it all meant, but not today. Today was her birthday, and she was going to lie on her couch with her dog and adopted cat and wait for Veronica to come over.

Book Club Questions

1. Would you have given the book a different title? If yes, what would your title be?

2. How did the book make you feel? What emotions did it evoke?

3. What did you like most about the book? What did you like the least?

4. Were there any plot twists that you loved? Hated?

5. How did you feel about the ending? How might you change it?

6. Who is your favorite character and why? Who is your least, and why?

7. What do you think will happen next to the main characters?

8. At what point did you start to figure things out?

9. What (if any) questions do you still have about the plot?

10. Did you think it was believable or too far-fetched?

Author Bio

A.K. Ramirez is a mystery writer tucked in a corner of the Pacific Northwest. She likes to weave mystery, family drama, and a little bit of romance all in one. She has participated in NaNoWriMo on and off for years, reaching her goal three times with three different novels, in both the mystery and fantasy genres. When she isn't writing, she runs a dog training, boarding, and daycare facility or spends time with her husband, kids, and pack of dogs. You can find her and all her socials at www.akramirezwrites.com

Author Bio

MORE BOOKS FROM 4 HORSEMEN PUBLICATIONS

COZY MYSTERIES

ANN SHEPPHIRD
Destination: Maui
Destination: Monterey

CRIME, DETECTIVE, AND NOIR

JOE DAVISON
Journey to Hell

MARK ATLEY
Too Late to Say Goodbye
Trouble Weighs a Ton

HORROR, THRILLER, & SUSPENSE

ALAN BERKSHIRE
Jungle

AMANDA BYRD
Trapped
Moratorium
Medicate

ERIKA LANCE
Jimmy
Illusions of Happiness
No Place for Happiness
I Hunt You

MARIA DEVIVO
Witch of the Black Circle
Witch of the Red Thorn

MARK TARRANT
The Mighty Hook
The Death Riders
Howl of the Windigo
Guts and Garter Belts

DISCOVER MORE AT 4HORSEMENPUBLICATIONS.COM